MOTHERLOVE

HOPE ANDERSEN

MotherLove: an unconditional, deep and nurturing affection that a mother has for her child.

"To describe my mother
would be to write
about a hurricane in its
perfect power.
Or the climbing, falling
colors of a rainbow."

–MAYA ANGELOU

ISBN: 978-1-966343-09-7 (hard cover)
        978-1-966343-10-3 (soft cover)
Andersen. Hope
Edited by: Amy Ashby

Published by PipeVine Press, an imprint of Warren Publishing
Charlotte, NC
www.warrenpublishing.net
Printed in the United States

For Nicholas, Haldis and Kylie with all my love

PROLOGUE

St. Croix
December 19, 2022

A mile offshore from the coast of St. Croix is a small yacht, inconspicuous among the other yachts, small and large, that frequent the island. Unlike most of the other luxury boats, this one is not harbored at the marina, as you might expect in the middle of the night, but is anchored off the coast. There's a party going on. Loud music. Inevitably drugs. Beautiful people on board doing what beautiful people do to pass the time and forget their boredom. Drink. Snort. Pop pills.

And traffic girls.

The woman in the wetsuit who is swimming out to the boat knows all this. She is prepared for what she must do. What she has been called to do. It is her mission. Her purpose in life. As she makes her way silently through the water, she is glad of the overcast night, the lack of moon and stars. She is grateful that the water is calm so that she can save her energy for what may become a strenuous fight, although it is her intention to simply slip in, do the job, and be done. She has done this before. She can do it again; of that, she is sure.

She treads water as she watches a handful of guests disembark into a taxi boat that will take them back to shore. The party is slowing down. Now it is just the man left to conduct business under the cloak of dark. She waits, watches as the taxi boat drives away.

As the swimmer draws closer to the boat, making sure her Glock is accessible, she sees a young woman jump off the starboard side of the boat and into the water. Seconds later, a head emerges and then arms, and the girl is swimming toward the ladder back into the boat. The girl lifts herself up onto the ladder, her bright white bikini glowing in the dark, and begins to ascend, struggling a little to pull herself onto the deck. Her waist-length hair falls like ribbons down her back. The man is waiting for her. He helps her up, kisses her, pops something into her mouth, pats her on her ass, and disappears. That man is the one the swimmer has come for.

Several minutes later, she ascends the ladder herself. The girl in the white bikini is standing next to the port railing, swaying, almost toppling. She is clearly high. The swimmer has no time to stop her mission and deal with the girl. She lifts herself onto the deck where the man is seated, smoking a cigar. The swimmer aims at the man and shoots two shots that pierce him between the eyes. There is a splash as the girl in the white bikini falls into the water. Then the sound of girls screaming nearby.

The swimmer walks past the dead man into the interior of the yacht. The instrument panel in the cockpit casts an eerie light. She heads toward a cabin in the bow, opens the door. A group of young Haitian girls, eight or nine, are bound together, terrified. The swimmer unties one of them, the oldest looking of the group. "Parlez-vous anglais?" she asks.

The girl nods.

"Untie your friends while I lower the dinghy in the water. Can you drive a boat?" The girl nods again.

"Good. Take them to this address. You will find help there," the swimmer says as she puts a slip of paper in the girl's hand.

The girl nods, and the swimmer disappears to set up the boat. Using the davit, hand over hand she lowers the dinghy into the water. She helps the young girls into the dinghy and watches them putt away. Then she drags the body of the dead man to the aft, places the body on the swim platform, and dunks it. Satisfied that the corpse has floated away, she looks for the young woman in the white bikini, but the girl is nowhere to be seen. Accepting that the girl will probably be collateral damage, she pulls down her mask, lowers herself into the water, and vanishes.

PART ONE

CHAPTER ONE

Hopewell, New Jersey
December 21, 2022

Rebecca Winslow lies in the darkness, listening to the silence and pulling herself out of a troubled sleep. She heard him come in at 4 a.m., stumbling over furniture in the dark, waking her; though, to be fair, she had been sleeping fitfully. She has been sleeping fitfully since they split off into separate bedrooms six months ago. It is too dark and too cold for her to go back there now, to the reason why.

She needs a drink. Water. Maybe coffee and orange juice to dispel the dull headache she has woken with. She lifts the heap of comforters off herself. The air in the guest room is frigid. Goosebumps rise on her arms and legs. She breathes in the cold through her nose, sensing it flow down her throat and into her chest. If she stays focused on every moment, every moment as it comes, she may stave off the memory. But there, she does it. She remembers Juliet's tiny, cold, dead body in her arms and Royce's face, filled not with grief but disgust, as if their daughter's death has somehow been her fault.

She wipes the tears that have fallen involuntarily on her cheeks, takes hold of the fuzzy robe at the end of the bed, and wraps herself in it. Quietly, so as not to disturb him in the next room, she opens the door to the guest room and makes her way down the dark hallway to the stairs. The wood creaks under her weight, splitting the silence. She cringes, hopes the noise will not wake him, tiptoes carefully down the rest of the stairs to the kitchen, stops in the living room to plug in the Christmas lights on the mantel and the tree. She needs their soft light to warm the darkness.

The silence is palpable. Standing in the glow of hundreds of white flames, she wonders what she might have said to him when he came in. Nothing comes to mind. Rebecca is past caring how he spends his evenings without her. She assumes he was at a bar drinking with his friends, closing it out, and tells herself she doesn't care. There must be other women. She is actually grateful that he has found a way to take care of himself that does not involve her having sex with him.

Just then, she sees his shirt on the floor, glowing in the dark, and walks over to pick it up. The scent of perfume overwhelms her, almost as though someone has poured a bottle out and doused his shirt in its sickly, sweet stench. She drops the shirt like it is on fire, feels vomit rising in her throat. "How dare you," she will tell him when he wakes, "bring a woman home with you. Rub my face in it." But she knows she will say nothing, do nothing, because that has been their agreement. As long as she is sleeping in the other room, refusing to have sex with him, he is free to take care of himself as he chooses. But his cruelty, the "fuck you" attitude he has adopted, comes as a surprise. She knows he blames her—for Juliet's death, for the months of abstinence, for her inability to bounce back from grief and despair. He is also to blame, for not allowing her the time to grieve before he sought out other women for comfort. Tears begin flowing again.

She needs air.

She slides her feet into a pair of boots by the back door and walks out into the dark morning. The sky is pewter and a light snow falls. She breathes deeply, practicing what she has learned from her therapist. In, two, three, four. Out, two, three, four. It is the solstice. The shortest day of the year. Less time to dwell on sorrow. She tries to shake off the negative emotions of the morning. In, two, three, four. Out, two, three, four. Only three days until her parents arrive for Christmas. How is she going to entertain them for the weekend? When had she thought this might be a good idea? She remembers it was not her idea but Royce's. He thought this would help all of them heal from it, the big IT that had been living with them since Juliet died just months after Rebecca's sister Natalie disappeared. She hates that the two events have been grouped together—one a tragedy, the other a predictable drama. Natalie was always the one to steal the limelight. Now Natalie, the younger sister, has appropriated their mother's grief so there is no emotional support for Rebecca as she mourns the loss of her own child.

In, two, three, four. Out, two, three, four.

Too late to call the visit off. Her parents are already making their way up the East Coast from Florida.

So she will endure, comply as she always has, acting the part of the dutiful daughter. She will shield herself from their bad advice or disappointment by pretending that she is fine, that she and Royce are recovering nicely from their loss, even though she feels desperately lost and unhappy. The question now is not when her life is going to fall to pieces, but how. What is going to push her from her indolence into taking the action to separate and divorce?

She is not ready to go there yet. She has been with Royce for twelve years, married to him for six. He is her best friend. She loves him. Despite this recent infidelity, she can't imagine life without him. Not to mention the house in Hopewell and the condo in the city. She, who grew up in a middle-class home, has become used to the lifestyle he provides. She would never be able to make it on her own as a journalist. She is not even sure the paper will take her back after her long absence.

The snow falls heavier now, coating her in white. Her hair is frosted, and moisture forms where the warmth of her body meets the cold flakes. Her lips tremble as though she is saying a silent prayer. She stands like a statue in a garden, shrouded in white, frozen.

The back door opens and Royce looks out.

"What are you doing, Becca? Are you trying to kill yourself? You are going to freeze to death out there. Come in. I'll make a fire."

Obedient, she steps out of the snow.

"What were you thinking?" he says as he takes off her snowy robe and wraps her in a warm blanket and massages her back. She rubs the snow out of her hair with a towel. She is so cold, she feels dizzy and drunk.

"Coffee. I need some coffee," she says through chattering teeth.

"I'm on it. Let me get the fire started first."

She watches him crouch down near the hearth, crumpling papers, laying down fatwood, building an intricate pattern of logs as though he is playing Jenga. He strikes a match and the flames rise, slowly at first and then catching, rearing and sparking until the blaze has taken hold. She is mesmerized by the orange licks of light, by his half-naked body in the dark. But then she remembers the shirt, and when he puts his arms around her and draws her close to him, she recoils.

He raises his hands in surrender, rolls his eyes, snorts. He strides into the kitchen, fills the electric kettle with water, and dumps coffee into the French press, his actions clipped and deliberate. When the water boils, he pours it into the press and comes back into the living room.

Rebecca is too cold and tired for his angry energy. She braces herself, hugging her ribs tightly.

"How about I give you a foot rub while we're waiting for the coffee? I bet your toes are ice," he says, kneeling before her, removing her boots, and taking her right foot in his hand. "Yup. Ice. Sit." He clasps her elbow in his hand and leads her to the sofa.

She sits.

He massages her foot, caressing it with his fingers, stimulating the blood in it so Rebecca can feel her toes again. His touch is gentle and soothing. Then he does the same with her left foot. When he is finished, he rises and walks to the kitchen. He returns with a mug of coffee for her.

"This should warm you up. I've got to be in the office early for a meeting. Are you going to be all right?"

She nods, though she knows she is not all right. She is confused by his tenderness. How can he be so sweet and yet so cruel? She wonders if she is losing her mind.

"I've got Margot this morning," she says, remembering her appointment with her therapist.

"That's good. Can you get there on your own?"

His thoughtfulness crackles in the air, like the marbles she and Natalie used to fry in a hot pan and then dunk in ice-cold water. Natalie would claim the most beautifully cracked ones. When Rebecca objected and a quarrel ensued, Natalie would go crying to their mother, who always sided with the younger sibling, reprimanding Rebecca for not taking the higher ground. What their mother really wanted was silence so she could be left alone and drink as she pleased, without the hassle of two young girls.

Back then, despite their three-year difference, she and Natalie had bonded. They had played dress-up together, imagining themselves to be princesses and gypsies, and built fairy villages in the mossy woods behind their house using mountain-laurel blossoms as teacups, not knowing they were poisonous. They had jumped in piles of leaves in the autumn and sledded and skated together in the winter on half-frozen ponds. They had a secret world, full of unknown dangers, away from their mother, until Natalie turned five and the temper tantrums began.

Rebecca felt as if her soul had been ripped out of her. Natalie was suddenly the sole object of her mother's attention, as if she had been diagnosed with a fatal disease and her mother was trying to make up for wasted years. She even managed to get and stay sober throughout Natalie's youth and teenage years. From the time Rebecca was eight until today, including today, all eyes were on her younger sister. No matter that she disappeared a year ago, breaking her mother's heart.

Rebecca was left with the collateral damage. Grief. Loss. Powerlessness. She was left to take care of herself when she desperately wanted someone—her sister, her mother—to be there for her.

"Earth to Rebecca," Royce says, breaking into her thoughts. "Did you hear a word I said?"

"I'm fine. You don't need to worry about me," she snaps.

"Just trying to help. You don't have to get bitchy."

"Speaking of bitches—who were you with last night?" She can't help herself for asking but immediately regrets her words.

"For Christ's sake, Becca, you can't have it both ways."

"Then don't bring your souvenirs home with you," she says.

"What do you—"

She points at the shirt lying on the floor.

He picks it up. "So? It's my shirt."

"It reeks of her. It's like she poured a bottle of perfume on you. Who is she?"

He runs his hands through his thick, dark hair. "Becca, I honestly don't know. She was just a woman in a bar."

"And you picked her up and had sex with her."

"Becca—"

"Stop saying my name! Did you or did you not leave that shirt there purposefully to upset me?"

He looks at her, both exhausted and defiant. "I did not. Look, she must have poured perfume on it. I was drunk. I would never set out to hurt you. I thought when we agreed I was free to, you know, take care of myself elsewhere that you were okay with that."

She grips her coffee mug in both hands, brings it to her mouth and takes a sip.

"I was. I am. I thought I was. I'm so confused. Maybe I'm just crazy."

He comes over to the couch and sits beside her. "You are not crazy, Becca. Well, maybe you are a little bit crazy, but we can get through this. I know we can. It is just going to take time. I love you." He lays his hand on her inner thigh, starts to caress her.

She feels nothing. Not a stir of love. Not a flutter. She wonders if she has lost the ability to love him altogether or if she has put up a wall so thick that nothing can penetrate it. Maybe Margot can help her. At least piece her together so she can face the holidays with her family. She moves his hand away.

"She would have been seven months old today. Do you know what babies are doing at seven months? They can roll over, scoot around, sit up; some even crawl."

"You are torturing yourself. Stop."

"Don't you ever think about her?"

"I do, but I try not to."

"That's where we are different. I think about her every day. I never want to forget her. I want her to live in me always."

He takes her hand and rubs it lightly with his fingers. "She will always be a part of us. But she is gone, and we need to move forward. Maybe this is a good time to try again."

"Never," she says, pulling her hand abruptly out of his. "I'll never put myself through that again."

"Stop making everything about you, Becca."

Rebecca feels her jaw clench, her stomach tighten. And then that old, all-to-familiar feeling of shame. She blames herself for the two miscarriages she had early on in their marriage, for Juliet's being stillborn. If only she hadn't starved herself into anorexia when she was a teen. Over the past ten years, she has tried to treat her body well, but there seems to be no forgiveness for the damage done. She could blame this all on her mother who didn't get sober until Natalie was eight. As a young girl, Rebecca had lived with the active "isms" of her mother's disease, and the trauma had left a mark. So many marks. So many scars. So much work to be done.

"I'm trying, Royce. I really am."

"Try harder." Royce rises from the couch, looming over her. He grips her shoulder with his hand, digging into her flesh. His blue eyes are dull and menacing. "I have got to get ready for work." He leans down and kisses her brusquely on her mouth. "I'm keeping up my end of the deal, Becca. It's time you kept up yours."

Only when he leaves does she take a breath.

CHAPTER TWO

Princeton, New Jersey
Later that day

"Rebecca, come on in," a lean woman in jeans and knee-high Uggs motions to her. The woman's shoulder-length soft gray hair rests on the shoulders of her Icelandic sweater like a cloud over water. Rebecca enters an office with which she is very familiar. She knows the plump velour couch that greets her like a hug, the picture windows overlooking the now-frozen pond, the abstract paintings on the walls—great chunks of brown and blue and beige swimming together. The artwork contrasts with the homier décor of the room, the voluptuous lamps with rosy shades, and wrought iron statuettes of Buddha. Margot, her counselor, is nothing if not eclectic, and maybe that is why they get along.

Rebecca sits down, stares at her hands for a moment, scolding herself for the torn cuticles, the bitten nails. She lifts her head to look Margot in the eyes.

"I don't even know where to begin," she says, quickly extricating a tissue from the box on the table in front of her as her eyes begin to overflow with tears.

Margot watches patiently in silence as Rebecca blows her nose, wipes away the tears, and collects herself.

"Why is it that as soon as I come in here, I start crying? Every time."

"You feel safe."

Safe. She hasn't felt safe in months, not at home. She walks on eggshells around Royce, around herself. She is afraid that the slightest thing—an overcooked egg, a dripping faucet, laundry folded the wrong way—will upset the equilibrium they have created and send her world toppling, the Jenga blocks all falling down. She sees the fire he built this morning, herself standing outside in the snow, and the shirt reeking of perfume. She feels herself jerked from one emotion to another—tenderness, loneliness, rage—like she is on a subway train that is speeding around corners and sending her reeling, clinging on to the metal bars.

"He brought another woman home with him last night. This morning, really." She twists the soggy tissue in her hands, knowing she has purposefully told only half the truth.

"Go on."

"His shirt stank of perfume. From her. Whoever he was with."

"And that upset you?"

"Of course it did. Wouldn't it upset you?"

"Didn't you tell me you had an agreement with him that he could live his life however he chose, as long as you didn't have to have sex with him?"

Rebecca's shoulders tense, her jaw clenches. "Yes. I said that. We agreed. But I didn't expect him to rub my face in it."

"Yet you are the one who set the rules. You can't have it both ways. Either you are going to give him permission or you are not."

Rebecca tightens her fist around the wad of tissue, tosses it toward the wastebasket and misses. She starts to rise to pick it up but Margot puts out her hand.

"Leave it. I will get it later."

Silence slams a door shut between them. Rebecca wants to crawl under the covers and disappear, only there are no covers, no soft bed in which to hide. There are minutes left, ticking by, and she feels obliged to get her money's worth. Royce's money's worth because Royce pays for everything, keeps track of all she spends, dictates what she can and cannot purchase. She has turned her life over to him in an effort to keep him happy. But still, he is mercurial—at times he treats her like a princess, showering her with gifts and putting her on display before his friends, making her feel so special; but sometimes he is so mean and ugly, accusing her of things she never did, never even dreamed of doing. Blaming her for so many things that are out of her control.

"She would have been seven months old today. She would have been sitting, maybe crawling. I could have had her picture taken on Santa's lap. We all could have worn matching pajamas."

She is sobbing now, sniffing as she pulls more tissues from the box.

"But that is not what happened, is it?" Margot says. "She was stillborn."

Stillborn. Hearing those words come from Margot's mouth pierces Rebecca's heart. She wonders if she will shatter into a million pieces.

"When is it going to get better? When am I going to stop feeling like this, like it is all my fault?"

"You didn't do it, Rebecca. And you are not alone. Did you know that one in every one hundred and seventy-five births is stillborn? That each year more than twenty-one thousand mothers and fathers in the United States alone will go through what you are going through now?"

Rebecca looks at Margot fiercely. "That doesn't make it any easier."

"Of course not. I'm just saying that you have got to stop blaming yourself."

"Who do I blame then? God? What did I ever do to piss Him off so much that He would do this to me? To us? It's ruined my life. It's ruining my marriage. All I ever did was follow the rules, win all the prizes, marry the right guy. I have tried so hard."

Margot reaches across the table and takes Rebecca's hands into her own, looks deeply into her eyes.

"At some point, Rebecca, you are going to have to forgive yourself."

"For what?"

"For being born."

***

Driving back home from her counselor's, Rebecca does not feel a sense of relief. If anything, Margot sided with Royce, condoning his behavior and blaming Rebecca for bringing it on herself. And the baby, her Juliet? Margot reduced her to a statistic, diminished the impact that such a devastating event could have on a life. Her life. She told the receptionist she had forgotten her calendar and would need to make a follow-up appointment at another time. She has no intention of going back to

Margot. She served her purpose, getting Rebecca through those first six months of grief. But now, Rebecca can see where Margot's therapy will take her, down the slippery slope into her childhood, to root causes, and frankly, she doesn't have the energy or the desire to go there. She is going to handle this herself, as she has always done. She is smart. She is capable. What if she is a little crazy? Who wouldn't be after losing a child? She tells herself that everything is going to be all right. No one is going to hurt her anymore.

As soon as she gets home, she puts on her running gear and takes off on a run at Sourland Mountain. Gradually, over the past few months, she has been working her way back into fitness. The process has felt, at times, impossible because she has been so wracked with depression that some days she can barely get out of bed. But Royce has commented on her extra weight and made it clear that he expects her to reclaim her petite body if she hopes to be seen in public with him again. Not that she wants to attend the galas and openings he attends—with his eye toward making the society page. If she never rubs elbows with another celebrity or CEO, she will be fine. When she married Royce, she knew there would be socializing. What she hadn't anticipated was that he would treat her like a trophy, another victory in his catalog of successes. He expected her to look the part. If she didn't, if she were anything less than perfect, he would threaten to dump her, to replace her with a brighter, shinier version of her.

Why don't I share these thoughts with Margot? she asks herself as she finds her stride and the sweat begins to flow. Why does she keep the darkest parts of her life with Royce a secret? She tells herself that Margot won't understand, that she will take Royce's side and that will only exacerbate the feeling of shame that resides within her. She doesn't feel safe with Margot at all. But now, where can she turn? Who can she talk to? She knows enough to realize she can't keep this all bottled up in herself. Her mother used to talk about a Higher Power when she was active in Alcoholics Anonymous. Rebecca knows that "HP" is just a euphemism for God, and she is definitely not having anything to do with that. Not now. Not after all that has happened. She remembers a friend of her mother's saying that she believed in Nature. Rebecca can go with that. She only has to look at the light sparkling on the snow, which has covered the fields and piled up in the niches between the branches of the trees. A bright red cardinal darts by against the stark landscape. The air is still and peaceful; the only sounds are her running shoes crunching on the snowy road and the beating of her heart. She can definitely go with Nature. It is hard to stay depressed when she is running through all this. Still, she would love a friend to talk to.

When she lived in the city and worked for *The New York Times*, she had colleagues with whom she would spend time after work. One in particular, Lorelei Sanders, a seasoned investigative reporter from Long Island, took Rebecca under her wing. She mentored the cub reporter both professionally and socially. The efforts paid off. The Newswomen's Club of New York conferred the Front Page Award on Rebecca when she was twenty-eight. That was a golden time. But Royce grew jealous and became protective of their time together. He whisked her away to New Zealand, culminating in a week in Fiji; he distracted her with almost daily gifts—first editions of Jane Austen's novels, paintings by Marc Chagall, tickets to the Metropolitan Opera.

Royce had always been generous, since they first met. He bought her expensive gifts like cashmere coats and gold necklaces, sent extravagant bouquets of flowers that were the envy of the girls in the dorm, took her to the best restaurants for dinner. Rebecca, having been raised more modestly, was not used to such largess. She felt ambivalent about all the attention he showered on her. She asked herself, could she, *should she* be taken in by his material gifts? Wasn't love more than *things?* And the things he gave her reflected him, not what she truly loved or wanted. Except the flowers. She loved the flowers. How ungrateful she had felt questioning his generosity.

Over time, Royce had studied her, familiarized himself with her interests. His gifts became more attuned to who she really was, what she would really enjoy. She became addicted, in a way, to his presents. Every day was like opening a window on an Advent calendar. He wooed her and wowed her. Dizzied by his generosity, she let go of her career goals. Then he insisted that they marry, and her world became increasingly small and compact. He bought the farmhouse in Hopewell for her when she got pregnant the first time. When she miscarried, he demanded she slow down, take on a less exacting job, so she quit *The Times* and went to work for a local paper in Princeton. Lorelei warned her that she was committing professional suicide, but Rebecca was caught in the web of pleasing her husband, who provided for her so lovingly and well. She lost touch with her friends and focused only on satisfying Royce, trying to get pregnant again, and then work. After the second miscarriage, she began to lose hope of ever having a child, and yet she was so determined to give Royce the heir that he desired. She stopped following friends on Facebook because she couldn't stand to see the images of their new babies, month after month, and then second ones on the way.

When she became pregnant again, Royce demanded that she stop work entirely. He hovered over her when he was home, but many nights he chose to stay in their condo in the city. He said it was for work, but she suspected he was having an affair because he had ceased to request sex from her on the off chance that it might cause another miscarriage. He seemed to love watching her body grow, feeling the baby kick inside her belly, and yet there was disgust there too. He called her his "fat Mama" and spoke about the regimen she would need to follow to get back to her prepartum weight. Still, he showed her off with her baby bump at parties and boasted about another Winslow on the way. To carry on the family name. When he found out the baby was a girl, he was not thrilled. But he grew accustomed to the idea and even picked out the name Juliet for their child. He wanted her to have an auspicious name, with star quality: Juliet Winslow. What better choice than to name her after one of Shakespeare's most famous heroines? How could he have known that tragedy would ensue? When she was stillborn, he blamed it on Rebecca and withdrew, busying himself with work and leaving her to grieve on her own.

For six months they have been living like this, in a state of separation. Any time Rebecca says she's not ready to have sex again, he replies, "I know why you said that." But he really has no clue. He could not possibly know how confused she has been by his behavior, which has become more erratic and controlling over the years. He could not know how he made her feel when he blamed her for the baby's death. He could not know how lost and out of touch with herself she feels, as if she has no self at all.

A breeze shakes the trees, and a whiff of snow, which feels like gauze on her cheeks, brings her back into the moment. Nature. She can find peace in this moment if she only allows herself to be here, now. Margot asks her that a lot. "How is your now?" Now she is running on a quiet mountain road in the snow. There is light shining through the trees and making diamonds dance. She sees them sparkle. She enjoys their beauty. She is not captive of the depression that has held her prisoner for so many months. Not in this moment anyway. Fine particles of snow shaken from the trees fall on her face. She remembers trying to catch snowflakes on her tongue as a little girl. She smiles. A little girl. She wants a little girl.

Rebecca stops in the middle of the road, bends at her waist, and puts her hands on her knees. Without meaning to, she has given herself permission to hope, which rises in her like bubbles in a vintage Christmas light. She wants more than anything in the world—more than being loved unconditionally by her mother, or understood and adored by her husband; more than rising to the top of her career, or achieving fame and fortune—a baby. A baby would change everything.

Maybe Royce is right. Maybe they *should* try again. An offering for a new beginning. Her throat tightens as a lump forms and tears begin to flow. *Surely Juliet will forgive me. Surely she will understand.* Just as surely, she will forgive Royce his dalliances if he will help her overcome her fear of losing yet another child. Her doctors have told her stories of women who have suffered multiple miscarriages, even stillbirth, and gone on to carry healthy babies to term. Maybe that is the problem, *her* problem. She couples sex with pregnancy and that with loss. Maybe if she can just have sex with Royce for the sex of it, without intentions or outcomes, they can come together as partners again. But that is just it. They were never partners for sex. He has his fuck buddies for that. Her sole purpose, in Royce's eyes, is to provide an heir. One day, she *will* hold his baby in her arms. She can hope.

The cold sweat on her body chills her, but she feels warm, energized. She knows Royce won't be home for several hours, but she will use the time to prepare his favorite meal—boeuf bourguignon. She will pick up filet mignon from the butcher in town. Hopefully the market will have fresh peas to accompany the meal. She starts the long run home.

But when she gets home, Royce has left her a message. He forgot about the office Christmas party and expects to be late.

The message, though short, is layered with innuendo. This is the first Christmas party, in the twelve years they have been together, that he has not insisted she attend. In the past, he has always made a fuss over what she wore. He would come home from the city with a gown from St. Laurent or Gucci, with jewelry from Tiffany's to match, making sure she was dressed to the nines. Though she never felt like herself in these costumes—she preferred to wear sweats and T-shirts—she obliged him, hanging on his arm and making small talk with the other guests. That was the part she hated most—making small talk. She had nothing to offer the shallow conversations. Engage her in a literary discussion or an existential debate and she could shine, but Royce discouraged her from expressing her views about life, let alone anything that bordered on politics. They came from very different schools of thought on that, so they left subjects like politics alone and focused on the surface. The way she looked. How many of his cronies told him he was lucky to have such a "hot" wife. Funny to be thought of as hot. For so many years, Natalie outshone Rebecca's beauty.

She wonders who he will attach himself to tonight, for he is sure to find some woman to accompany him. He cannot be seen in public without some beautiful female on his arm, as if it is both his duty and his badge of manhood. Bette, Royce's mother, warned her early on in their marriage that she had better adjust to this reality about Royce or leave him while she still had little invested in the relationship.

"Royce is an attractive man, a very wealthy, attractive man. He is entitled to the attention he deserves from women. He has a lust for life that may not be satisfied by one woman alone. You should know that about him if you plan on continuing in this relationship," she said.

Rebecca had hoped that Bette was wrong, that she would be the one woman to whom Royce would dedicate himself. She believed when they took their vows that he would forsake all others for her. But *lust* was the operative word. A leopard can't change its spots, and when Rebecca swore abstinence from sex, Royce immediately sought pleasure elsewhere. At first it was endless hours of porn and jerking off, which he would report back to her as if to punish her. Then there were the nights when he was "working late" and, of course, the stinking shirt. Rebecca can see the writing on the wall. If she doesn't provide him with the heir he feels entitled to, then she is useless to him. At thirty-five, she is dangerously close to being past her prime for childbirth. She is sure he will replace her, throw her out on the grounds of irreconcilable differences, and she will be penniless in the street. Charles Dickens's narratives float past her consciousness. Is she like some character in a nineteenth-century novel? Will she end up like Jo in *Bleak House*, sweeping crossings to survive?

Anxiety rises in her like mercury rising in a hot thermometer. She needs to talk to someone, to move from triage into stability. The truth is, she has no friends. Once, long ago, there was Lorelei, and for a brief time, Royce. Now she has Margot, a woman she pays to listen to her sorrows, which seems pitiful. But though she swore she would not call Margot, she finds herself dialing the emergency number.

"Hello?" a voice says at the end of the line. It is Margot.

Rebecca immediately hangs up, praying that Margot didn't recognize her number. She doesn't really want to talk to Margot, who will only spout off some platitude or statistic. What she really wants is a friend who she can confide in. Someone she truly feels safe and comfortable with and to whom she can speak her truth. But what is her truth? The truth is she doesn't feel safe and comfortable with herself, her skin no longer fits, so how can she possibly feel relaxed around anyone else? She has learned this much from Margot: She needs to take responsibility for her own happiness. But how?

The words of Eleanor Roosevelt echo in her mind: "No one can make you feel inferior without your consent." That was Lorelei's mantra. She knows she needs to make it hers. She hears the words in her head, believes them intellectually, but realizes they have not yet made the transition to her heart. Her heart is hard and broken. What is it going to take to soften, to put the pieces back together again?

She stands up and looks out the living room window. The sun is setting and casts a silver sheen on the snow. The house is as cold and quiet as a tomb. The grandfather clock chimes the half hour, and she startles. It is going to be a long night.

CHAPTER THREE

St. Croix
December 22, 2022

The news of the dead man and the girl found by a morning jogger on one of the island's favorite beaches travels fast. Conversations in the marketplace are laced with speculation encouraged by the media, who swooped in to feed on the situation like a flock of carrion birds.

The police chief, an imposing man in his late sixties who towers over his peers, stands on the beach with two policemen, one the chief's age, the other much younger. They are surrounded by orange cones delineating where the bodies were found. The chief is not happy, and not just because he had been woken from his bed at an ungodly hour. Murder is not good business for a tourist spot like his island. He had hoped to keep reports of the murder toll to two for the year and dispel St. Croix's previous reputation of having a higher homicide rate than any nation in the world. He crumples the empty paper coffee cup in his hand, thrusting it at the young policeman.

"Dispose of this."

The young policeman jogs over to a metal trash can as the chief marches between the cones, making his way to the shore.

A strong breeze blows in off the water, the blue, blue water which kisses the white sand of the crescent-shaped beach. The midmorning sun is already high and blazing, tempered by the wind. He has lived in St. Croix all his life. He never grows complacent about its beauty, never takes it for granted. But then, something like this.

He knows that he will have to act quickly to banish the rumors that are already flying. That is his job—to preserve the surface peace, to protect grim reality from soiling the fantasy for which people pay dearly. Looking around at the tourists approaching the site, laden with beach umbrellas, totes, and coolers, he feels a sense of urgency to get things back to normal. But there was nothing normal about the black body bag strapped to the coroner's gurney. The other body, the girl, still alive, though barely, covered in a white sheet, her face concealed by an oxygen mask. Her long blond hair that hung down over the sides of the gurney as the first responders lifted her into the ambulance, closed the doors, and drove away. The scream of the siren that sounded so incongruous on such a beautiful day.

"Pick up the cones," he instructs the young policeman standing next to him.

"But Chief, what about the crime scene?"

"There is no crime scene. This was an unfortunate boating accident."

"Shouldn't we wait for the autopsy?"

"Are you telling me how to do my job?"

"No, sir."

"Good. Pick up the cones and get rid of that tape. I will handle the media. But first, our guests." The chief strides over to the group of tourists, some anxious, others purely nosy. He smiles, his teeth as white as lightning against his dark skin. "Friends," he says, extending his arms wide, "I regret that your day has been interrupted by such an unfortunate accident. These things happen. But now, our beautiful beach is yours! Enjoy the sunshine and the water! It is perfectly safe, I assure you. Such accidents are an anomaly on our island."

Satisfied with the chief's explanation, the crowd heads for the beach, intent on making the most of their vacations. The children gallop ahead, squealing, running straight for the water while parents laden with beach paraphernalia scout out a prime location to claim as their own. Umbrellas are planted and dot the white sand like bright flowers. Waves lap up onto the shore, propelled by unseen forces. The breeze, invisible to the eye, provides just the right temperature. Another day in paradise.

The chief knows differently.

CHAPTER FOUR

Princeton, New Jersey
December 23, 2022

Rebecca goes to the grocery store to pick up the provisions she will need to feed her family over the holidays. She is glad for the distraction of shopping lists and scouring the produce for the best-looking fare. The mundane act of filling her cart with rib roast, brussels sprouts, potatoes, beets, apples, and onions for Christmas dinner does not bring her joy, but it does give her space to experience a moment's peace.

But then there are the breakfasts and the lunches to be considered, and Christmas Eve dinner. She had a plan when she entered McCaffrey's—she would make shrimp scampi for Christmas Eve and a big green salad. However, the idea of peeling shrimp and yanking their little heads off disgusts her, and she decides to make a vegetarian chili instead. Surely they will have their fill of protein on Christmas.

She pushes her cart up and down through the crowded aisles, assaulted by the Christmas carols blasting from the store's audio system, which compete with the noise in her head. To make a trifle or not to make a trifle? Will her mother notice anything or will she be off the wagon again? Will Royce say anything, about the office party, the fact he never came home last night at all? Should she get a bottle of wine for Royce and her father? Should they even have booze in the house with her mother there? These thoughts circle round in her head, loud; a thousand voices are screaming at her.

There is no way she is going to get through this holiday without upsetting someone, she knows that already. She dreads their coming. She dreads the questions, the sorrowful looks, the hopeful hints that they should try again, that it's not too soon.

Most of all, she dreads her mother. Her father will spend the days reading or watching the sports channel. Accommodating as he is, he will indulge Royce by admiring her husband's newest acquisition—a custom shell to row in on Lake Carnegie. Royce was an Olympic-level rower in college, a fact that his mother, Bette, brings into any conversation. But most conversations Bette has revolve around Royce, his accomplishments, his achievements, as though he is a demigod. And always, there is the twisted barb at the end of the sentence that implies he settled for less when he married her. A girl from a middle-class family, no pedigree, and her mother a recovering alcoholic. No matter how many awards she wins for her writing or how many amazing holiday spreads she prepares, in Bette's eyes, Rebecca will never be good enough for Royce.

Now there is this: She can't even give him a child. Why Rebecca is thinking about Bette baffles her. Her mother-in-law isn't even going to be around for the holidays. She and her husband, Bill, will be with friends in Vienna, Austria, an invitation that trumped Royce's suggestion that they join the festivities at the farm. Rebecca is sure that when her mother-in-law heard Rebecca's parents would be there—

"Excuse me, miss, can you move your cart? I'd like to get in there." A young woman with a baby in the front of her shopping cart breaks into Rebecca's reverie. "I wouldn't normally say anything, but you have been standing there awhile, and this little guy is getting antsy."

Rebecca does not even know why she has stopped in front of the cold cereal boxes. Neither she nor Royce eats cereal.

"Are you all right?" the girl asks. "You look awfully pale, like you might faint. Can I get you some water?"

"No, no. I am fine. It is just overwhelming, you know. The holidays. My parents are coming."

The young woman nods knowingly as she reaches out and takes a giant box of Cheerios from the shelf.

"How old is he?" Rebecca says, looking at the baby in the cart. He has the face of a cherub, plump and dimpled, and a head of red hair. She smiles at him, and he breaks into a goofy smile, two small teeth showing.

"He's nine months. Can't get enough Cheerios."

Rebecca begins to tear up and quickly wipes her eyes. "He is beautiful."

"We think so. Do you have kids?"

"I did. She died."

The young woman's face crumples with concern. "I'm so sorry. Well, we had better get going. Merry Christmas."

Rebecca watches the young woman push her cart away as fast as she can, as if Rebecca's tragedy is contagious and she is afraid of catching the disease.

Sighing, Rebecca looks back at the cereal and remembers it is her father who likes almond granola in the morning, with honey and yogurt. She takes a box off the shelf and heads down the aisle toward checkout. She has had enough of this shopping for one day. If they need anything else, she will ask Royce to pick it up on the way home. All she wants to do is to sleep.

"Snap out of it," she says aloud.

An older woman, who happens to be passing by her as she speaks, looks at her suspiciously and moves her cart down the aisle.

Rebecca cringes, so uncomfortable is she in her own skin that she wants to tear off the outer shell of her being and replace it with something new.

Why can't I just be happy? she asks herself. *I should let go of these sad feelings, this constant reminder of Juliet's death. I should have sex with Royce again and make a trifle for Christmas Eve. I should—* She stops herself, hearing Margot's voice in her head. "Don't should on yourself." *I should not should on myself,* she tells herself, then laughs at the irony of the statement.

Another shopper looks at her askance, giving her a wide berth.

She wants to assure the stranger that she is not crazy, but honestly, she is not so sure of that herself.

Whatever.

She pushes her cart around the store, picking up ladyfingers, lemon curd, and custard for the trifle. Raspberries, kiwi, and heavy cream. She feels her heaviness lifting as she imagines the dessert coming together. She knows her father will be pleased.

Over the loud speaker, she hears Mariah Carey singing "All I Want for Christmas is You." What Rebecca wants this Christmas is for her life to stop aching, for everyone's lives to stop aching. The past year has been a nightmare with Natalie disappearing, Juliet dying, her mom picking up drinking again. Who would have thought last Christmas, when they were all together, when she was four months pregnant and Natalie was home from rehab, that life would look like this now? For one moment they were a happy family.

Life has a way of changing so suddenly, of taking such abrupt turns. For Rebecca, change is paralyzing. She thrives on routine. Actually, she is stifled by the need to control, and when things began to unravel in her life—when Natalie took the only job she could find, as a waitress at the Crazy Horse, and was soon using drugs and alcohol again—she felt life pulling at the frazzled edges of her reality.

What was her reality? Rebecca had declined, at Royce's insistence, to let Natalie stay with them until she found a room in a sober house. Instead, her sister had found some not-so-healthy roommates. If she hadn't done that, Natalie might not have taken the job at the bar, might not have picked up again, might not have left for the islands with that mystery man. Rebecca might not be the villain her mother made her out to be, as though she had been personally responsible for Natalie's fall and subsequent disappearance. Rebecca's reality was based on other people's interpretations of what had gone on. It was not fair. Nor was it based on the history their family shared together.

Growing up, Rebecca was always quiet and obedient. Her father teased her that she was old before her time. He said she was "so ripe she would fall off the vine." She didn't know what he meant at the time, but she knows now that her seriousness, her overdeveloped sense of responsibility, and her desire to control stem from the fact that her mother was an active alcoholic when she was young. That much she has learned in her conversations with Margot. Then Natalie came along. The baby of the family. She was, from birth, a wild child. She had tantrums as a young girl, setting everyone's nerves on edge with her rants and screaming.

One day, when Natalie was just eight years old and acting particularly belligerent and defiant, her mother threw a glass of wine in her face, just to stop her. Rebecca could still see the blood-red stain on Natalie's white mock turtleneck and the shock on her mother's face when she realized what she had done. Shortly after that, her mother went away on "vacation," her father told them, though Rebecca later learned her mother had been admitted to a treatment center for alcoholism in Minnesota and stayed there for twenty-eight days.

Mom came back sober and learned to handle Natalie's outbursts, which continued throughout her teen years. While Rebecca was applying herself in school and preparing to head off to Yale, the first in her family to enter an Ivy League college, Natalie was sneaking off at night, smoking dope in the bathroom at school, and engaging in sex at an early age. The thing was—she got away with it because she was beautiful. Model beautiful. Slender, with long golden hair to her waist and wide green eyes. Rebecca was attractive too, though she would grow into her sultry beauty as she aged, but she was not a traffic stopper like Natalie. Forget that Natalie's role model was Janis Joplin, that she stayed in bed on Saturday mornings until noon, waking only to light a Camel cigarette and pour herself a glass of bourbon from her secret stash. To her father, Natalie could do no wrong. She had him, and most of the men and boys she came into contact with, wrapped around her pinky finger.

Rebecca did not have it so easy. She had to work hard to be appreciated, even noticed.

Margot once asked her if she was glad Natalie had disappeared. In a way she was, yes. Before that, after Natalie had returned from rehab, their mother had once again devoted all her attention to the younger sibling. But after her sister left, for four months before Juliet's death, she did not have to compete with Natalie for her mother's attention. All eyes were focused on the baby to be born, the grandchild on the way. What Rebecca had not anticipated was the negative attention Natalie would claim with her sustained disappearance, the grief that would consume her mother and ultimately lead her back to booze.

When her father called and told Rebecca that her mother had "fallen off the wagon" and was going into treatment again, this time in Florida, Rebecca felt an anger well up inside her that she had not experienced in a long time. If ever. She was not mad at her mother. She knew enough about the disease of alcoholism from her brief stint in Adult Children of Alcoholics (ACOA) to accept her mother's relapse not as an inevitability but a probability. It was Natalie whom she was furious with, for placing her mother in a precarious state that led her to want to self-destruct. Maybe she was a little bit mad with her mother too, when she realized her mother had not fallen to pieces at Juliet's death. Instead, her mother had been the rock on which Rebecca had leaned for those first couple of months. But that support dried up as summer and fall came and went with no news of the younger daughter. Her mother grieved over her own loss and worried herself into a state of self-pity and isolation which only had one possible remedy: alcohol. Even after all her years of sobriety, she was still a victim of Natalie's power.

Rebecca wonders how her mother will be this holiday. Will she cast a pall over the celebration? Will she join Royce in bringing shame and regret to the Christmas table where there should only be happiness and joy? There will be no Hallmark moments to record; of that, Rebecca is sure. Sometimes she wishes the police would come to the door and tell her Natalie is dead. At least there would be closure.

"How can I be so cruel?" she says aloud. This is how far the depth of her anger and resentment goes. She had no idea she could be so unkind. But life can do that, chip away at you. Not every rock conceals a gorgeous marble statue inside. Sometimes, when the rock is struck, it just crumbles and leaves a pile of rubble behind. That is what her life feels like now—a pile of rubble. A heap of stones she wants to hurl at the universe for being so unfair. A boulder she would launch at Natalie were she to walk in the door.

CHAPTER FIVE

Rebecca is vacuuming the living room rug when she gets a call from her father.

"Hey, sweetheart." It is her mother's voice, though the call is coming in from her father's phone. "We have made good time, better than we expected. We are only an hour or so away. Do you mind if we descend on you a little early?" Her mother's voice sounds bright, sober. If she is feeling any shame over her relapse, she is not letting on.

"Of course not," Rebecca says. "Just be aware I may not have everything ready …."

"I can help you. I'd like to help you."

Her mother's offer makes Rebecca cringe. They have very different ideas about how to do anything in the kitchen or around the house. Her mother is the kind of cook who thinks recipes are just suggestions and who does not wash her hands after throwing something in the garbage. She does not make beds with tight hospital corners but rather just pulls the covers up, pats the duvet smooth, and calls it done. She is not a slob; she is a free spirit who believes that all children should eat a little dirt every day to build up their immune systems. Rebecca has even caught her mother slicing mushrooms into a spinach salad before wiping the dirt off of them. And practicing the sixty-second rule. Rebecca imagines that, to her mother, she must seem neurotic with her fastidious cleanliness, her attention to detail. She hopes her mother will not be hurt if she refuses her help, suggests that she sit in a chair by the fire.

"That would be nice, Mom. I would like that," she hears herself say.

"Great! We'll see you soon!"

Why does she do that? Say what she doesn't mean to say just to keep the peace? Margot calls her a people pleaser, a common symptom of an adult child of an alcoholic. Great. Now she will have her mother in the kitchen with her chopping vegetables into large, healthy chunks instead of tiny, diced squares for the white bean chili she is planning to make for dinner. What will they talk about as they stand shoulder to shoulder, women doing women's work while the men step outside in the snow to smoke cigars or do whatever it is they do to amuse themselves? She will not know what to say to her mother. She cannot ask about her stay at the rehab in Florida. Her father has cautioned her not to bring up the subject of the relapse unless her mother brings it up first. And what does she have to share about her own life? *I am not doing anything. I am not working. Not writing. Not having sex with my husband. I am grieving, and it is eating me alive.*

"Oh my God, I am so tired of *me*!" she yells over the whining roar of the vacuum. "Can't somebody help me?"

She wishes she were Freddie Mercury, up on stage in front of thousands of fans, able to scream her heart out. "Why can't *she* find somebody to love?" She turns off the vacuum and drops it on the floor, picks up her phone, and types QUEEN in her browser window. She listens to the chords of the piano, the harmony of the voices, and Freddie belting out the refrain. But it is not loud enough.

She shouts at her smart speaker. "Play Queen 'Somebody to Love'!" When the music comes on, she feels an ache in her heart that is different from the excruciating pain she felt when the baby died. "Increase the volume to eight!" The music blasts out of the speaker; she feels the bass throbbing inside her, a painful throb where once she held a child. She aches, longs for something to fill the void. The truth is, she does not want someone to love. She wants someone to love *her*. To pour their heart and soul out for her. To put themselves at death's door for her. She has never felt that she was really valued, that she ever really mattered to her sister, her mother. Even her dad, because he seemed to spread his love equally between them in a distracted sort of way. What she wants from her mother when she comes is her undivided attention. She wants her to listen, to hear all the anguish Rebecca is going through. But Rebecca knows that such a conversation will never come to pass.

She will put up her old defenses against being hurt by her mother's indifference. She will ask questions, place the focus on her mother as she retreats further and further back into the dark cave where she lives, invisible.

The phone rings. It is Royce.

She turns off the music and answers the phone. "Hello?"

"Hey there. What are you doing? You sound all out of breath."

"Vacuuming."

"I told you we should have hired a cleaning lady. You don't need to be wasting your time and energy on that shit."

Rebecca prides herself on the care she takes of her own home. It is the one thing she does and does well. For him to call it "that shit" hurts her. She recognizes he does not value anything she brings into the relationship.

"I'm sorry. That came across differently than I meant," he adds. "I know you pride yourself on the way you keep the house, and I am appreciative. It's just that we can certainly afford a cleaner. I'd rather you spent the time taking care of yourself."

"It is not about the money, Royce. Anyway, let's not get into that now. Mom and Dad are going to be here in an hour."

"That is way earlier than expected." There is a stiffness in his voice.

"They made good time. You are not going to be late again, are you? You promised …."

"No. I am leaving the office now. I just wanted to see if there was any last-minute thing you wanted me to pick up."

She bites her lip to keep from crying. She has been here, in this exact place, so many times before. He does something cruel, unthinkable—like not coming home, which raises so many fears in her mind—and then he becomes all sweet and helpful, glossing over his bad behavior. In the past, she has fallen back into the trap, let her guard down, trusted him—until he has slammed her again with some explosive outburst over an inconsequential thing like not stacking the dishwasher the way he thinks it should be done or forgetting to fill up the gas in his car.

"You know I rely on you to keep the tank filled," he shouts as he stomps around the house, slamming doors and kicking furniture out of his path. "It's a simple thing. I don't ask much of you. Even a moron can check the gauge and see that it's close to empty."

His words sting her. He becomes so volatile over the littlest things. She has learned to tread lightly around him, follow his instructions, meet his demands so she does not upset him.

She hates it when he yells at her. She wants to put her hands over her ears and scream. Run away. And yet, she stands there frozen as he fumes, spit flying from his mouth, telling her she is crazy, lazy, stupid, useless. Invisible.

His rages have become worse since they stopped having sex. She knows that she used to appease him. A blow job or some rough intercourse could diffuse the explosion. But since she has kept him from her bed, she has watched his anger rise, the way she watches the electric kettle in the morning, the bubbles rising slowly from the bottom until they erupt at the top, a roiling mass. That is why she gave him "permission" to find someone else to screw: so he could let the steam off elsewhere. Though she suspects he has been doing that all along.

Of course, he had to rub her face in it, leaving his shirt on the floor that way. He likes to watch her get upset and thrown off balance. That is his way of keeping the upper hand. He takes perverse pleasure in causing her pain. She has seen his expression, an artificial Buddha-like smile as he watches her rant and rage at his behavior. It's the look she imagines is pasted on his face when he watches porn and has just cum. This is emotional porn. He takes pleasure in hurting her just so he can make up and get all sweet again, as he is now on the phone. Acting as if nothing has ever happened between them. The only silver lining she can find in this dark cloud is that he has never abused her physically. Not yet, anyway.

She grips the phone so tight that her fingertips turn white. Her jaw is tight. Her jaw is always tight.

"Becca? Are you still there?" he asks.

"Yes. Just thinking."

"Don't exert yourself."

"I have everything covered."

"Are you sure? The stores won't be open tomorrow. You don't want to be caught short."

"I have it covered."

"All right then. I'll see you soon. When did you say your parents were arriving?"

"In less than an hour now."

"I'll plan accordingly." By which he means, she is certain, he will take the long way home.

***

The winter sky is silver dappled with pink clouds illuminated by gold as the day closes in on itself, casting a rosy glow on the newly fallen snow. The view from the picture windows in the living room could be a Wyeth painting, as idyllic as it is—the snowy fields with stalks of golden grass jutting through, the big red barn with a frosted roof, the gnarled apple trees with a few withered apples dangling like Christmas ornaments.

"You have a lovely place here," her mother says as she stands by the fireplace, looking around.

"You have been here before, Mom."

"Yes. But I still find it lovely, maybe lovelier than before. It must be the snow. The sunset. The Christmas tree."

Rebecca pours hot water into a mug to brew a cup of hibiscus tea for her mother. "Christmas does have a way of doing that."

"Doing what?"

"Helping you experience magic."

"I'm so glad you still believe in magic."

Rebecca does not want to tell her mother that for her, the magic is gone. She has only gone through the exercise of making the house look "holiday perfect" to satisfy Royce.

Looking around, though, she sees why her mother might be taken in. Rebecca has lit a fire in the fireplace, and it crackles merrily. The tree, decorated in white lights and gold-and-silver ornaments, is classy. Tasteful. As are the lighted swags over the doorways, on the mantel, and curling up the banister to the second floor. Classical Christmas music plays softly in the background, and balsam candles send a woodsy scent into the air. She has created a holiday oasis.

"So Mom, how are you doing?" she asks.

"Well. Very well. As much as I wish I hadn't relapsed, I can see the value of the experience. I gained some insight into things."

Rebecca is not sure she wants to go deeper into this conversation. Her mother has been in the room for five minutes, and already the discussion is trending toward group therapy. "Where is Dad?" she asks.

"He's bringing in the bags and the presents from the car."

"Presents? Mom, I specifically asked you not to bring presents," she says, yanking the teabag out of the hot water.

"I know, Rebecca, but I couldn't resist. They aren't big presents. Just a few little things to put under the tree."

Rebecca brings the tea over to her mother. "I wish you had not done that, Mom. Royce and I are not even giving each other presents!"

"What's this about presents?" her father's voice booms as he walks in the door, laden with luggage and shopping bags filled with brightly colored packages.

"Mother! Daddy! Did you have to?" she scolds.

"Well, hello to you too, sweetheart! How about you give your old dad a hand with all this?"

"You should not have done this."

"We wanted to," her mother says as she rests her mug of tea on the table and begins to unpack the gifts, arranging them under the tree. When she is finished, she stands up and puts her hands on her hips. "There," she says. "Much better."

Rebecca takes her father and the suitcases to the guest room on the first floor.

"I hope you don't mind the smaller room," she says to her father. "I thought I'd save you from climbing the stairs."

"Not a problem. And I hope you don't mind all the fuss. I told her not to. I told her you wouldn't like it."

"It's all right. I would not expect anything else from her."

"She's doing well, Rebecca. She's trying very hard. Be gentle on her."

"I will."

"You seem tired. Is everything all right?"

"I am. Both tired and all right."

"Well, don't think you need to entertain us. I'm good with a book in front of the fire."

"Thanks, Dad."

"Oh, and that's another thing. Your mother wants you to start calling us Dorothy and Jack."

"What?"

"It's some therapy thing she picked up in rehab. She says it's time to break the bonds of parenthood and all become adults together."

"Whatever you say, Jack. Though that feels really awkward and weird."

Her father puts his arm around her. "Attagirl. I knew I could count on you."

Rebecca does not want to be counted on. She wants someone *she* is able to count on for support, especially her mother. That is really all she has wanted throughout her life—a mother who will erase all the bad feelings she has about herself. Her inferiority. The feeling that she has never been enough, that she is damaged goods. Only a mother's unconditional love could smooth out those wrinkles in her personality and leave her feeling whole. Is that asking too much? Perhaps. She knows that her parents, her mother especially, are flawed human beings. They stumble. They fall. And she tries to forgive them. But can she forgive herself for needing them to be her anchor, to provide stability, security, and hope? If her parents are suddenly to be just friends—with all the accompanying impermanence and superficiality that implies—she will never experience the mother love she has longed for all her life. That door will be shut forever.

CHAPTER SIX

Hopewell, New Jersey
Christmas Day

The snow has been falling all night and the day before, and a foot of white stuff covers the ground. Rebecca looks out the bedroom window across the fields where now, just tips of grass peek up through. She takes off her pajamas, puts on her running gear, and heads downstairs as quietly as she can so as not to wake Royce. But the old floorboards on the stairs are creaky, and her steps echo like shots in the morning stillness.

Royce appears at the top of the stairs. "Where are you going?" he says.

She feels called out, like she has done something wrong. "I'm just going out for a run."

"What about breakfast? It's Christmas."

"I will make it when I get back. No one will be up for a while, I imagine. I won't be long." Her words slice at her throat; she winces, struggling to speak her truth.

"Be careful out there," he says. "Even though Rafael plowed, it's likely to be pretty slick."

"I will be," she says and leaves.

She heeds his warning and steps gingerly down the stairs by the back door. She stretches, reaching as far as she can into the gray sky, and then bends over her shins, pushing them out behind her. Then she eases herself into a lazy gait as she takes off down the long driveway to the road that cuts up into Sourland Mountain. The snow has stopped, but a light breeze blows puffs of sparkling flakes across her path and into her eyes. The sun is just coming up, lending strokes of peach to the gray background behind the stark silhouettes of the trees. She runs, more quickly now, feeling heat build in her arms and legs, even as the freezing air turns her cheeks a rosy pink. This is what she has needed—to get out into the air and breathe, deeply, so deeply it hurts her chest. She needs to start the day off on a positive note, to counter all the negatives that fight to take her over. It's Christmas. The first Christmas since Natalie vanished. Every Christmas for years has been overshadowed by a celebration of her younger sister's birthday. Growing up in a nonreligious home, they had made this day a different kind of special. Why couldn't she have grown up in a normal family with traditions like stockings and presents opened on Christmas Day? Instead, December 25 was all about Natalie. She is sure her mother will be feeling the loss of her little girl today. The loss of her own little girl ...

Don't let yourself go there. Look at the road covered in a thin layer of snow from where the plow has gone through. A path without blemish, only the footprints you leave behind. Look at the snow sifting down off the trees, shaken by winter birds that dart and rest and fly again in the quiet of the woods. Breathe in the cold and exhale warm air through your nostrils that pinch closed every time you breathe in. Focus on this moment. Find peace.

She runs along, practicing her meditation, seeking illusive serenity to fuel her for the day. She is sure her mother will have moments today when Rebecca will be asked to listen and support, even though she, too, is suffering. But if she can just stay neutral, stay as quiet as these woods are now with only the squeaky sound of one branch rubbing on another, or her feet meeting the snow, she will make it.

The woods are lovely, dark and deep,
But I have promises to keep,
And miles to go before I sleep,
And miles to go before I sleep.

She loves that poem, "Stopping by Woods on a Snowy Evening," by Robert Frost. And so many others that give her solace. W. B. Yeats's "Lake Isle of Innisfree" comes to mind. But it doesn't fit the season, so she turns back to Frost instead.

The only other sound's the sweep
Of easy wind, and downy flake.

She determines that she will focus on cooking and cleaning and cooking some more. They can play board games and watch a holiday movie. There are a hundred ways to stave off the holiday blues, and she is emersed in one of them right now. What is it Margot says? "Move a muscle, change a mood." Right now, she is awed by the beauty around her as the sun makes its way higher into the sky. The snow all around her sparkles like jewels. *I can do this. Nothing is going to ruin my day. Not Royce. Not Mom or Natalie.* She runs back down the mountain road toward home. As she does, the sky clouds up and more snow begins to fall.

When Rebecca opens the back door, stomping the snow off her feet, she is greeted by Dorothy, who walks into the living room in her red plaid pajamas and green chenille robe. "Good morning," she yawns. "What's going on? Where were you?"

"Merry Christmas, M—Dorothy. I just took a run."

"In this snow? That's dedication." Dorothy comes over to Rebecca and stands next to her. "Hug?"

"I'm sweaty."

"I love you just the way you are."

Rebecca feels her stomach tighten as her mother wraps her arms around her. *Is this love really for me, or is it for the empty space Mom must feel inside?* Rebecca wishes she could just turn off her head and accept the hug as a hug, not turn it into an opportunity for psychological evaluation.

"Jack still sleeping?" Rebecca asks.

"Like a baby. Don't you hear him snoring?"

"He always was a walrus. Coffee?"

"Love some."

The electric kettle heats in minutes. Rebecca pours boiling water into the French press. "Give it four minutes."

Dorothy walks over to the paperwhites and leans in to smell them. "I love these. Especially at this time of year."

"Me too."

"Now those phallic amaryllis you can keep … What the fuck is up with those?"

Rebecca shakes her head at her mother. "Here, sit. Have some stollen."

"You're breaking into the stollen now? Don't you want to wait for breakfast?"

"No. Royce hates stollen. He 'discourages' me from making it. Won't allow it at the Christmas table. He must have his Wolferman's cinnamon buns."

"He certainly is bossy."

Rebecca takes a sip of her coffee. "It's Christmas. Let's talk about something happy."

The two women sit on the sofa next to each other, sipping coffee from Christmas mugs that sport red gnomes. The fire Royce built while she was out crackles nicely in the fireplace. Rebecca gets up, adds a couple of logs, sets the blaze burning higher, and then settles herself on the sofa again. At first, she is at peace with the silence—the muffled whiteness of the world outside, the quiet of the world within, but after a few minutes, thoughts begin to swirl in her head. Something happy. It hasn't been a happy year. Losing Juliet and Natalie. Her mom's relapse. Her own depression and decline. She is determined not to go there, not to dwell on that today. But today is Natalie's birthday, and there is no way around that. Surely her mother must be feeling something.

"So how are you doing, Mom? Really."

"You don't need to mother me, Rebecca. I'm fine. Good. Really good."

"Are you really, Mom?" She hesitates to bring up the elephant in the room but plows ahead anyway. "It is her birthday today."

Dorothy's smile vanishes. She sighs, exhaling any joy that she had been grasping on to. She suddenly seems very old and very tired.

"I just wish I knew if she was still alive. I want to believe she is."

Rebecca grips her coffee cup tightly. "Of course she is, Mom. Dorothy. We would have heard something if she wasn't. Someone would have gotten in touch."

"You think? On TV shows, maybe. The FBI always manages to figure out who the parents are. But how many kids are out there who die as a John or Jane Doe? Dead from overdoses in back alleys? Anonymous? The statistics are shocking."

"What about the detective you hired? Hasn't he found out anything?"

Dorothy shakes her head. "Nothing. It's a dead end." Dorothy wipes at tears that have begun to flow.

"Maybe we shouldn't talk about this right now. Not this morning," Rebecca says.

"No, it's good. I need to face the truth. To accept that she may be gone forever. It's not like we didn't see this coming. She always was such a wild child. Not like you. You were always so good, Rebecca. You never gave us any trouble. I don't know that I have ever told you how much I appreciated that. How much both your father and I appreciated that."

Tears spring to her eyes, and Rebecca heads out toward the kitchen.

"More coffee?"

"I'd love some."

Her mother gets up from the sofa and follows her daughter. They stand by the counter, waiting for the electric kettle to boil. Rebecca stares at the ring of blue lights at the base of the glass kettle, feeling her mother's presence so close to her. She is anxious over what her mother might say next.

"You know, Rebecca, I never was a very good mother to you because you were so self-sufficient. You didn't seem to need me. But Natalie, my God, Natalie required so much attention. I tried my best to be there for you at all the important moments, but I realized in treatment that you needed me there for the moments in between too. I'm so sorry I wasn't there for you. Can you forgive me, baby?"

Baby. Her mother hasn't called her baby. Ever. Rebecca looks at the little bubbles that have started to rise in the kettle. She waits for them to erupt into a rolling boil and for the kettle to click off before she pours the water into the French press. She does not know how to respond. She knows this is her mother making amends, taking a Ninth Step, a very important part of her recovery. But somehow, Rebecca had hoped that when her mother came to her, there would be more. More of a recognition of her own deficits and less laying on Rebecca that it was *her* fault, that she brought on her mother's indifference by her own self-sufficiency. Rebecca made it easy. She greased the path for her mother to slide into a preoccupation with Natalie by her own withdrawal and control. At least, that is what her mother is implying.

What Dorothy doesn't know, couldn't know, was that all throughout the sisters' childhood and adolescent years, all Rebecca yearned for was the attention that Natalie received. She tried to compensate for her sister's bad behavior by striving for perfection. She excelled in all areas of her life—academically, artistically, athletically. She was the lead in every school play, the solo in every recital, captain of every varsity team, and valedictorian of her graduating class. She went to Yale on a hefty scholarship and then to the Columbia School of Journalism. By the time she was twenty-five, she had landed a job as a writer for *The New York Times*. She married Royce Winslow, grandson of the billionaire Nicholas Winslow. Her life, from the outside, has been a fairytale.

But inside is the void, the hole that only love can fill. She has never felt that love from her mother. Her father was kind, but rarely home. Royce, her first and only love, has proven to be as cruel as he is charismatic. And God, if she believes in God at all, has cursed her with two miscarriages and a stillborn, denying her the chance to love another human being as she desires to be loved.

Forgive her mother? How can she find it in her heart to forgive her mother, or Royce, or God? Yet she finds herself hugging her mother, in the kitchen, as they both shed tears—one because she thinks she has made peace with her daughter; the other because the void she has felt all her life is still there, a black well with no bottom.

It is only a matter of time before she falls in.

CHAPTER SEVEN

St. Croix
Christmas Day

The chief is alone on Christmas, as he has been for the past twenty years since his divorce. Old memories visit him, as they do every December 25, the ghosts of Christmas past. He made choices then, bad choices, that lost him his wife and daughter. At the time, he saw no other way. He is not sure he could have done things differently.

Today he has a purpose: to watch the girl who lies in a coma in the hospital. It isn't really his job, but the young policeman on whom the duty fell has a family, with young ones at home. Let him believe that the chief magnanimously offered to fill in so he could spend the holiday at home. The truth is, the chief needs answers, and he wants to be in the hospital room should the girl wake up. He sits on a chair next to the girl's bed. He listens to the wheezing breath of the machines that are keeping her alive. The miracle of science—wires attached to monitors displaying waves of green that signify someone is still alive in there, behind the swollen eyes, beneath the bruises that have spread like blossoms on her cheeks. Even with the breathing tube, the discoloration, the pallid skin, he can see she is a pretty girl. More than pretty—beautiful. Such a downfall for a young woman. He has seen so many who vacation here, barely more than girls, naïve about the danger that beauty yields. They are easily seduced due to their own vanity, an infatuation with self that is smug and blind to the possibility of evil. They drink and drug and sex indiscriminately, heedless of the consequences.

"What were you up to?" he asks the girl, not expecting an answer. "How did you become involved with a such a man? Were you just there to party, or is there more?"

The machines bleep monotonously in the quiet room.

"What did you see?"

This is the question the chief most wants the answer to. He doesn't really care about the beautiful girl and what brought her here. He needs to solve the murder. They expect him to.

CHAPTER EIGHT

New York City
December 26, 2022

Christmas passes as Rebecca imagined, in an ebb and flow of preparing meals, doing dishes, setting the table, and making small talk to avoid the potentially hot issues of politics, religion, and sexual orientation. The following day, they take her parents into the city to look at all the window displays along Fifth Avenue. They taxi down to Rockefeller Center to see the Rockettes and gaze on the magnificent Christmas tree all covered in lights with skaters circling and swirling on the rink below. Then back up to The Plaza for tea. One final treat—tickets to *Hamilton* on Broadway. After an exhausting day of sightseeing, they spend the night in the condo, where Royce has arranged for a catered after-theatre dinner, which impresses her mother. Her father does not say a word. With each extravagant gesture on Royce's part, Rebecca's father clamps more tightly shut. She senses how uncomfortable her father, who has worked so hard all his life just to maintain their middle-class lifestyle, must feel. As if the Winslows are royalty and everyone else is commoners. Royce relishes lording his wealth over people and making them feel small. And he has done it again at Christmas.

"Rebecca, did you hear me?" Royce's stringent voice calls her back from her reverie. "Earth to Rebecca. Time to serve up dessert," he says.

Obediently, she rises from her seat and begins clearing the dinner plates from the table. Her mother rises to help.

"No, Mom, please don't. I can do this."

"I would like to help."

"It's best if you just sit down. I can handle this."

"She's right, Dorothy," Royce says. "Too many cooks in the kitchen, you know. Besides, this is part of Becca's job description." Royce laughs at his own joke, but no one joins in. Rebecca sees the fury in her father's eyes as Dorothy pats his hand gently.

***

She wakes the next morning—earlier than all the others—dons her running gear, and sets out for a run around Central Park. She is back in forty-five minutes, having done the requisite five miles. The condo is quiet when she returns, though it is now past eight. Early enough for her to call Margot, who is always in the office at the crack of dawn.

She pours herself a glass of water, grabs her phone, and heads into the den. If anyone does wake, she can still have privacy. Though if Royce catches her in there, he is sure to reprimand her. Her stomach churns with a curious excitement, as though she is about to do something bad, forbidden. Spilling the family secrets. Airing the dirty laundry in public. Well, not in public, exactly. Just to her therapist.

She dials the number, which rings several times. Then she hears Margot's voice. "Greetings! You have reached Margot Fischer, LCSW. I am out of the office until January third. If this is an emergency, please hang up and call 911. If you would like to leave a message, please wait for the beep. But be aware that I will not check my messages until January third. Happy Holidays!"

Rebecca waits for the beep. She considers leaving a message, but she fears it might sound too scathing or needy, so she just hangs up.

Royce's desk is covered in files, an indication of the number of projects he has going on, which he never talks to her about. She knows that she shouldn't pry, but her curiosity gets the better of her. She glances at some of the labels. As she suspected, they all deal with investment companies, real estate, philanthropy, import/export—except for one, which reads *Stables*.

Has Royce expanded his ventures into racehorses and betting? Rebecca wonders. *I wouldn't be surprised.*

She starts to open the folder when her mother appears in the door to the den.

"There you are. I was hoping to find a cup of coffee."

Rebecca quickly closes the file, replaces it, and leads her mother back into the kitchen to make coffee.

"Morning, Dorothy. I'll take care of that," Rebecca says as she fills the kettle with water from the tap.

"How's my girl today? Looks like you have already been for a run."

"Yes. Every morning. It's my therapy." That and other therapy. She doesn't need to go there with her mother, who will no doubt turn the information into a conversation about herself, but she finds herself speaking anyway. "I have a therapist," she says.

"You're in therapy?" her mother laughs. "Well, join the club! I think that is great. You can work through some of the baggage of your childhood—"

"Mostly we talk about Juliet."

"Of course," her mother says, sinking back into the sofa cushions. "Of course you do. That is going to take time. I know, because that is what I mostly talk about with my therapist. Losing Natalie. And how that excruciating loss can trigger our own most self-destructive behavior."

Rebecca clutches her mug tightly. "Mom. Dorothy. Can we not do this? Can we not dive deep into an agonizing conversation? We only have a couple of days together. Can we just focus on the fun stuff?"

Her mother looks at her, reaches out her hand and pats the sofa beside her, inviting Rebecca to sit down. "Of course. I'm sorry. I'm so intense at times. Of course, we can focus on just the happy stuff. You were always so good at that."

Her mother's comment pierces her like a knife. *You were always so good at that*, at that denial that there was anything wrong in her life, their lives, their relationships. She plastered a smile on her face as a young girl in order to survive the pain that she felt. That mask served her then, but it didn't serve her anymore, and the process of ripping it off—slowly, bit by bit, acknowledging that her life never was so rosy, nor was it rosy now—was possibly the most difficult thing she ever had to do.

"There's that crease between your brows, Rebecca. You know that makes you seem years older than you are."

Go to hell, Mother, she wants to say. Instead, she smiles.

"I'm going to go take a shower and wash it away."

CHAPTER NINE

Hopewell, New Jersey
December 28, 2022

When her parents have left them and the house is again painfully void of sound, except for the crackling of the fire in the hearth, Rebecca plops down into the deep cushions of the sofa in front of the fire, a glass of Chardonnay in her hands. Royce looks at her from over his reading glasses. He has been catching up on *The New York Times Sunday Edition* and is hard at work on the crossword puzzle, which he insists on completing in ink.

"You're drinking? Since when?" he says.

"There was just this little bit left over from the weekend."

"You never drink."

"I thought it might relax me."

"You had better watch yourself. I don't want you following in your mother's footsteps."

"It's just one glass of wine."

"Suit yourself." He turns back to the crossword.

The room is fiercely quiet, so quiet Rebecca feels it might implode. There is so much space between her and Royce, unspoken expectations and regrets, the air is electric.

"Mind if I play some music?" she asks.

"Suit yourself," he says again.

She sighs, setting the wine glass down on the coffee table. "Royce," she says, trying to get his attention. "I'm sorry if I have disappointed you."

He fills in several boxes on the paper.

She finishes the glass of wine in one large swallow. A warm sensation rises up inside her, throughout her body. Her muscles relax, her jaw loosens. No wonder her mother drank, albeit too much, if this was what one glass of wine could do. Imagine two or three. But no, then she would run the risk of losing control of her words, her emotions. She couldn't trust herself not to say something to Royce that she would regret. She doesn't want her world to come tumbling down.

She reaches over to the coffee table and takes a section of the paper, begins reading it. The news is all bad. The economy is bad. Putin still plunders Ukraine. More mass shootings in the United States. She quickly skims through the pages, as much out of habit from her years working in the field as anything else.

Then her eye catches a title in the bottom corner of the page: "Woman's Body Washed Ashore in St. Croix."

She stops, her breath catching in her throat. Thoughts explode in her mind. *Could this be Natalie? She left for the islands with the mystery man. Could this be the island she went to? What if he was a drug runner who got into trouble with the cartel? What if Natalie got involved? What if she is dead?*

Rebecca is afraid to read the article lest it contain unwanted answers to her questions, but she is equally afraid not to in case there is a happier ending than she imagines. She forces herself to make her way through the short article that offers little information except that a woman, approximately thirty years old, was found washed up on a beach in St. Croix. She had no identification, was unconscious but alive, and is now in a hospital on the island in a coma. Authorities are seeking any clues to her identity.

"Oh my God. I think it's Natalie," Rebecca says.

"Hmm?" Royce says without looking up.

"I think they found Natalie on St. Croix, and she's in a coma," she says, holding the paper up for Royce to see.

"Don't be absurd. You've just been around your mother too long."

"I am not being absurd. It makes perfect sense. Besides, I feel it in my gut. This must be Natalie."

"You really can't handle your booze, can you?"

"Stop it! Just stop it!" she cries. "Here. Read the article." She thrusts the paper at him.

He reads it, then tosses it down on the table.

"The only similarity I see between this girl and Natalie is that they are approximately the same age."

"And she was found in the islands! That is where Natalie was supposed to have gone!"

"That's a stretch, Rebecca. Even for you. There are a lot of islands. It's just another girl, probably a tourist who went down there for the holidays and got drunk and fell overboard."

"You don't know that. It could be Natalie."

"That's about as likely as me being Mark Zuckerberg. We are both male, about the same age. We both make a great deal of money. But come on, Rebecca, you can't be serious."

"I won't know until I see for myself."

"What are you going to do? Travel down there? By yourself?"

"If I must."

"Well, I can't go with you."

"I didn't ask you to come. But I am going. I have to go. You understand, don't you, Royce? If there is a chance …."

He turns back to his crossword puzzle. "I think you're going on a wild goose chase. Please tell me you're not going to get your mother involved."

How stupid did he think she was? She would never mention a word of this to her mother, until she was absolutely certain whether the woman was Natalie or not. She doesn't relish the idea of traveling alone. She wishes Royce had offered to go with her. But with or without him, she will see this through.

"I'm going, Royce. With your blessing or without it. Nothing you say or do can stop me."

She hears her mother's voice. *I tried my best to be there for you at all the important moments, but I realized in treatment that you needed me there for the moments in between too. Can you forgive me?*

Forgiveness. Can she let go of the rock she wants to hurl at her sister, return to loving her as she did when they played together as young children in the snow, making angels and fabricating angel names? Adrielle. Coraline.

The sunshine and blue waters of the island call her, give her hope. This is the new beginning she has been waiting for, the catalyst to help her let go of the past and move into a brighter future.

She leaves Royce to his crossword puzzle and heads upstairs to the guest room, sits on the brass bed, and looks out the window at the white sky. Where once the sheer blankness seemed to reflect her soul, now it feels like heaven calling. Her breathing is quick; her senses are on fire. She picks up her phone, searches for the number for the St. Croix Police, then holds the phone to her chest. Exhales. And dials.

CHAPTER TEN

Hopewell, New Jersey
December 30, 2022

Despite his earlier protestations, Royce becomes engaged in the preparations for her trip. He insists that she take a limousine from Hopewell to LaGuardia and call him on her layover in Miami, just to make sure she is safe. He books her reservations at the King Christian Hotel in Christiansted, one of the nicest hotels on the island. He arranges for a rental car. She appreciates his concern as she is feeling nervous about venturing off by herself, but she suspects he has an ulterior motive. No doubt he has already arranged a week-long tryst with some woman while she is gone. No matter. She is looking forward to a week away from the snow and freezing temperatures in New Jersey. She has checked the weather on the island. It is a mild seventy-five degrees.

Royce has encouraged her to look at this trip as a winter getaway rather than the answer to their quest to find her sister, and Rebecca is, uncharacteristically, open to his suggestion. She tells herself not to go with any expectations. The truth is, the closer she gets to following this lead, the less certain she is of her decision to do so.

What if the woman is not Natalie? Rebecca will have spent a week by a pool, relaxing. That is not such a bad thing. But what if the woman is Natalie? Then all sorts of complications will arise. How long will she be in a coma? Can she be moved in that fragile state from St. Croix to the mainland? Where will she go once she becomes conscious again? Will she have brain damage or will she recover fully? How did she end up washed up on a beach anyway? All of these questions are beyond Rebecca's control, like picking up the All Clad pot without a potholder and burning her hand, or missing the bottom step on the stairs and nearly spraining her ankle. Slicing into her finger when she was cutting cucumbers for salad. She feels suddenly inept, uncapable, and is concerned whether she can really pull this trip off by herself.

She catches herself mindlessly chewing her fingernails as she speaks to her mother, who calls as she is packing.

"Hi, Rebecca. We had such a lovely time at your place over the holidays. It was just great to see you," her mother says when she answers.

"You too, Dorothy. And Jack. So glad you came."

"Am I catching you at a bad time? You sound like you're in the middle of doing something."

"No. Just packing. I have you on speaker."

"Packing? That sounds exciting! Where are you going?"

"To the islands. For a week. Just a little winter getaway."

"To recover from us descending on you?"

"No. This is just for fun."

"Like a second honeymoon?"

"I'm going alone."

"Really? That sounds lonely. Is everything okay between you two? Not that it's any of my business."

"Everything is fine. He just has to work, and I wanted to get some sun after all this snow."

"Of course." Her mother is silent for a few moments. "You know, I would have gone with you. To keep you company."

"Don't take this the wrong way, Dorothy, but I really wanted to take this trip alone. I need some time away from everything. Everyone. We will go somewhere together another time."

"Promise?"

"Promise."

"You would tell me if there was something going on, wouldn't you?"

"Absolutely. You would be the first to know."

She says goodbye and hangs up. She doesn't like lying, but sometimes telling the truth can be crueler. No point in giving her mother false hope.

PART TWO

CHAPTER ELEVEN

December 31, 2022

The morning of New Year's Eve, she departs on her adventure to St. Croix. Empowered by her resolution to pursue this quest, she slings her handbag over her shoulder, hoists her carry-on bag in her hand, and strides down the front path to the waiting limousine, confident she is doing the right thing. Royce is not there to kiss her goodbye. He left for work much earlier.

A long day of crowds and lengthy lines at security checks exhausts her. At least she has the luxury of flying first class from New York with room for her legs and space to breathe. That won't be the case on the little island hopper she is taking from Miami to St. Croix. Now she is boarding the plane, after a several-hour layover, on the last leg of her trip. There is barely enough room in the aisle to carry her bag, so she holds it out in front of her like a shield. When she finds her seat, she has to hoist her bag into the tight space left in the overhead compartment. The plane is cramped, warm, and stuffy. By the time she is seated, she has worked up a sweat. She wants to take off her down coat, but she does not know where she would put it, so she eases her way into the window seat, careful not to step on the toes of the woman who has risen from her aisle seat to give access. "This had better be worth it," she mutters under her breath as she sits down, closes her eyes, and sighs.

The door to the cabin shuts and the engines rev ferociously as the plane prepares to take off. The little plane shakes, making its way down the runway. She grips the armrests and takes a deep breath.

The woman sitting beside her laughs. "You are not a traveler, I see," she says, her voice flavored with an accent Rebecca assumes is French, but she cannot be sure.

Rebecca exhales. "I am a reluctant traveler. I actually hate flying. Especially takeoffs and landings."

"Here. Take my hand. I have done this a thousand times. I can assure you that you will be safe." The woman holds her hand out to Rebecca. "I am Monique. Monique LaFleur."

"Rebecca. Rebecca Winslow," she says as she squeezes the woman's hand tightly in her own. The engines grow louder, the pressure builds in the cabin, and the plane seems as if it will explode. Rebecca squinches her eyes shut. Then they are taxiing down the runway, faster and faster until the plane lifts miraculously into the air. Rebecca opens her eyes, releases Monique's hand, and glances out the small window. She sees the tiny houses, the highways that meander like sentences, and the miniature cars like frantic punctuation points, seeking a conclusion.

"Beautiful, isn't it?" Monique says. "Though I am glad to leave the mainland behind."

Rebecca smiles. She does not want to twist in her seat to take a good look at Monique, but from the corner of her eye, Rebecca sees that she is a beautiful woman with tawny skin that appears as soft as velvet. Her black hair is piled on top of her head, an intricate labyrinth of braids, her long nails are painted bright red in contrast to the gold rings and bracelets that cuff her fingers and wrists. Rebecca knows a wealthy woman when she sees one, but this woman is not pretentiously so.

"Are you going to the island for 'oliday?" Monique says, in a voice as smooth and soothing as cream.

"Sort of. Maybe. Not really."

Monique laughs, a lusty trill that takes Rebecca by surprise. "What is it then? A family reunion?"

"In a way. I hope so anyway."

"My, this does sound mysterious. Tell me more."

Rebecca squirms in her seat, not certain she wants to reveal her family secrets to a stranger, no matter how charming she might be.

"First, you tell me. Why are you going to the island?" Rebecca says.

"My home is there."

"You are native to the island?"

"I was born there, but France is my home."

"So you live in France but vacation on St. Croix?" Rebecca says, trying to keep up.

Monique's smile reveals brilliantly white teeth, shocking against the red lipstick. "Actually, I live in Manhattan. I do still have an apartment in Paris though."

Very wealthy.

"And you?"

"Oh, my husband and I go back and forth between our farm in Hopewell, New Jersey, and a condo in the city."

"Where in the city? Perhaps we are neighbors."

Rebecca is reticent to reveal their address lest this stranger think her too snobby. She still has not adjusted, after all these years, to the reality that she and Royce have money. Lots of it. Enough to live in a building where Gilda Radner, Rudolph Nureyev, Roberta Flack, Lauren Bacall, John Lennon, Yoko Ono, and so many other celebrities have lived. She did not grow up like this. She grew up in a very middle-class home where every penny was accounted for and the family piled in the station wagon to set out on their one vacation a year. Now she can hop on a plane at whim, travel first class, and stay in five-star hotels. All of which she is grateful for but still seems foreign to her, accustomed as she is to having to work hard, to watching her parents work hard.

"Across from Central Park. In the Dakota. We have one of the smaller units in the building." Though this, she knows, is not the truth. Their apartment is one of the larger units.

"You needn't apologize for your good fortune. I myself am down on Bleeker Street. I am a singer."

"A singer! Should I know who you are?"

"Not necessarily. I have a few albums. Mostly I sing in cabarets. I am very popular abroad. But enough about me. Tell me about this mysterious reunion."

Rebecca looks out the window. They are flying high above the clouds, which lie like a comforter beneath them, illuminated by the sun. Should she tell this woman her secret? What harm could there be? After all, once they have disembarked, what are the chances they will cross each other's path again?

"I have a younger sister. She disappeared over a year ago."

Monique listens intently, her hands folded in her lap.

"We are pretty sure she ran off to the islands with some man."

"And you are trying to find her? There are a lot of islands, you know."

"I know. But I read this story in *The New York Times* about a woman whose body had washed ashore on Cane Bay Beach."

"I know that beach. It is not far from my villa, on the north side of the island."

"She is in a coma now in Juan F. Luis Hospital, and I am going down to see if she might be Natalie."

Monique is quiet for a moment. "Natalie. Such a pretty name, Natalie Winslow."

"Natalie Baker, actually. Winslow is my married name."

"Natalie Baker," Monique says, repeating the name slowly, savoring each syllable. "That is, what you say, 'a long shot,' is it not?"

"It is. I know it is. But I have to see for myself. If nothing comes of it, if there is no family reunion, I will have had a pleasant winter getaway."

"What will you do if it is your sister? You say she is in a coma. Surely she cannot be moved. That could go on for a long time."

"I guess I will cross that bridge when I come to it."

Monique reaches into her purse and pulls out a business card. "Here. Take this. If there is anything I can do to help you while you are on the island, do not hesitate to call me. I will be on the island until March."

"I hope I'm not here that long!" Rebecca says.

"*Ma chérie*, go with no expectations. That is always the best way."

The captain's voice comes over the loudspeaker, announcing their descent. Rebecca looks out her window. The clouds have broken, and the sun shines through. Far below her, she sees the thin island, surrounded by the dark blue of the deep ocean and a lighter bright blue closer to the shore. She takes Monique's business card and puts it in her purse, ready for whatever comes next.

As she tucks the card into the side pocket, she sees the sonogram of Juliet that she carries with her at all times. She realizes she has not thought about Juliet once during the whole trip down. Does this mean she is forgetting her child? Is she letting the memory of her fade into the distance as she becomes preoccupied with other matters—like the identity of the girl on the island? Rebecca hopes not. She nurtures the memory of the baby in her arms, no matter how painful, lest she forget it.

Margot told her the day would come when Juliet would not be in the forefront of her mind. Rebecca did not believe her, did not want to believe her. But the truth is, now that she has experienced the reprieve, she feels *relief*. She has not forgotten Juliet any more than those who lost loved ones on 9/11 would ever forget when the Twin Towers fell. But she cannot live in that heightened state forever, making herself sick and crazy with grief. There has to be room for other things. For change. And right now, Natalie—the woman she hopes is Natalie—is the other thing.

CHAPTER TWELVE

Rebecca steps off the small plane onto the long runway of the airport in Christiansted.

"Welcome to the Henry E. Rohlsen International Airport. This used to be the Alexander Hamilton International Airport until 1996. Then it was renamed after a St. Croix native who was one of the Tuskegee Airmen during World War II," Monique says to Rebecca, who is taking off her down coat and gathering it into her arms.

"Interesting. We just saw *Hamilton* on Broadway. Was Alexander Hamilton born here?"

"No. On Nevis, an island about a hundred and forty miles from here. But he spent the formative years of his childhood on St. Croix."

"That's so interesting. I imagine there's a lot more history to this place."

"Indeed. Come, let's go through check in, and then you can start your visit with our famous Cruzan rum punch."

They walk up to the open-air security check. Monique passes through quickly, smiling and chatting with the security guards. Then it is Rebecca's turn.

"Madame, your passport and vaccination cards, please."

Rebecca hands over the documents. The security officer looks at them intently, then speaks into a cumbersome walkie-talkie. He listens for a reply, keeping his eyes on Rebecca the whole time. "Madame, you must wait here."

Rebecca looks at Monique, who is standing by, chatting with another guard. Monique catches her eye and walks back over, speaking to the guard.

"Is there a problem?" she says.

"The police are on their way," he says.

"Police?" she says.

Just then, two police officers dressed in their blue uniform shorts and safari shirts, knee highs, and shiny black shoes stride out of the concrete building onto the runway. "Madame Winslow?" the older officer says.

"Yes?" Rebecca says. "What is going on? Is there a problem with my passport? My vaccines are up to date."

"Come with us, please," he continues, taking her by the arm. The younger officer picks up her bag.

"Wait!" Rebecca says. "I am a US citizen! You can't arrest me without a reason!"

"You are not under arrest. We are taking you to the station to answer some questions," he says, his voice flat, revealing nothing.

Monique walks with the trio as they enter the concrete building. She dials her phone. "Don't worry Rebecca," she says. "I'm calling my lawyer. She will meet us at the police station."

"Lawyer? My God, I haven't done anything!"

Monique looks at the officers. "You should be ashamed of yourselves. This is no way to welcome a visitor onto our island."

Rebecca tries to focus on what is around her to keep from panicking. The airport is not what Rebecca expected. She does not know what she expected, but this is not it. This large open room, painted coral, with huge ceiling fans that circle overhead like lazy buzzards, and dirt on the floor. She reminds herself that she is not in Kansas anymore. She is on an island. Where hospitality awaits them in the form of a rum swizzle, which they are offered immediately upon entering the room.

"No, thank you," Rebecca says as a young woman in a brightly colored skirt and blouse holds out a drink to her.

"Take it. It will help," Monique says.

"I don't really drink," Rebecca says.

"Don't really drink or never drink? If you never drink, I understand. But if you don't really drink, you should try this." Monique sips her cocktail through a straw.

"All right." Rebecca takes the drink and sips it, hoping it will help her relax. The rum immediately courses through her.

"Now that is the way to welcome someone onto the island," Monique says to the officers as they propel Rebecca toward the tiny police car.

The whirring lights. The nasal siren. The island around her flashes in a blur. Rebecca is fighting back tears. Royce was right. She never should have come. Now she will be locked up in a cell for a crime she didn't commit.

The younger officer turns around in his seat and speaks to her.

"This is just a formality. There is nothing to worry about. We will have you at your hotel in no time."

Easy for him to say. He has not been escorted out of an airport with no explanation, stuffed into a police car, and treated like a criminal.

"Can you at least tell me what this is all about?" Rebecca says.

The officer turns back around in his seat without a word.

CHAPTER THIRTEEN

The police station is as rustic as the airport, a concrete box painted white with hot pink bougainvillea climbing up the exterior walls. The interior is painted a bright yellow. Huge fans swirl around. Several wooden desks are scattered throughout the open space, and the older officer leads Rebecca to the farthest one, pulls out a wooden chair for her to sit.

"The chief will be here momentarily," he says, taking his time over that last word as though he is saying it for the first time.

Rebecca's heart is pounding in her chest. She is no longer frightened. She is angry. That she is being detained without an explanation infuriates her; it triggers something inside her that, at this moment, she cannot name. What could she have done to warrant this treatment? She wonders if the call she made to the police, inquiring about the woman in the hospital and telling them she was on her way down, raised suspicion, was responsible for the way she is being treated now. If anything, she thinks they should be glad for any leads they could find into identifying the Jane Doe. Instead, they are treating her as if she has done something wrong.

The younger officer brings her a glass of water with a slice of lime. "It won't be long now, madame. Thank you for your patience."

At least this younger officer is showing some respect. She takes the water and smiles at him. "Thank you. Do you have any idea how long this is going to take?"

Just then, a large man in a uniform dappled with medals strides into the room. At the same time, Monique and a white woman in a power suit and six-inch heels walk through the door of the station. The chief stops abruptly.

"Monique! I didn't know you were on the island," he says.

"It is of no concern to you."

The electric lights suspended from the ceiling flicker and hiss.

"Is your mother—"

"I am not here for a family reunion," she says.

The chief snorts. "I gathered that when I saw you brought your lawyer with you. Just why are you here?" he asks, any tenderness gone from his voice.

"We are here for her," Monique says, pointing to Rebecca. "Just what are the grounds on which you are holding her?"

"We are not holding her. She is free to leave at her will. We simply brought her here to ask a few questions."

"About what?" the lawyer says.

"It is a sensitive police matter."

"My client has the right to know why she is being detained. If you aren't going to charge her with anything, then I think this interview is over."

"Calm yourself, Ms. Nave. All in due time. Now," he says, turning to Rebecca, "I am Chief of Police Louis Montmart."

"And I am your attorney, if you wish. April Nave." The woman holds her hand out to Rebecca.

"I assure you, Madame Winslow, you will not need an attorney. We merely have a few questions for you regarding your inquiry into our murder investigation," the chief says.

Rebecca's heart hammers rapidly in her chest. "Murder! No one said anything about murder. I thought you said the woman was alive, in a coma."

"Calm yourself, madame. She is. But there was another body that was found at the scene. This one, a man with two bullets in his head." The chief points two fingers trigger-like at the center of his forehead. "Execution style."

Rebecca's head grows light, and the room swirls around her. Surely the woman cannot be Natalie if murder is involved. It is one thing to fall off a boat, drunk. It is another to jump off a boat, fearful for your life, escaping an assassin's gun. How could she even do that? Natalie was wild, that is true, but was she wild enough, foolish enough, to get involved in something like this? No, it cannot be Natalie.

Rebecca knows she has made a foolish mistake coming here, only now to find herself embroiled in a murder investigation.

"I'm sure I was mistaken in coming here," she says. "I'm sure this woman is not my sister. She can't be my sister. My sister wouldn't get involved in something like this." Yet even as Rebecca speaks, she recognizes in her heart that she does not know Natalie.

"Your sister never spoke to you about a man who might be involved in criminal affairs?" the chief asks.

"Criminal affairs? No. All I know is she disappeared to the islands with some man she met in a bar. I never heard from her again." Rebecca's voice echoes. *Can this be real?*

"She just said this woman could not possibly be her sister. Is that not enough for you?" Monique says.

"Monique." April Nave lays her hand on Monique's arm. "Let me handle this. Chief, it seems to me you are making a premature leap here. We do not even know if the woman in the hospital is Mrs. Winslow's sister. Should we not establish that first before we go down the rabbit hole of questions about an alleged murder?"

"Perhaps," he says.

"The first place you should have brought her was to the hospital, not to the police station," Monique says, her annoyance with the chief evident in her tone.

Rebecca is grateful for Monique's support. She is thinking the exact same thing.

The chief continues. "So Madame Winslow—"

"Please, call me Rebecca."

"Rebecca, are you prepared to identify the woman in the hospital?"

"I will if I can. If she is my sister. But honestly, at this point, I hope she is not."

Monique puts her hand on Rebecca's shoulder, giving it a squeeze. "We will be here for you, whatever the outcome. You have nothing to fear."

They drive to the hospital in the police car, Monique and April following behind. This time, the sirens are silent and the whirring lights are still. Rebecca looks out the window at the island beyond the glass. Palm trees sway in the breeze. They drive by clusters of small shopping malls—hardly what Rebecca expected to see. She wonders how far they are from the beach. Given that the island is only five miles wide at its fattest, it cannot be far. She imagines walking down the beach, looking for shells, diving into the crystal blue water. Then she sees Natalie's body washed up on shore next to a man with a bullet hole in his head. Her imagination paints the picture in exaggerated detail: Natalie's long golden hair is muddied with sand and seaweed as it spreads around her face like a fan. The man she is with wears a suit, a black suit with a black shirt and black socks and shoes. He has a black ponytail tied behind his head. The bullet hole in his forehead is precise and smooth.

She shakes herself from her daydream. Day-nightmare is more like it. "How much longer?" she asks.

"We are almost there," the young officer says.

Nervous dread fills her body. She questions why she even has come. She and Natalie were never close. They were like water and oil; they just didn't mix. Rebecca was jealous of the attention Natalie demanded and received not only from her mother but from friends at school. And Natalie made it clear that she resented Rebecca's goody-two-shoes personality. The superachiever. The one who could be counted on. Then Rebecca realizes that is why she is here: because she can be counted on to do the right thing. Even when the right thing costs her, as it is costing her now. She has been in a heightened state of anxiety since she boarded the plane in New York. She is worried what Royce will do while she is gone. She is anxious over the identity of this girl. She is concerned that if it is Natalie, her sister may have been involved in a dangerous game.

The only time Rebecca has not felt like puking during the past twenty-four hours is when she is talking to Monique. Monique soothes her, calms her. She is so grateful they met.

"Here we are," the young officer says.

They disembark and walk toward the hospital. Rebecca is immediately struck by how shabby the structure looks. Then she notices a large sign with an image of a new structure to take the old building's place.

"Yes. It is a shame," the young officer continues. "This hospital was new twenty-five years ago, but in 2017, Hurricane Maria did some serious damage. They are going to rip it all down next year and build a whole new hospital."

Monique takes Rebecca's arm. "Are you ready for this? Whatever may come?"

"I think I am," Rebecca says, though inside she is shaking.

They walk up the steps into the building. The chief tips his hat to the receptionist at the front desk. She flashes a brilliant smile and waves him on, a ritual which Rebecca supposes has occurred a number of times. The aqua walls show stains from water damage, and the once-white floors are colored a yellowish gray. A few nurses in crisp white shoes pad by on silent feet. Rebecca realizes she is looking down at the floor, relying on Monique to guide her. She looks up.

A long corridor splashed with artificial light unfurls in front of her. She is reminded of *The Green Mile*, a few dozen agonizing steps to the final, awful injection. The lights flicker overhead. The putrid stench of death and bleach fills her nostrils. Dread grips her as she makes her way past the rooms of sick patients, lying in their beds. The only sounds are the quiet hushes of doctors' voices and the repetitive pulsing of machines. What will she find when she gets to the room? Who will she find?

They round a corner and make their way down another long corridor, this one with windows looking out one side onto a walled courtyard. Nurses in their starched scrubs push patients in wheelchairs. A few people in gowns propel themselves along using walkers. Rebecca wonders if Natalie will have to go through physical therapy when she wakes up from her coma. If she wakes up. If it even is Natalie.

At the end of the hall is a policewoman seated on a wooden chair. Rebecca braces herself.

Monique gently lays her hand on Rebecca's back, encouraging her to enter the room. A sun-bleached gray curtain conceals the woman in the hospital bed from inquisitive eyes. Behind the curtain, machines wheeze and beep, breathing life into the comatose patient. Rebecca's heart pounds in her chest and ears; she wonders if Monique can hear it. She wants to rip back the curtain, reveal the Great Oz. But this is no fantasy. And whether or not there will be a happy ending is not in her control. Right now, she just needs courage to take the next step, to see if the woman really is Natalie.

"Please, Madame Winslow, are you ready?" the chief asks her.

She nods her head. "As ready as I will ever be," she says, though secretly, she feels like vomiting on the floor.

He draws the curtain back.

As she stares down at the young woman who is attached to multiple wires and tubes—face bruised, eyes closed and swollen—Rebecca's tears begin to fall. This is, indeed, Natalie, her beautiful little sister, now disfigured and unconscious, kept alive by the pulsing hiss of the machines. She wipes her face with her sleeve. Monique hands her a tissue.

"Well, is this your sister?" the chief asks.

"I think so," Rebecca says almost inaudibly.

"I'm sorry. I didn't hear you," the chief says.

"I think so. Let me see her ankle."

The nurse pulls the sheets back and reveals a thin, tan leg. Right above the ankle is a tattoo of a starfish.

Rebecca nods her head. "Yes. This is my sister. Natalie Baker." Rebecca remembers the day she got the tattoo. They were on Cape May for vacation. She was fifteen, so Natalie was just twelve. Their parents had given them money to spend at the arcade and sent the girls on their way. Natalie couldn't have cared less about playing games to pass the time. She had it in her head that she wanted a tattoo. So she dragged Rebecca with her in search of a tattoo artist. They finally found one in a seedy-looking shop on the boardwalk. They flashed their fake IDs, which Natalie had conned out of some college boys, unnecessarily it turned out. The tattoo artist barely gave them a look. The trouble was, Natalie's money wouldn't cover the ink. She demanded Rebecca pool her money in order to purchase the tattoo. Not wanting her sister to create a scene, Rebecca complied. An hour later, Natalie returned to her parents on the beach, sporting a starfish on her ankle. Rebecca remembers how mad her mother was that she had allowed her little sister to be subject to ink poisoning. But to Natalie, her mother only oohed and aahed, commenting on what a great choice of art it was. A starfish for her little star. Too many memories were like that. Rebecca being reprimanded. Natalie being manipulative and ending up on top.

Suddenly, Rebecca feels dizzy, as if she might faint. "I need to sit down. Could I have some water, please?"

Monique pours Rebecca a glass of water from a carafe on the bedside table and hands it to her.

Images flash across Rebecca's mind of Natalie bounding down the stairs in a miniskirt and heavy boots, laden with black leather bracelets and chains, her eyes heavily lined in black. Her mother asked, "Are they really going to let you go to school like that?" or something disparaging, and Natalie stormed off as she always did, so sure of herself. Her style softened over the years. She transformed from goth into vintage hippie. Rebecca assumed it had something to do with the drugs her sister had turned to. Natalie was high on pot every waking hour of the day, and she enhanced her high with alcohol and other substances, Rebecca was sure. Their parents did nothing until one night when Natalie nearly overdosed on cocaine and alcohol at a party. Frightened by the close call, they sent her to treatment, diving into their retirement fund and hoping that the twenty-eight-day stay would be the cure. But it was not. Natalie picked up again and, once again, began to run with the wrong crowd. By then, her parents had enough AA and Al-Anon under their belts to know they had to detach with love. They kicked Natalie out of the house, an action that almost broke her mother's heart, telling her she would be welcome back when she was clean and sober.

Now here she was. Embroiled in a murder investigation. Possibly on her way to jail. Where was the beautiful little sister who insisted on wearing dresses made of silk and tulle when she was five? Where had she gone? Why this?

"Well, you are not going to stay in any hotel; that is for sure." Monique's voice breaks into Rebecca's thoughts.

Her mind is like a dense fog. She can barely comprehend what it is that is being said.

"We will need you to answer some more questions in light of this," the chief says.

"After she has had some rest," April Nave says, rising to her full stature in front of the chief.

"May I remind you that this is a murder investigation?"

"A murder that my client had nothing to do with. She is in shock right now, is exhausted from traveling, and needs some time to pull herself together before she can be of any use to you."

"Very well. But I want her at the station first thing in the morning."

"I will bring her there myself," Monique says. "Come now, Rebecca. I am going to take you home."

"But—Natalie! I can't leave her. What if she wakes up? I need to be here," Rebecca says.

"She is not going to wake up, *ma chérie*. The doctors are keeping her under observation until she is stronger. She will be fine. You need to take care of yourself."

Monique starts to lead Rebecca from the room, but Rebecca breaks free and goes to Natalie's bedside. She takes her sister's limp hand in hers, leans over, and whispers in her ear. "Natalie, I don't know if you can hear this, but I forgive you. For everything. I am here for you now. I won't leave you. I will take you home. Everything will be all right. I promise."

Monique lays her hand on Rebecca's back. "Come. We must go now."

As they pass out of the room, Rebecca looks at the policewoman. "Is Natalie in danger?"

"I am sure it's just a precaution," Monique says.

"But what if the person who killed the other guy comes back to kill my sister?"

"Let the police do their work. I'm sure there will be no problem."

"How can you be so sure?"

"One can never be sure, but one can pray," Monique says. "Can you pray, Rebecca?"

"I can try."

CHAPTER FOURTEEN

The drive to Monique's house seems long, made longer by Rebecca's exhaustion and the fact that she has no idea where she is going. She is in a daze, her mind blurry with all that has happened in the past twenty-four hours. It hasn't even been twenty-four hours since she left Royce, not knowing that within a day, her life would change forever.

"Royce," she says aloud. "I have got to tell Royce."

"What is that, *ma chérie*?" Monique says as she maneuvers the small car along dirt roads that are pocked with deep ruts.

"My husband. I need to let him know I found Natalie."

"There will be plenty of time for that when we get home," Monique says. "The reception out here is very poor. It won't be long."

They continue past small houses, up into the hills, until they reach a steep driveway covered on both sides by dense underbrush. Up the drive they go, climbing, climbing, until they reach the top. There, at the side of the circular drive, is Monique's villa—a modern structure made of stone and glass, it seems incongruous in the rough tumble of the undergrowth. But as she looks more closely, Rebecca notices that the landscaping around the house is beautifully manicured with short, trimmed grass, flaming pink bougainvillea, statuesque palm trees, and bright flowering hibiscus.

As Rebecca steps out of the car and onto the drive paved in sun-bleached broken shells, she feels the heat but also a cool breeze that blows the palm leaves, making them knock against each other. A delicate, salty sweetness fills the air. A sign over the pastel-blue front door reads Tranquility, and Rebecca is glad Monique has invited her here. She needs tranquility. She needs a reprieve from being on edge and being bowled over by life's surprises. She wants, more than anything, just to lie down somewhere and go to sleep.

"Come, let's take you inside."

For one split second, Rebecca is filled with doubt. Should she really be going into this stranger's home? What does she know about Monique, really? Just that the older woman befriended her in a time of need. What if Rebecca is walking into a setup, a trap? What if Monique lures unsuspecting female tourists into her home, drugs them, and then traffics them? What if she is somehow involved in the murder and what happened to Natalie? Monique could be a drug dealer, for all Rebecca knows. She is certainly rich enough. Maybe she is trying to get close to Rebecca so she can find out what Natalie knows before taking her out too? She needs to let Royce know right away where she is, in case anything happens. *Before* anything happens. Hasn't enough happened already? She doesn't think she can take much more.

"*Chérie*, are you all right? You look pale, like you might faint. Come inside. I will get you something to drink," Monique says as she takes Rebecca's arm.

Rebecca follows obediently, as she always does, despite the anxiety she feels gnawing at her.

The interior of the house is as modern as the exterior—wide, open rooms with recessed lights throughout and a glinting steel-and-black kitchen. All very sparse and classy, minimalist. Of course, the furniture is white.

"Drink?" Monique says, heading for the kitchen. "We have white wine, chilled, or if you prefer something nonalcoholic, limewater. Or I can make you a Bloody Mary."

"Limewater," Rebecca says, then reconsiders. "On second thought, I will have that glass of wine."

"A good choice," Monique says as she pours two large glasses of Chablis.

Rebecca hopes the wine will make the call to Royce easier. She knows he will be critical of the way she has handled things so far. Were he here, she is sure he would already have arranged to have Natalie flown back to the States. He would have put the police in their place and not have been intimidated. But he is Royce, and he always gets what he wants. That is not the way she rolls. Besides, it is not his sister lying on that hospital bed, battered and bruised, practically dead.

She takes a swig of wine, knows she must make the call before it gets too late and she loses nerve. "Monique, is there somewhere private I can go to call my husband?" she asks.

"Of course, *chérie*. Let me show you your room. You will have fine reception from there. Or you can sit out on the balcony if you prefer."

They mount the freestanding wooden staircase to the second floor and take a left down the hall to an end room. When Monique opens the door, Rebecca gasps. The room is expansive and filled with light. Rebecca is enchanted by the white rattan furniture and the colorful floral comforter and matching curtains, which frame the sliders leading out to the balcony. But mostly, she is stunned by the view. She steps onto the balcony and looks out toward the water, sees gulls swirling around below her. A staircase comprised of hundreds of wooden steps zigzags its way down the mountain and disappears in the trees. She imagines there must be a beach beyond. Out in the distance are the silhouettes of neighboring islands.

"Will this do?" Monique asks.

"Oh yes, very much so. Thank you."

"Make yourself at home. My house is yours. Now call Monsieur Winslow and put his mind at ease."

"Oh, my husband is never at ease. He is always working."

"What is it that your husband does?"

"A little bit of everything. Real estate development, investing, import/export. Mostly Royce just makes money. Lots of it."

"Royce Winslow?" Monique's eyebrows lift, questioning.

"Do you know him? That would be too wild, if you knew my husband."

"No, I don't believe we have met. But I do recognize the name. Funny, it is such a small world. I'll fix us something to eat."

"Thank you so much, Monique. For everything," Rebecca says. "I don't know what I would have done without you."

"It is my pleasure. Now make your call. Come down whenever you are ready to eat," Monique says as she closes the door gently.

Rebecca nestles herself onto a chaise lounge on the balcony. She wishes she didn't have to make this call. She wants this moment to go on forever—the peace, the beauty. Looking out over the water, she notices the tiny specks of boats cruising along the shore and, even smaller, miniature sails blown by the wind across the sea. This is not the house of a serial killer or a drug lord. She feels too many positive vibes coming from this place. She laughs at herself for her momentary dive into panic, then gives herself a virtual pat on the back for having recovered so quickly. Margot would be proud. Maybe she should call Margot? No. Margot is out of the office ,and besides, she needs to call Royce. She closes her eyes, takes a deep breath, picks up her phone, and dials.

"Hello?"

"Royce?"

"Who else would it be?"

"I don't know. You answered so quickly."

"I have been waiting for your goddamned call for hours. Did you make it to St. Croix?"

"Yes. I am sorry. I should have called sooner. It's just that—"

"No problem. I was just worried about you, that's all, when I hadn't heard anything. I'm probably being overprotective. Forgive me?"

"There's nothing to forgive."

"But you know, if you had just called me sooner, like you were fucking supposed to, I wouldn't have had to be short with you."

"I'm sorry. A lot has happened. First of all, the woman in the hospital is Natalie."

"Jesus, Rebecca. That's good news, I guess. Have you made arrangements for her transport?"

"That's the thing. The police won't agree to release her."

"The police? How did they get involved?"

"Evidently there was another body at the scene. A man. With a bullet in his head. Execution style. They are investigating this as a murder."

"Christ! Leave it to Natalie to get involved in something like this."

"They have her under guard. They think she may have had something to do with it or at least know something about what went on. I'm sure it is not her fault. I'm sure she's an innocent victim."

Royce is silent for a long time.

"Royce? Are you there? Hello?"

When Royce speaks, his voice is level and stern. "Rebecca—I want you to come home immediately. And I don't want you to talk about this to anyone."

"I can't do that, Royce. Now that I've found her, I can't abandon her."

"You might be putting your life in danger."

Rebecca looks out over the mountains. The sun is sliding down in the sky and will soon disappear. Already streaks of pink and peach stretch out across the horizon. "I am not coming home until she can come with me."

"Well, that is going to get pretty damned expensive at twelve hundred dollars a night."

"You don't have to worry about that."

"What do you mean?"

"I met someone on the plane. A singer named Monique LaFleur. She is letting me stay in her villa. She has been very supportive."

"Rebecca! Listen to yourself! Strange women taking you home. Police. Murder. You can't be serious. Have you totally lost your mind? I want you to get on the next plane home."

Rebecca feels anger welling up inside her. Who is Royce to tell her what to do? He doesn't trust her, doesn't think she can take care of herself, handle this difficult situation. Then again, maybe he is truly concerned for her well-being.

"I appreciate your concern, but I can handle this. I will handle this."

"I'll give you three days. Then I am coming down there to get you."

"Fair enough."

"Three days, Becca."

"I love you too."

She hangs up.

Rebecca stares at the silent phone in her hand. She wishes she had not told Royce she could handle it because really, she wonders if she can. She wishes she had asked him to come down immediately to help her with the doctors, the police. It all feels like more than she can manage on her own, yet something inside her tells her she must move forward. She should be able to do this. She is tired, so very tired; she just wants to go to sleep.

She walks into the bedroom, takes off her jeans, top, and undergarments, and pulls back the covers on the bed. The sheets are pleasantly cool. She lays her head down on the pillow, closes her eyes. Suddenly, her mother's face appears in her imagination. "FUCK!" Rebecca says and pulls a second pillow over her head. "Not now. Not tonight. Just leave me alone until tomorrow."

Before a shooting star crosses through Orion, she is asleep.

CHAPTER FIFTEEN

The next morning, she is woken by a rooster's call, which sounds more like a New Year's horn blowing than a cock-a-doodle-doo. The sound is so loud, it seems to be coming from inside her room. She rolls over, pulling the pillow over her head. Her stomach growls noisily, reminding her of the pipes in the farmhouse before its renovation. She reaches out her hand, patting the bedside table for her alarm clock. Then she realizes where she is. Not in New Jersey in her home but in Monique LaFleur's house on St. Croix. She sits up in bed, pulls the sheets up to her chest, and tries to piece together the jagged pieces of the puzzle.

Outside, the sun is high and shining. She figures she must have slept for at least twelve hours. Now she has much to do. She needs coffee and some food and then to go into town back to the police station to answer their questions so that she can begin to make arrangements for Natalie to go home. But first, coffee.

She sees her bag on the floor beside the sliders, opens it, and takes out a robe. She puts it on and heads downstairs. The house is very quiet. She wonders if she is alone. She hopes not. She needs Monique's help to get her where she needs to go. But then she catches herself, tells herself that she is on her own here. She can't rely on Monique to do everything for her.

She walks into the kitchen, sees the impressive espresso maker on the counter, and stops short. She has no clue how to use it. She misses her electric kettle and French press. How difficult can it be to make a cup of coffee? She starts opening canisters and cupboards in search of beans or grounds.

Just then, Monique walks in, carrying a handful of fresh cut flowers. "Good morning, *chérie*. You had a good sleep?"

"Too good, I think."

Monique laughs. "Yes. I was wondering if we were ever going to see you again."

"I apologize for ditching you last night."

"Ditching?"

"You made us dinner. I was exhausted, and I just went to sleep."

Monique trims the ends off the flowers with a pair of heavy shears before placing them in a vase. She is smiling. "You amuse me, how you worry about such trivial things when there is so much more to be concerned about. But you must be hungry, no? Now what can I get you? Coffee?"

"Yes, please. That would be lovely."

Monique places the flowers in the vase and then proceeds to make coffee with the machine.

"You will have to teach me how to use that," Rebecca says.

"Oh, it is most easy. It is not unlike the Mr. Coffeemaker in the States. The water goes in here. Coffee in the filter. Push a button and voila."

The hiss of the coffee brewing and smell of the brewed beverage fill the air.

"Now how about something to eat? An almond croissant, perhaps? With an egg?"

"You are going to spoil me."

"Just for today. Tomorrow, I will send you to the market on your own."

A shiver of guilt cuts across Rebecca's heart. She does not want to be a burden on anyone. Perhaps she should check in to the hotel where she was originally booked.

"Relax, *chérie*. I am only teasing you. I would not have asked you to stay here if I did not want you to be my guest."

Rebecca takes a bite of her croissant. It is perfectly flaky and buttery, the almond filling sweet and nutty—just what she needs to begin this day. She sips her coffee, which is hot and rich. If she can only stay in this moment, she will be okay.

As soon as she tells herself that, she sees Juliet. Grief ambushes her, and she puts her cup of coffee down so abruptly, the liquid splashes over the edge, leaving a dark puddle on the white marble counter. "I am so sorry," she says.

"What is troubling you so?" Monique asks.

"It's a long story. Maybe for another time. Right now, I need to focus on Natalie. Answering the questions the police have for me. Getting her released. I need to take her home."

Monique puts her hand on Rebecca's back and massages it gently. "When you are ready, we will talk. Meanwhile, I will take you to the police station. The chief is anxious to speak with you."

Rebecca inhales, exhales, deliberately calming herself. She forces herself to think about her surroundings. The quiet house. The sounds of the birds. Wind chimes tinkling in the breeze. If she can just stay in the moment, she will be all right. She will make it through the interview. She will convince the chief to let Natalie go. "I only have three days," she says.

"What do you mean?" Monique asks.

"Royce said he will come get me in three days if I don't have everything figured out."

"Does Royce always 'call the shots,' as you say?"

"Pretty much."

"Well then, let's see if we can't get this figured out as soon as possible." Monique looks Rebecca in the eyes. "You can do this."

Rebecca is encouraged by Monique's words. The anxiety she previously felt about the interview and Royce's ultimatum melts away and is replaced by sprouting confidence. She can handle the chief, and when she is done, she will put on her jogging clothes and take a run in the hills. She knows she will feel better after she has had a run.

***

Monique insists on driving Rebecca to the police station for her interview with the police chief. Though Rebecca feels slightly guilty over the inconvenience, she is grateful for the offer.

"Buckle up now. The roads are rutted, and my little Charlotte feels every bump," Monique says, tapping on the leather steering wheel as she starts up her classic Fiat 124 Spider.

Rebecca complies.

As they start down the drive, Monique wastes no time in introducing a conversation. "So tell me, *ma chérie*, what is it that has you so troubled?"

Rebecca is taken aback by the sudden question. "Troubled? I am not troubled."

"*Chérie*, the face cannot lie. Nor the hands."

Rebecca looks at her fingers, her nails chewed to the quick, and self-consciously balls her hands into fists. She is mortified that Monique has noticed the results of her bad habit. "Well, I suppose I do have a few things on my mind. I mean, wouldn't you? My sister is a suspect in a murder, for God's sake."

"There is more. Yesterday, you said you had something to tell me."

Rebecca thinks back to the previous day. Did she insinuate she had something to share? If she did, it would have been about Juliet, she is sure. Can she trust this woman to understand her grief and not to judge her for holding on so long, as Royce does? Is this a secret she is willing to share? She is surprised when the words begin to spill out of her mouth. "I had a baby girl, a stillborn, this past May. My husband doesn't understand how I can still be grieving. He wants to try again. But I had two miscarriages prior to Juliet's death, and I just don't feel ready to make myself vulnerable to more hurt again. I'm scared to lose yet another child. My husband thinks I should be over it. He wants an heir."

Monique listens to Rebecca's story intently while maneuvering the road. She stops the car suddenly as a doe and her two fawns step out of the underbrush, pausing in their tracks in front of the car. The deer look at the car inquisitively and then disappear with a flourish into the bushes on the other side.

"Losing a child is such a tragic thing. I, too, lost a baby once, though she was already a little girl. Eleven years old. Her name was Marie-Claire."

"I am so sorry. What happened?"

"I put her on a plane to see her grandmother in Paris. She never made it there. The police found her body in an alley, brutally raped and beaten."

"Oh my God! That's awful! That has to be even worse than losing a baby at birth. At least my baby didn't suffer." Rebecca immediately regrets her words, which she fears may have come across as insensitive. "Did the police ever find the man who did it?"

"Not the police. But he was found later. Dead by execution."

The reporter in Rebecca wants to know the details of the case, but she isn't going to take Monique on a journey down a path of sordid memories. That the older woman has experienced such grief in her own life solidifies the bond between them. "Men can be such monsters," she says.

Monique steers the small car adroitly around potholes that pock the road. "Your husband is a man. From the sounds of it, a selfish man. Men who have power and wealth are often that way."

Rebecca is silent. She is not sure she likes this woman taking her husband's inventory, even though she does agree and has often told herself that Royce is the most selfish man on earth.

As if reading her thoughts, Monique says, "*Excusez-moi, chérie.* It is not my place to criticize your 'usband. But you, I see, are in distress. I feel that you could use a friend where you might not have one at 'ome."

Truer words were never spoken. "You are right about that," Rebecca says, feeling a lump begin to swell in her throat.

"There is something I see in you that is very special. I would like to be your friend, if you will have me," Monique says, "to be the mother I fear you never had."

Now Rebecca bursts into tears, her heart aching from both the pain of her past and the promise of this new future.

Monique hands her a box of tissues from the glove box. "Wipe away those tears, *ma chérie.* We can't have the police chief think I have been abusing you. He will do that well enough himself."

Rebecca blows her nose and wipes her tears away, swallowing the cocktail of emotions that have arisen inside her. She knows she must be composed with the police chief; she must not break down or appear weak. She must channel Royce's selfish confidence if she wants to get Natalie released. Still, she is glad she will have her new friend there beside her to give her emotional support as she faces the interrogation.

***

The chief wastes no time in getting to the heart of the matter. "So we know from the toxicology report that there were drugs in your sister's blood as well as a high concentration of alcohol."

Rebecca sits stiffly in the wooden chair in front of the chief's desk, neither affirming nor denying Natalie's culpability. The chief puts his hands together as if in prayer, fingertips touching.

"Tell me, how long has your sister been an addict?"

Rebecca is not certain how much to reveal of Natalie's past, nor does she see the relevance Natalie's using might have to the murder investigation.

"Answer the question, please."

"My sister has been known to use drugs and alcohol." Rebecca takes a breath and counts to four.

"Expand, please."

"You know, in high school. She was like any other kid. Then it got a little out of hand. But she recently went into a rehab program for treatment. Frankly, I'm surprised to hear she was using again." Rebecca knows this is a lie, but she is not going to let this man bully her. She has put on her big-girl pants, and she is ready to fight him as Royce would to get what she wants.

"This man she was found with? Was he her drug dealer?"

"I have no idea who or what that man was." Rebecca squirms in her seat, worried that the chief is looking for a way to incriminate Natalie in some nefarious dealings and to make her, Rebecca, a part of it.

"Didn't you say yesterday that she traveled to the islands with a man she met in a bar?"

"I don't know if that's the same guy. I never met the man."

"If I were to show you a picture—"

"I already told you, I never met the man. How could I possibly identify him?"

The chief lays his hands on the desk in front of him, splays his fingers wide. "It is imperative that you be completely honest with me. There are laws against perjury."

"I am being honest! I never saw the man or met him. Nor did I talk to my sister about him other than her mentioning she was going away with some man to the islands." She breathes heavily through her nostrils, like a bull preparing to charge. "I don't see how you can assume this was the same man."

"We are following all leads."

Rebecca knows he is grasping at straws. She has heard that same line before, as she listened to the police interview her parents one time when Natalie ran away at fourteen. For one whole day, her parents were suspected of deliberately holding their own daughter hostage, some kind of weird syndrome that was all the buzz in the news at the time.

"Do you have any evidence to suggest that my sister was involved in a drug ring? Because if there is no evidence, then I assume I am free to go." She starts to rise from her chair.

"Sit down. We are not finished, Madame Winslow."

Rebecca sits back down, her heart pounding. She knows she must not let her emotions take over. Or her fear. She needs to advocate for Natalie, for herself, but she suddenly feels weak. The energy she felt a moment before has vanished.

"Now what's this about a drug ring? Who said anything about a drug ring? But she did have drugs in her system," the chief continues.

"Has it ever occurred to you that she might be the victim of foul play?" Monique says quietly from the corner of the room where she is standing.

Rebecca is startled by her voice. She had forgotten that Monique was even there but is glad now to have an ally. Her courage, nearly extinguished, is rekindled.

"Foul play does not lead to her level of alcohol consumption," the chief replies gruffly, irritated by his daughter's interjection.

"That just means she was drinking. And so what if she was using? People do drugs all the time. It doesn't make them criminals," Rebecca says.

"We are not accusing your sister of anything. We hope she may be able to help us determine who the players are in the situation."

"What exactly is the situation, Father?" Monique asks as she walks toward the desk.

"Even if you were Madame Winslow's attorney, which you are not, I am not at liberty to say at this time."

"You are holding my sister prisoner! I'd say that gives me the right to know the situation," Rebecca says, forcefully.

The chief deliberates for a moment. Rebecca is shaking, unsure if she has gone too far, but she believes that unless she pushes, she will not learn the truth about why they are holding Natalie. If they have any reason at all.

"What I am about to share with you is entirely confidential. You must not share it with anyone. Can you do that?"

Rebecca nods her head, suddenly silenced by the solemnity of the chief's tone.

"Monique, you must excuse yourself as you are not next of kin."

Reluctantly, Monique turns on her heels and walks out the station door.

The chief turns to Rebecca.

"The man we found on the beach was a known sex trafficker. Peter Robinson. Does that name mean anything to you?"

Rebecca shakes her head. Inside, a million voices are screaming. *Drugs. Murder. Now sex trafficking. What the hell has Natalie gotten herself into?*

"There were girls found on a boat, young Haitian girls, who identified him as their abductor. But he was not the leader of the ring. He was only a cog in the wheel. Maybe this will jog your memory."

He lays a photo of a man on the desk in front of her.

"Have you ever seen him before?"

Rebecca glances at the photo of a man, his face bloated and distorted, with two star-shaped bullet holes between his eyes. She looks away quickly as bile begins to rise in her throat.

"Is this Peter Robinson?" she asks.

"Yes."

"No. I have never seen this man in my life. But you think this may be the man who Natalie came to the island with?"

"We don't know. This is why we must talk to her."

"She's in a coma! Who knows when she'll come out of it? It could be days, weeks, months. Are you going to keep her a prisoner in the hospital just so you can interrogate her when she comes to?"

"Calm yourself, Madame Winslow. I am only doing my job."

"And I'm doing mine, which is to protect my sister. I want to take her home, and I want to take her home now."

The chief sits up stiffly in his chair. "I am afraid that won't be possible. She is a witness in a murder investigation. We have the authority to keep her here until we have the opportunity to question her."

Rebecca's body melts into her chair. "You know, when she comes out of the coma, she may not even know who she is. She may have a long recovery ahead."

"That is a bridge we will cross when we come to it. Meanwhile, we can hope for the best. Thank you for your time, madame."

He rises out of his chair and motions toward the door. Together they walk out into the sunlight. Monique is standing outside the police station, waiting.

"We will be in touch. I assume you will be staying on the island?" the chief asks.

Rebecca turns to Monique, who squeezes her shoulder and smiles.

"For as long as you need, *chérie*. For as long as you need."

As they leave the station, Rebecca turns to Monique and April, who has joined them after a morning in court. "So that's it? That's all he wanted? To know whether Natalie used drugs? He already got that from the toxicology report."

April slings her leather bag filled with documents over her shoulder. "My guess is he was scoping you out to see if you might have any connection to this."

"Me? I've never done drugs in my life. Not even pot."

"And sex trafficking?" Monique adds.

Rebecca chokes on a laugh. "Get serious! Do I look like someone involved in sex trafficking?"

"Looks can be very deceiving. The police just need to be thorough," April says.

"They don't want our little island getting a bad reputation as some others have," Monique says.

"Well, they should direct their energies toward something more useful," Rebecca says.

"Speaking of energy, I have an arraignment at eleven. I will see you back at the house this afternoon?" April asks.

"I want to spend the day with Natalie. I can play her some of her favorite music. Read to her. Just be there in case she wakes up," Rebecca says.

"That sounds like a good plan," Monique says. "I will drop you there and pick you up when you are ready."

"You don't need to bother. I can get an Uber home."

"Are you sure? I would love to have the afternoon to myself, lying by the pool, doing nothing."

"Absolutely. You have done so much already."

"It is no problem, *chérie*. This is what we are supposed to do for one another, is it not?"

Rebecca thinks about Royce, whose only concerns seem to be selfish. How much is this all going to cost? When will she return so he no longer has to worry about her safety? But maybe she is not giving Royce the benefit of the doubt or enough credit. Maybe he really does want her back home so they can be together. Maybe his idea that they try to have another baby—no, she is not ready to go there yet. It has been too soon since she held Juliet in her arms. She isn't prepared to go through that again, to give her whole heart, her whole body and soul, up to the anticipation of a baby only to have her heart shattered in a single moment. It is more than she can bear.

CHAPTER SIXTEEN

She sits next to Natalie's bed, listening to the breathing apparatus cycle through its lullaby. The intake-exhale of the machine mesmerizes her, and she finds herself matching her breath with its steady rhythm. She looks at her sister—eyes closed, bruised face, golden hair. Natalie looks so small and oddly peaceful. Rebecca wonders if her sister is willing herself to stay asleep, if she is afraid to enter back into the real world, afraid of what she might have to face, have to remember.

"It is going to be all right, Natalie. No matter what you did or what you were involved in, I forgive you. I am going to take care of you. You can come and live with Royce and me for as long as it takes for you to recover. Who knows? You two might actually get to like each other. Just come back to us, Natalie, and I promise, I will be there for you, no matter what."

As she speaks these words out loud, tears fall onto the starched white sheets. Rebecca feels something for her sister that she has never felt before. Gone is the competition between them. Gone is the jealousy over "Mom always liked you best" and the petty rivalry over their father's affection. Rebecca lets go of her resentment toward her sister for having ruined her adolescent years, forcing Rebecca to be the dutiful daughter while Natalie acted out as she pleased, rebelling as any normal teenager does against authority. Of course, Natalie took that liberty to the extreme, creating chaos for the household. But Rebecca releases her anger now as she looks at her little sister, so frail and helpless, dependent upon machines to keep her living.

She feels her shoulders relax, as though a heavy weight has been lifted. Her jaw is slack, free of tension. Her hands, once balled into fists filled with fury, are open. A bird could alight in them, or a butterfly. Rebecca is infused with love and is determined not to let the chief of police upset her sister's recovery.

She opens the book she has brought with her to read to Natalie, one of the few in English that Monique had on her shelves. *Love Warrior* by Glennon Doyle. Rebecca knows nothing about the book except that she likes the title, and she likes the epigraph: "I set out to write the story of my marriage. The first time I wrote it, I started with my wedding day because that is when I thought my marriage began. This assumption was my mistake. We'll get back to my wedding day and all the terrible magic that followed, but for now let's begin at the beginning. It's our only choice, it turns out."

Rebecca read these words when she first picked the book off the shelf in Monique's guest room earlier today. It seemed no coincidence that she selected this book to read to Natalie, because isn't she questioning her marriage now, trying to ascertain in what direction it is going to move, what the next steps in her relationship with Royce should be? If Glennon Doyle could help her figure that out now, while she was trying to lure her sister back into consciousness, then more power to the universe for its sly trick of putting the right message in front of her at the specific moment she needed it.

She turns to page one and begins to read. "I was loved. If love could prevent pain, I'd never have suffered. My leather baby book with *Glennon* branded on the front is one long poem written by my father and filled with pictures of my tender-faced mother ...." Maybe the universe is playing a cruel joke, because this has not been her experience at all. Her reading is interrupted by a knock on the door.

"May I come in?" the chief says, his large frame eclipsing the doorway. "How is our patient?"

Rebecca notices that he makes his presence known without permission. She wants to say something, to tell him to go away, but she does not have the nerve. The polite little girl inside her closes the book and gives the chief her attention.

"The same. Still unconscious."

"That is unfortunate. We were hoping there might have been some improvement."

"How long has it been? Five days since you found her?"

"Yes, five days since the jogger came upon her body on the shore."

"Hopefully she will come to any day now. Meanwhile, I will be here at her bedside. I will be in touch if there is any improvement."

"I trust that you will," he says as he turns to head out the door. Then he turns back around and faces Rebecca. "This must be very difficult for you, Rebecca. You mustn't let yourself get exhausted. Take a walk in the courtyard. The fresh air will do you some good." Then he is gone.

Rebecca is surprised by his concern. She had pegged him as a crusty old man set in his ways, with a single vision toward getting what he desired. And there seemed to be no love lost between him and Monique, which contributed to Rebecca's judgement of him. This little spark of humanity he showed has pushed the hidden door in her heart open ever so slightly, letting more light into her soul. She does not want to like him. She wants to categorize him as bullheaded and leave it at that, but there is something in her that is prompting her to see gray rather than black and white. She has no idea why the change is coming or where it is coming from, just that she feels something breaking up inside her like ice floes shattering into a thousand pieces. Maybe she is losing her mind. Or maybe she is finding it again.

Whatever. She doesn't want to read any more of this book. Not now. The thought of baby books reminds her of her own. How her mother had filled in every milestone in her journey of the first three years ... until Natalie was born. And then the pages went blank. The years passed by, unrecorded, invisible, as Natalie occupied all her mother's space, claiming all her mother's love for herself.

She wishes she had brought another book, something else to read so that her voice might reach Natalie somewhere in her subconscious, drawing her out of her deep sleep. Deep sleep. "Miles to go before I sleep." Frost. Poetry. She has memorized so many poems; surely she can reach into her reserves and pull out one now that might help Natalie wake up and participate in her life.

As that last thought crosses her mind, Rebecca is aware that she is really talking to herself. It is time for her to wake up and participate in her own life. To let go of the past. To move forward. Who says that better than Mary Oliver in "The Journey"?

She begins to whisper the words of the poem softly to her sister. To someone passing by the room, if they happened to look in, they might assume that Rebecca was praying as she sat in the chair next to Natalie's bed, leaning over and holding her sister's hands, her lips moving slowly, steadily.

Rebecca pauses, takes a sip of water from the glass on the bedside table. She tries to remember the next lines, but her mind is blank. Something about leaves and stones. Then pieces of the poem come back to her. She picks up when she recalls the last lines, which she speaks aloud as she presses her hands gently on Natalie's face, careful of the tube and wires, their foreheads touching.

determined to do
the only thing you could do—
determined to save
the only life you could save.

She pulls back, looks at her sister, attached to the wires and monitors, listens to the steady bleep of the machines. Is it Natalie's life that she wants to save? Or is it her own?

***

After several hours of sitting at Natalie's bedside with no perceptible changes in her sister's condition, Rebecca decides to take the chief's suggestion and get some fresh air. She would like to walk on the beach, but one look out the bedroom window tells her that the ocean is too far away and inaccessible by foot. She doesn't want to be gone too long. So she makes her way down the hallways to the walled courtyard, which is now void of wheelchairs and nurses. She sits on a bench that backs up against the white stucco wall, closes her eyes, and lets the sun warm her. After sitting in the air-conditioned hospital for so long, her body is stiff and cold.

She looks around, confirms that she is alone, and rises, stretching her arms high above her head and bending from side to side to loosen her tight muscles. She leans over and touches her toes, feeling the stretch all the way up her legs and into her hamstrings. She jogs in place, taking deep breaths and exhaling, as she swings her arms by her sides. She stops, leans forward on bent knees and then straightens up, the blood now coursing through her body.

That is when she sees him. A man standing in the second-floor window, looking out at her. She wonders how long he has been watching. He has something in his hands, which he brings to his face. A camera. He is taking photographs of her.

A cold shiver snakes up along her spine as her mind floods with questions. *Who is this man? Who sent him? The police? Royce? The men who killed Peter Robinson? What if that had not been a camera but a gun?* Her heart beats wildly in her chest, and she races toward the courtyard door, back into the relative safety of the building. Her next thought is Natalie. *Have they done anything to Natalie?*

She climbs the stairs, taking two at a time, not patient enough to wait for the elevator. She sprints down the maze of halls, past open doors where patients lie wheezing, coughing, dying. She passes the nurses' station and bolts into Natalie's room, half-expecting to find her dead.

But she is not. She is still lying there—eyes closed, golden hair outspread against the crisp white sheets—attached to the apparatus that keeps her breath rhythmic and steady.

Rebecca collapses in the chair by Natalie's bedside, with more questions now than answers. Just what has she gotten herself into? She thinks about calling the chief to tell him about the figure in the window. But then she hears Royce's voice—chastising her for being silly and emotional, leaping to conclusions and not living in reality. She knows this was real. Her instincts tell her she may be in danger. She just doesn't know who she can trust.

Doubt, like a pebble thrown into a lake, ripples out, making her question everything, everyone. Including Monique.

What is real? She has no clue except that she knows she must stay in the moment. Take things one step at a time. Deal with each event as it comes. If she can just do that, she will be all right.

CHAPTER SEVENTEEN

When one of the nurses comes in at 4 p.m., the time when shifts change from day to night, and suggests that she might do her sister more good if she takes care of herself and goes home to get some rest, she readily complies. She is tired, drained from sitting all day by Natalie's side, listening to the steady rhythm of the machines. The stale air of the hospital, the fluorescent lights, the smell of sickness and, probably, death have sapped her of her energy.

Her strange experience in the courtyard momentarily jolted her from her lethargy but then left her feeling even more depleted as she sank deep into a sense of isolation. Alone. That is how she feels. Completely alone.

The nurse assures her that if there is any change in Natalie's condition, they will call, adding that Rebecca needn't wait expectantly by her phone. She should live her life, pray for her sister, and hope for a happy outcome. It could still be days, weeks, months before Natalie comes to, if she ever comes to at all.

Rebecca calls a taxi to take her back to Monique's villa. She is pragmatic. She knows she can't make Natalie wake up any sooner than she will. But Rebecca also knows that the clock is ticking. Almost twenty-four hours has passed since Royce issued his ultimatum. He will be down to St. Croix in two days if the situation has not changed, and he will expect her to leave the island with him.

She does not know if she will be able to do that. She knows she cannot abandon her sister. All Rebecca can do at this moment is pray that she wakes up within the next twenty-four hours so Natalie can be absolved of any part in Peter Robinson's death.

***

Rebecca climbs into the silver van that serves as a taxi. She is the only passenger in the spacious vehicle, which adds to her loneliness. Though she is glad, too, that no one is there for whom she must keep up the pretense of being all right. She is not all right. Her mind grinds over the same questions, the same scenarios she has been anxious over all day. Her head throbs with the effort. She feels tears spring from her eyes. She swallows down a gasp that threatens to erupt into weeping.

The taxi driver looks at her in the mirror. "Is everything all right, miss?" he says. She wipes her eyes with the back of her hand. "I'm fine. Just exhausted."

When they reach the house, the air shimmers like a glass of wine with light shining through it. She will ask Monique for a glass of Chablis as soon as she walks in. It will calm her down, help her to relax after this emotionally draining day.

The critical voice in her head asks, *Is this how you become an alcoholic? Does it start with depending on one drink to help you relax?* She counters the negativity quickly. Just because her mother is an alcoholic and her sister is an addict/alcoholic does not necessarily mean she is going to go down that road too. Look at her father. He drinks in moderation. He has never needed to go into treatment.

For most of her life, Rebecca has told herself she must not drink because she might have inherited her mother's genes. She reasoned that the female gene that carried on into her sister and created Natalie's addictive personality must also be present in her because she is female too. Now she is beginning to doubt her reasoning. Since she has been at Monique's, she has enjoyed a glass of wine. A single glass of wine. She hasn't snuck down to the kitchen at night to swig a drink. She has refused the offer of a second glass, knowing that the first one made her woozy. But wouldn't her mother tell her that the fact she was laboring under all these questions ought to be a red light flashing?

To hell with what Mom thinks. To hell with everyone telling me who I ought to be and what I ought to do with my life. Rebecca has an overwhelming desire to break free. She is not sure what it is she wants to break free from, but the iceberg image comes back into her mind. The ice being shattered into a thousand pieces.

I am losing my mind. Or maybe, just maybe, I am finding out who I am.

Without Royce, without the heavy yoke of being a wife under his scrutiny and direction, subject to his moods, she has a new freedom. The wine is just a part of it. There is also her whole attitude toward Natalie. That, too, has changed, and she does not know why or how. She does not need to know why or how. She just needs to know that it has.

She opens the blue front door, not certain whether she should knock. To knock seems such a formal thing to do. And hasn't Monique said, "My house is your house"?

When she enters, the house is dark except for one light over the stove in the kitchen. "Hello? Monique?" she says, taking a few steps forward into the living room. She switches on a lamp that rests on a glass end table and sees a pad of paper that she assumes is a shopping list, but when she looks more closely, she sees PR, RW, NB, and then the word <u>stables</u>, underlined. What could this mean? Rebecca's heart throbs in her chest. She has no idea why she responds to the note this way. All she wants at this moment is to get Natalie off the island safely and back home. She turns out the lamp and walks into the kitchen to pour herself a glass of wine.

That is when she notices the lights outside, illuminating the infinity pool. The water is so blue and inviting. She sees two figures in the water. Monique and April. They are standing in the water facing each other, laughing, talking. The next thing she sees is Monique taking April's face in her hands and pressing her lips on April's lips. Rebecca feels her face turning red. She turns away, embarrassed. How could she not have seen before that Monique and April were lovers? She has been so into her own world with her concerns over Natalie, Juliet, and Royce that she has not noticed what is going on in the world around her. Surely there have been clues. But she has missed them. What will Royce say if he finds out she is staying in a house with two lesbians?

Royce is like his mother—homophobic, conservative. He will probably assume her sexuality is in question by proxy. But she knows that is not so. Seeing the two women together does not shock her, nor does it stimulate her. It just is. As far as her own sexuality goes, she feels as if she has dried up and withered away. The way she feels now, if she never has sex again, it will be all right. But touch—the loving touch of someone who cares—that is different. She could use that now.

She puts her handbag down on the kitchen counter, opens the fridge, and takes out the bottle of white wine. She opens the cupboard, retrieves a glass, and pours herself a drink. Then she makes her way over to the glass sliders.

"Mind if I join you?" she asks.

"Rebecca! Where is your bathing suit? The water is divine," Monique says.

"I just got back. The water does look good, but I needed this first," she says, raising her glass. "I hope you don't mind."

"Not at all. How is your sister?" Monique asks.

"The same. Still unconscious. They said they would call if there was a change."

"Of course. Do you mind me asking—don't you think you should tell your parents? Or perhaps you already have?"

"I thought about it, but I want to wait until Natalie is in the clear. My mother is a bit … unstable. I don't want to give her more to worry about. Right now, she has accepted that Natalie is gone. The last thing she needs is Natalie back, in a coma, with a murder charge on her head."

"Never underestimate a mother's resilience," Monique says. "But I see your point. Perhaps it is best to wait. For a bit anyway."

Rebecca sits down on a chaise lounge beside the pool, stretches her legs out. "The police chief came by."

"This does not surprise me," Monique says. "I hope you said nothing to him."

"Just pleasantries."

"Good. If he bothers you again, let me know," April says. "We'll sue him for harassment."

Rebecca's eyes open wide as she takes a sip of wine. "Please God, no! I can't take any more excitement!"

"I'm just teasing," April says. "But really, he has no place showing up at the hospital uninvited."

Rebecca thinks back to the morning and how the old man had encouraged her to take care of herself. "Maybe he's not such an old goat. I think he has a soft side."

Monique lifts herself up onto the side of the pool, wraps herself in an oversized terry-cloth towel, and lies down on a chaise beside Rebecca. "He can be very charming. But I caution you—he is not what he seems."

Rebecca takes a long sip of her wine. "Well, I'm just glad he didn't put me in the clinker."

"The clinker?"

"Jail."

"But you have not done anything," Monique says.

"Sometimes that doesn't matter," Rebecca says.

"She's right, you know. Do you realize how many innocent people are locked up every year?" April says as she floats on her back.

"And how many criminals go free," Monique says quietly.

Rebecca rests her empty glass on the tiled floor. She ponders whether or not to tell the women about the man in the window but decides against it. She tells herself that maybe she just imagined the whole episode. She doesn't want to sound hysterical. And there is the issue of trust. Instead, she asks, "Do you think they'll arrest Natalie once she wakes up?"

"That depends on what she tells them, doesn't it?" April says.

"If anything, she's the victim, not the perpetrator," Rebecca says. "I can't believe this is happening."

Monique rises from the chaise, taking Rebecca's glass with her as she heads toward the kitchen. "How about another glass of wine, Rebecca, while I prepare dinner?"

Before her inner critic has the chance to object, Rebecca says, "Sure. Why not?" Rebecca likes the way the wine takes the edge off her anxiety. It helps her handle all these scenarios that keep bombarding her from left and right. She tells herself she will be careful. She won't let herself drink any more than two glasses. She will not get drunk. She wonders what Royce would say now if he could see her relaxing with a glass of wine with two women in string bikinis. She follows Monique into the kitchen.

"What is so amusing?" Monique says as she chops up vegetables for a salade Niçoise.

"Nothing. Just my husband. I was imagining how he would react to all this. He is very conservative."

"He would disapprove?"

"I'm afraid so."

"Poor man. Such a puny world view. But you, you seem quite liberal. How did you two find each other?"

Rebecca thinks back to when she first met Royce. They were in a class together in college—Introduction to World Mythology. It was an easy elective that all the premed and prelaw students took to satisfy their humanities requirement. Rebecca, an English major, was there because she genuinely wanted to learn about mythology in different cultures.

She had no idea that Royce liked her, had any interest in her. He seemed infatuated with another girl in the class. They always sat together and kissed each other when they departed to go their separate ways. The kisses were deep and long, and Royce's hands would travel over the girl's body until they landed on her ass and he gave her a mandatory squeeze. "See you later," he would say and then wink. How obvious was that. Rebecca imagined they were into kinky sex and drugs and all those things Rebecca kept herself separate from.

Still, when she looked at the couple fawning over each other, she wished it were she, not the other girl, whom Royce was kissing. She thought about him when she was not in class, his thick, dark hair always cut short and neat; his tall, muscular body which he kept trim and tight. And his eyes, deep blue as the deepest waters of the ocean, that penetrated her when she caught him looking at her across the classroom. She had a crush, to be sure.

One day, Royce came up to her after class. His fuck buddy was nowhere to be seen.

"How are you doing?" he said.

She held her books tightly against her chest, trying to mask the fact that her breasts were heaving in her blouse and her heart was pounding like a jackhammer.

"I'm good. You?" she said.

"I would like to take you to dinner," he said.

"What about your girlfriend?"

"She's not my girlfriend. We're just hooking up. I'm looking for a nice girl. You seem nice."

Rebecca could not believe her ears. He was admitting to using the poor girl for sex and stating outright that she, Rebecca, was not the type of girl who he assumed engaged in that type of thing. She half expected him to ask her if she was a virgin—which she was, but he didn't need to know that. Part of her wanted to turn him down, knock him down from the arrogant pedestal on which he stood, but she looked in his eyes, his deep blue eyes, and she found herself agreeing to join him for dinner that evening.

Royce was charming. He took her to Joe Tecce's, a famous Italian restaurant in Boston, and encouraged her to order the linguine with garlic and oil because it was the best thing on the menu. A taste of heaven. Never mind the smell of garlic lingering on her breath or the golden oil dripping down her chin. He reached over and wiped it away gently with his linen napkin, without judgement, without making her feel self-conscious. From their very first date, he seemed to treasure her, a feeling she had been longing for all her life.

Months passed by with Royce courting her in secret while carrying on his double life. If he had not been so thoughtful, sending her flowers and bringing gifts on the occasions when they got together, she might have resented his dalliances. But always he assured her that she was his soulmate, the woman with whom he wanted to have a family. The other women meant nothing. They simply scratched an itch. He made it clear that he wanted to marry a virgin, and she was probably the only one on campus. She was the chosen one. Rebecca, who had never been the chosen one growing up, drank up his words and actions like they were golden nectar from the gods.

Let him compartmentalize, she told herself. *Let him sleep with other girls and treat you like Sleeping Beauty.* One day, when they were married, he would awaken her from her trance, they would make a baby, and they would all live happily ever after.

They dated for the rest of the year, never engaging in sex, just serious petting. When he went off to Wharton, he promised her that she would be set for life if she would keep herself pure for him. He sealed that promise with an expensive engagement ring, which she wore with pride during her senior year.

When she brought Royce home one weekend in the fall to meet her parents, her mother took her aside in the kitchen.

"Are you sure he's the one, Rebecca? He seems so rigid. So inflexible. There's something strange. I just can't put my finger on it."

Rebecca felt herself getting defensive. "He just has very good posture."

"Does he ever laugh? Smile?"

"Of course he does! He's just very serious. And a little nervous about meeting you and Dad. Honestly, Mom, you put up with all kinds of losers that Natalie brings home. I bring home a really nice guy, and you get all weird. There's no pleasing you."

"I just don't want to see you make a mistake, that's all."

"The only mistake I've made is bringing him home to meet you in the first place. Discussion over."

Now she sees how her mother was right.

"Rebecca! Rebecca!" Monique's voice calls out and breaks through into her consciousness. "My goodness, that is a serious look you have on your face. Here, have some wine."

Rebecca sighs. She takes the glass from Monique.

"So this husband of yours—he is giving you trouble?" Monique says, as she arranges the vegetables and tuna on ceramic plates.

"Not trouble exactly." *Unless you call sleeping with other women trouble.* But Rebecca reminds herself that she was the one who opened that door. "Nothing that any marriage probably doesn't go through."

"Were you married in a church?" Monique asks.

Where else would we be married? Rebecca wants to ask, but she knows it is a legitimate question. She had actually wanted to be married by a justice of the peace out in a field somewhere or on a beach, but Bette would have none of that. She wanted her only child to have a wedding to end all weddings, one that would make the society sections of all the snobby magazines that filled their pages with photographs of the Beautiful People, the 1 percent that Rebecca secretly despised. Not because they were such bad people but because she felt so much shame around them. As if she were not good enough, would never be good enough, even if she did marry into Royce's money. She would always be considered an outsider.

Royce's family footed the bill for the wedding, though Rebecca's mother insisted that she and Rebecca's father pay for Rebecca's wedding dress. Rebecca and Royce were married in Trinity Church, a beautiful stone church in the heart of Princeton, on a beautiful spring day when the air was still cool, the sky a brilliant blue, and the yellow bonnets of daffodils danced in the breeze. There were more than three hundred guests, most of whom Rebecca did not know but Bette had insisted attend. It was all "picture perfect" except for Natalie, her maid of honor, who showed up high. Rebecca could still remember how cold her hands were as they gripped her bouquet while she walked down the aisle toward Royce. Her heels resounded on the slate floor, and the organ music throbbed throughout the lofty church. She knew that, as a bride, she would have jitters, but these were more than butterflies in her stomach. These were doubts that had been brought on just minutes before she took her father's arm and processed down the aisle.

Her mother had made some last-minute adjustments to her dress, and as she took a loose strand of Rebecca's hair and tucked it into her daughter's chignon, she said, "You know, you don't have to go through with this." Rebecca was startled by her mother's comment. Here she was, marrying an extremely wealthy, handsome, and successful man in a wedding that was gorgeous in the extreme, and her mother was saying, "You know, you don't have to go through with this." Rebecca sloughed her mother off angrily, saying, "Stop it, Mother. Just stop trying to ruin my day."

The vows she took were solemn and binding. To love, honor, cherish, and obey. Over the years, she tried her best, but once they were married, and she and Royce were finally living together, she began to get a taste of what he was like as a human being—big on the honor and obey, not so much on the love and cherish. Except she should love and cherish *him*, worship him really. To him, she was just the virgin he had found to bear his children. When she miscarried the first time, his disappointment was evident. The second time, he accused her of doing something wrong. When Juliet died, he made it clear that he found her to be damaged goods.

Over the years, she had experienced a kind of emotional waterboarding by Royce. His on-again, off-again mercurial moods. She could never be sure which Royce would wake up next to her that day or come home to her in the evening. She suspected he had some kind of personality disorder. Bipolar, perhaps? But she would no more suggest to him that he go into therapy than she would have told her mother, who exhibited the same kind of behavior when she was drinking, to get sober.

"Rebecca, you are one of the most pensive people I have ever met," Monique says. "Where do you go in that brain of yours?"

Rebecca smiles. "You don't want to know."

"Come, let's eat, shall we? A little food will do you some good. Sit. I will call April." Monique places the plates of food on the dining room table and walks away in search of her companion.

Rebecca sits at the table looking out the slider windows. A beautiful sunset is gathering in the clouds on the horizon that rise up like frothy spinnakers. There is sure to be an afterglow, as her parents call it. Her parents. She wonders what is the best action to take with them. Should she let them know Natalie is alive, or should she wait until her sister has come out of the coma? It does not seem fair to withhold the news from her parents, but does she really want them coming down here? She knows they will be on the next plane as soon as they get the news. She does not think they will handle the possibility of Natalie's being involved in a murder very well. It could be the trigger that sets her mother off again. So she decides the best course of action is to let the next two days play out until Royce is due to arrive, see what happens with Natalie, and just handle everything herself in the meantime. This is the kindest thing she can do not only for her mother but also for herself. She closes her eyes and rubs the space between her eyebrows, which has creased in worry, inhales deeply, and sighs.

"What do you say tomorrow we take a little excursion?" Monique says between bites of her salad.

"You mean, leave the hospital?" Rebecca says as she spears some tuna and lettuce on her fork. "I don't know if I ... I don't know how I feel about that."

"You know what they say: All work and no play makes Jack a dull boy."

"Or Jill a dull girl," April says. "Though I am afraid I won't be able to go with you. I have to be in court all day."

"Would we be gone all day?" Rebecca's hand is frozen in midair, her eyes startled. "What if she wakes up?"

"She will still be awake when you return. I'm sure the nurses will take good care of her," Monique says.

"You can't live your life on the expectation that she will come to," April says, pouring herself another glass of wine, then refilling Monique's glass. She offers some to Rebecca, who puts her hand over the top of her glass.

"What is that supposed to mean?" Rebecca says.

"Just that she will wake when she wakes. You can't make it happen a minute sooner. Meanwhile, you need to take care of yourself. Enjoy the island. Have some fun."

"I didn't come here to have fun."

Monique lays her hand over Rebecca's. "No one is suggesting that you forget your sister or ignore her. Just that time might pass a little easier if you take a little break from your vigil and relax." Monique breaks a long baguette into pieces, handing each woman a chunk. "Besides, I have been dying to go to Buck Island for months, and I need a companion to come with me. You would be doing me a favor."

"Buck Island?" Rebecca says.

"Yes. There is a spectacular underwater trail there. It is an experience not to be missed."

"You will see coral reefs, fish of all kind, manta rays, maybe even sharks," April says.

Rebecca considers her options: say no and appear rude and ungrateful to this woman who has gone out of her way to be supportive, or say yes and possibly miss the moment when Natalie wakes up. Of course, there are no guarantees Natalie will wake up. And even if she does, she may not be lucid enough to even recognize Rebecca as her sister. Does Rebecca really want to sit in the hospital for another day, watching time pass slowly on the clock in the corridor above the nurses' station? Wouldn't it be more fun, healthier, to take a little break and enjoy the island and all it has to offer? Even the chief said some fresh air might do her good.

Rebecca cannot believe she is even thinking this way, putting her own wants and needs ahead of someone else's. But hey, it is Natalie, and her little sister is just about one of the most selfish people Rebecca has ever known. She is sure that if the roles were reversed, if it were she lying in a coma in a hospital on a remote island, Natalie would not even bother to look her up. Not give her a second thought. She would pursue her own plans as she has done all her life without regard for who she has to step over or run through to execute them.

"You're right. I should take some time for me. I would love to go snorkeling with you tomorrow, Monique. And I will even have a little more wine to celebrate." She passes her glass to April, who refills it.

"A toast," Monique says, raising her glass. "To Rebecca, who is emerging from the shadows."

"To Rebecca."

"To me," Rebecca says, clinking glasses with the two women. She doesn't know exactly what Monique meant or how she arrived at that observation, but the phrase does have a certain ring to it that strikes Rebecca as true. She is coming out of something. She is headed somewhere. She just doesn't have the slightest idea where she is going. Or why.

CHAPTER EIGHTEEN

The next morning, Monique wakes Rebecca early, bringing a cup of hot coffee to her bedroom at what feels to Rebecca like the crack of dawn.

"No sleeping in this morning," Monique says brightly. "We will want to get to the island before all the tourists arrive."

"How far is it?" asks Rebecca as she sits in bed, clasping the sheets to cover her nakedness and sipping on the hot, rich brew.

"Not far. The island itself is about one and a half miles north of the northeast coast. It won't take us long to get there. I assure you it is worth the trip. President John Kennedy designated the island a national monument in 1961. He wanted to preserve what he called 'one of the finest marine gardens in the Caribbean Sea.' The area was added on to in 2001 by President Bill Clinton. Because of their efforts, we can enjoy 176 acres of uninhabited paradise, most of which is underwater."

"And who said the Democrats never did anything good?"

"*Pardonne-moi?*"

"Nothing. Just a little political sidebar in my brain. Buck Island sounds wonderful. I'll just get dressed and wash my face, and we can be on our way." Rebecca waits for Monique to leave the room before she gets out of bed.

"*Bien,*" Monique says, "but a croissant first before we go. You will need your stamina for the swim."

***

The morning she spends snorkeling with Monique at Buck Island is like a dream. She could never have imagined how breathtaking the underwater scenery would be. The underwater tour lasts only an hour, but in that hour, she is transported to another world. Memories of the first time she saw the movie *Avatar*, with its surreal landscape and unparalleled beauty, flood her. Branching elkhorn coral creates fortress-like walls forming a lagoon between the island and the surrounding seas. Within the lagoon, fish of all sizes and colors swim, sometimes in pairs like lovebirds. They skim through the water, often bonded together in a giant balloon of silver sequins flashing in the light. The bigger fish look grumpy, wearing scowls on their pointed faces. Sea turtles rest on the reef floor while elegant rays spread their wings, fanning the water as they glide silently by.

The underwater world is a silent one, disturbed only by Rebecca's breathing. So caught up in the transcendent experience, she forgets, for an hour, her troubled marriage, her unconscious sister, her unresolved grief. She feels an overwhelming sense of peace as she follows behind Monique, whose blue flippers act as a beacon, and whose hands direct Rebecca's vision toward one breathtaking sight after another. She is in *awe*. There is no other way to describe it. Monique has taken her to the edge of the eternal. How could she have ever doubted her? She feels herself physically loosening, letting go, and not just because she is being held up by the water. She feels as if new space has been created in her soul. She is filled with gratitude for Monique, who suggested they engage in this adventure. *So much better than talk therapy*, she says to herself. But then Nature always was her go-to place for peace. Peace—that's what she experiences as she lets her legs move her gently through the water. A peace she hasn't known for a long time.

"That was amazing," she says as they climb back into Monique's little Spider to return home. "And that is not a big enough word."

"Sometimes there are no words," Monique says.

Rebecca leans back in her seat, closes her eyes, and sees an image of a bright pink angelfish swimming before her. An angel. That is what Monique is. Her angel.

"Thank you," Rebecca says. "You are an angel."

Monique laughs her throaty laugh. "*Mon Dieu, chérie!* If you only knew. I am no angel. But I am happy to help you, to be here for you, however I am able."

***

As luck would have it, or fate, or karma, if one were so inclined to believe in that sort of thing, Natalie did come to while Rebecca was swimming with the manta rays and getting sunburned on her back. By the time Rebecca received the news that Natalie had woken up and was suffering from situational amnesia, the police had already swarmed the hospital to interview the now-conscious girl. News of the girl's awakening has reached the media, who, with their glinting cameras, swarm the entrance to the hospital like piranhas. Now Rebecca and Monique race up the corridor in the hospital, maneuvering their way through an obstacle course of wheelchairs, walkers, and nurses, to catch sight of Natalie's face.

Where before Natalie had looked angelic and peaceful as she lay comatose in the bed, her face is now worn with fatigue, her eyes reflecting her confusion.

"How many times do I have to tell you? I don't remember. I don't remember anything," Natalie says.

"You must remember something. Look at this photograph again. Carefully," the chief says as he looms over her, shoving the picture of Peter Robinson in her face. "Have you seen this man before?"

"I tell you, I don't remember. I don't remember anything."

Rebecca elbows her way in, planting herself by the chief's side. "If she says she doesn't remember, she doesn't remember."

"Rebecca?" Natalie says. "Is that you?"

Rebecca reaches over and takes her sister's hands in her own. "Yes, Nat. It's me. I'm sorry I wasn't here when you woke up. I meant to be. I should have been."

"But how? How did you find me?"

"It's a long story. It doesn't matter. I'm here now."

"Mom? Dad? Are they here?"

"No."

"Why not?"

That would be the question Natalie would ask. *Why not? Why are they not here?* As if the whole world revolves around her. But even as she thinks it, Rebecca realizes that Natalie has a legitimate question. *Why aren't her parents here?* Because Rebecca made the decision not to share any information with her parents until she was absolutely certain the woman on the island was Natalie. But she has been certain for forty-eight hours. She could have called her parents, and they might have been at Natalie's side when she woke up. Why didn't she call? She tells herself that it was to save her parents from all this—the interrogation by the police, the suspicion of foul play, the connection between Natalie and the murdered man.

"I didn't want them to know. Until you were cleared of any wrongdoing."

"Wrongdoing? What are you talking about?"

Rebecca looks into her sister's eyes and sees that she is genuinely confused, alarmed.

"Oh my God, was I in a blackout? What did I do?"

"Didn't they tell you?"

"Tell me what?"

Rebecca turns to the police chief. "Well, are you going to say something, or shall I?"

"We were just getting there. The matter is sensitive, you know. There is a way to do these things."

Rebecca directs her attention back to Natalie. "There was another body that washed up on shore. A man. He had been shot."

"Oh my God! Is he all right?"

"Actually, no. He's dead."

"And the police think I had something to do with that?" Natalie looks at the chief. "You think I had something to do with that?"

The chief flicks some invisible threads off the sleeve of his shirt. "We don't know. That's what we're trying to ascertain."

"You can't be serious!" Natalie laughs. "I may be a little wild sometimes, but I am no murderer."

April strides into the room, her big leather bag slung over her shoulder. "Not another word, Natalie. I'm your attorney, April Nave. This interview is now over."

The chief shakes his head and motions for the other two officers to leave the room. "We will get to the bottom of this. Keep this," he says, tossing the photo on Natalie's lap. "It may jog your memory."

"Not today, you won't," Monique says, poking her father in the chest. "Shame on you! This woman is just hours out of reviving from a coma, and you are already questioning her? The doctors tell us she may have situational amnesia. What could you hope to get? A coerced confession perhaps? You will stop at nothing to protect your own ass!"

The chief waves his hand above his head as if swatting at flies. "Enough, Monique! We will be back later." He marches out the door, leaving the four women in the room.

When Rebecca sits back down, Natalie's eyes are closed and tears stream down her face. Rebecca takes her sister's hand again. "Don't worry, Natalie. We will get you through this. We will get you out of here." She slips the photo of Peter Robinson into her purse next to the sonogram of Juliet.

"How? They think I murdered someone, and honestly, I don't know. Maybe I did."

"Don't say that! For God's sake, don't say that!"

"But I don't remember anything."

"What is the last thing you remember? The last picture that comes to mind?"

Natalie pauses, reflecting. "A boat. A boat, a yacht, I think. And climbing a ladder."

April takes notes as she says, "That is good. Anything else? Do you see anyone with you?"

"No, just me, climbing the ladder. And then … nothing."

"Does the name Peter Robinson mean anything to you?" April asks.

"No. Should it?"

"What about the man who brought you to the island?" Rebecca says. "Do you remember anything about him?"

"My head hurts. I have a terrible headache. Can we do this later? I just want to rest," Natalie says.

"Of course," April says. "But we mustn't wait too long. This is a murder investigation, and as long as you are a suspect, the police can keep you here indefinitely. Better to clear your name."

"What if I can't clear my name? What if I can't remember?"

"Don't worry, Natalie. You have the best lawyer on the island. She'll get you off, won't you, April?" Rebecca says.

"As it stands, there is no concrete evidence against you. I think the chief is just trying to put the pieces of the puzzle together. You have nothing to worry about."

Natalie looks at her sister. "Tell Royce thank you. I assume he is paying for all this."

Royce. When Rebecca called Royce to tell him she had found Natalie, he was hardly supportive. In fact, he issued an ultimatum. Why did Natalie assume Royce would come to her rescue and foot all the lawyer's fees? Pay the hospital bills? Just because he, they, have money does not mean they are obligated to pull Natalie out of the mess she is in. In fact, Natalie has been in messes before—never quite as dramatic as this—and Royce has always stood firm about not bailing her out on the principle that "she made her mess, let her lie in it." He has some Puritanical notion that helping others who are in distress only causes them to be weak and robs them of the chance to build character. Spoken like a true 1 percent Republican who has always had the means to buy his way into or out of any situation.

Rebecca wants her sister to know it is *she* who has orchestrated her rescue, although she realizes it is not entirely true. Yes, she read the newspaper article that prompted her to get on a plane to St. Croix, but who put that article in front of her face, and why did she choose to read it? Chance? No. Something more. She was drawn to the article by something outside herself. Who had her sit next to Monique LaFleur on the plane and made her such a supportive and generous friend? Who ensured that Monique's partner was the most badass lawyer on the island? Rebecca couldn't have come up with all this if she had scripted it herself. Surely there was something greater at work. The "coincidences" were too blatant for even Rebecca to ignore.

As she sits with her sister, Rebecca wonders if Natalie will remember that she was five months pregnant when Natalie left for the islands with the mystery man. The first trimester was awful; her hormones raged and she was moody and exhausted. Then, like magic, she entered the second phase of her pregnancy. It was as if the moon had risen in the night sky and shone full down on her, casting shadows and creating moon paths on the water. She felt peaceful, serene, complete. She remembers going out with Natalie once during that fourth month, for lunch. Her appetite was back, full on, and her sister laughed at all she was eating. Natalie teased her that she would have to name the baby Grilled Chicken because she had such a craving for grilled chicken sandwiches with plenty of mayonnaise. That was a carefree day. Natalie was still clean and sober, or so Rebecca thought, and the two of them enjoyed light conversation about the baby to come. Impulsively, Rebecca asked Natalie to be the baby's godmother. Natalie seemed genuinely pleased. But was she? Or was she secretly jealous now that their mother had turned so much of her attention to the grandchild to come? Because it was not too long after that when Natalie ran off, out of their lives, without a word.

Rebecca wants to tell her sister about Juliet. About the grief she felt in losing the baby when life seemed to be going so well. Juliet had become the focus when Natalie disappeared. It was as if the baby had taken the place of the missing sister—daughter—in everyone's eyes. Where Natalie and her bad choices had pierced their mother's heart, Juliet gave them hope. She was the new generation, the bright light that eased their mother's pain. But when Juliet died, the pain became too much. Loss piled upon loss, their mother retreated again into the bottle, unable to deal with her feelings, whatever they were. Rebecca imagined they were mostly feelings about how she had failed both her daughters somehow. Her mother made it all about herself while Rebecca quietly disappeared, left alone as she was without anyone to confide in.

Natalie can't possibly know the grief she has brought on the family, Rebecca thinks now. *Nor does she need to know. Not now. But Mom and Dad need to know she's alive. That I have found her—even if she is a suspect in a murder investigation. Mom deserves to know the truth.*

"Will you be all right if I step out for a moment? Monique and April will stay with you. You can trust them," Rebecca says.

"Just promise you will come back."

"I promise."

Rebecca walks outside into the enclosed courtyard. A few patients are soaking up the sun. Rebecca glances up at the window on the second floor to see if the man with the camera is there.

He is not.

The air is sweet and warm, filled with the scent of jasmine. She finds a stone bench and sits down, feels the cold stone under her legs. She closes her eyes and wonders how she should break the news to her parents. Should she tell them everything? She decides to play it by ear and dials their number.

On the third ring, her mother picks up. "Rebecca! What a nice surprise!"

"Hi, Mom. How are you?"

Her mother laughs. "You just can't let go of that 'Mom' thing, can you?"

"What?" Rebecca says, confused.

"Remember? Your father and I asked you to call us by our first names."

"That's right. Dorothy. Jack. I'm so sorry. Old habits are hard to break."

"It's not a problem. I just find it amusing."

"Honestly, it feels a little awkward."

"Then don't do it, Rebecca. 'Mom' will do just fine. I like being your mom. Is everything okay?"

Rebecca sighs, takes a deep breath before she begins. "I found her."

"Found who?"

"Natalie."

"Natalie? You found Natalie! Where? How? How is she? Oh my God, Jack! Rebecca found Natalie."

"She is fine. She is in a hospital on St. Croix."

"St. Croix? How did you ever—"

"It's a long story. She was unconscious and now she is awake, and she wants to see you and Dad."

"Of course she does. Are you there, on St. Croix, now?"

"Yes. I came down two days ago."

There is a profound silence on the phone. Rebecca knows what is coming next and braces herself.

"You should have told us."

"I know, Mom, but it was complicated. I wasn't sure it was her. And then, there is another issue."

"Is she brain-dead? Paralyzed?"

"No, no. Nothing like that. She is fully conscious. But she is being held by the St. Croix police."

"The police? What on earth for? Don't tell me. Drugs were involved."

"Possibly. But more than that. Someone was murdered."

"Murdered! Natalie is not a murderer!"

"Calm down, Mom. I know. I have an attorney down here who is working with us to get Natalie released. We should be home in a few days."

"I think we should fly down."

"Honestly, Mom, there is not a lot you can do for her right now. I have got everything covered."

"Nonsense. I am hanging up and making flight reservations right away. We should be down there tomorrow. If not sooner. Tell Natalie I am on my way." There is another pregnant pause. Once again, Rebecca braces herself. "And Rebecca, I wish you had included us from the start. You really had no right to keep this to yourself."

"I just thought—"

"You didn't think. You acted. Selfishly. But what is done is done. We will see you tomorrow."

Rebecca holds the silent phone in her hands. *Selfish.* Her mother has called her selfish. And yet, what she has done, is doing, seems to her to be anything but selfish. She has gone to great expense—and right there, she catches herself. This "outing" to St. Croix has cost her nothing. Royce paid for the airline tickets, and beyond that, she has had free lodging and meals. An attorney who is working *pro bono*. She wonders if the police might charge her for Natalie's stay at the hospital, but so far that seems to have been taken care of. This trip has cost her nothing—financially.

Emotionally, she is paying the price. Standing up to Royce and walking out on him, against his wishes, was a huge step for her and took a kind of courage she did not know she possessed. Trusting Monique, and then April, took her to a new level—of what, she cannot name. She just has this sensation of breaking into a million pieces. Letting go of her obsession with Juliet and focusing on Natalie is an unexpected gift that she could not have predicted. Her feelings for Natalie—compassion and love—are new and unlike anything she has felt for her sister in the past. She does not know where all these new feelings are coming from, she just accepts them and is glad they are present.

Now her mom is calling her selfish. Maybe she was holding the cards too closely to her chest. But she believes her motivation was pure. That she really only wants what is best for her parents, for Natalie. And for herself. It is still very hard to put herself in her parents' shoes, to see this from their perspective, because she is so focused on her own.

"Well?" Monique says when Rebecca reenters the room.

Natalie is once again sleeping.

"My parents will be here tomorrow."

"Are you all right with that?"

"It is what it is." Rebecca looks at her sister sleeping in the bed, watches her chest rise and fall slowly, rhythmically. She wonders whether Natalie is telling the truth, that she really does not remember anything, or if she is pretending to have no memory of the events of that day in order to protect herself. If she is lying, surely the police will draw the truth out of her during their interrogation. Natalie will be helpless against their tricks. If she is innocent of the murder, they might twist the truth out of her about some sex trafficking ring and she could be locked away for years. Her parents will be no help against the police. Her mother will be too emotional, and her father is fairly clueless when it comes to situations like this. She remembers how he couldn't even talk the judge out of lessening Natalie's fee on a speeding ticket when she was sixteen. Suddenly, she wants Royce.

Royce may have many difficult traits, but he is authoritative, and he can cut through the tangled web of bureaucracy and get the job done. "I am going to call Royce and ask him to come down."

"Are you sure? April can handle this for you."

"I appreciate all you have done," Rebecca says, addressing April, "but I think Royce will be able to handle the police chief ... uh, your father, Monique." *Better than you*, she wants to say but doesn't. April has not done a very good job at keeping the chief at bay so far. Rebecca catches herself being judgmental. That was an old habit she worked on with Margot—the tendency to tear something or someone apart in order to detach emotionally. She wants to do better. April has done nothing wrong. It is just that Royce is a man, a very wealthy man, and he may be able to "convince" the police chief to let Natalie go without any more ado.

"Let's see what tomorrow brings," she says. "Why don't you two go home. I will stick around here for a while to see if she wakes up."

"As you wish. Just remember, you need to take care of yourself too."

Rebecca smiles, grateful for the reminder, but inwardly she wonders just how in the name of hell she is supposed to do that when people like her mother make impossible demands.

CHAPTER NINETEEN

The next day, Dorothy, Jack, and Royce arrive on the same flight, which makes it convenient for Rebecca, who is meeting them at the airport. She wonders what their conversations might have been like flying down, if there were any conversations. Royce is not particularly fond of her parents, nor they of him. Their interactions are usually strained, with Rebecca acting as mediator. She is curious how it went without her.

At Royce's insistence, she has rented a car and moved her belongings out of Monique's villa to the lavish Buccaneer Beach and Golf Resort where Royce has reserved a luxurious two-bedroom villa to accommodate the four of them. It will mean a longer ride to the hospital, but Royce insists they book rooms in the most expensive hotel on the island. Rebecca suspects this is his way of insulating himself from the poverty on the island, the shanty homes and half-naked children running in the streets. Royce will want to get Natalie off the island as soon as possible. Rebecca anticipates the interaction between Royce and the police chief as if she were going to a fight, though she knows already who will come out on top. Royce always comes out on top.

As the four of them drive to the hospital, no one speaks. The silence is so thick, Rebecca almost feels blinded by it. There is so much she wants to say to reassure her parents that Natalie is all right. That this inquiry by the police is nothing more than a nuisance. That Royce will take care of it. But she knows if she opens her mouth and speaks, she will give them permission to voice their opinions about how she has handled this situation. She imagines the disappointment her mother will express. The vitriol Royce will spew because he has been torn from his routine for several days. The disdain he feels toward her because she seems unable to solve any major problems on her own. She does not feel up to handling their criticism or outrage; she is dealing with her own demons. The guilt she feels over not telling her parents sooner. The anger that roils in her over her submissiveness to Royce. There is so much about herself that she would like to change, but she does not know how or even where to begin. Driving in such close proximity to these three people—two really, her dad is almost invisible—is like being squeezed in a vise. Pain shoots up the small of her back. Her ribs feel compressed, almost to the point of breaking, so much so that she can barely breathe. Her head throbs, threatening a migraine.

She rolls down her window to let some fresh air into the car. The hospital is only a few more miles away. She takes a deep breath. Exhales.

"Becca, do you mind? Close that window. We've got the air conditioner on," Royce says.

Immediately, the vestige of peace she felt is gone. She rolls up the window.

"How much farther?" her mother asks.

"We are almost there," she says. "The hospital is just a few more minutes away."

The reunion between Dorothy and Natalie is teary, as Rebecca expected it would be. Natalie's parents, because they are *Natalie's* parents in this moment, have ceased to remember that Rebecca is in the room. They receive their younger daughter back like the prodigal child she is, oozing gratitude over the miracle that somehow she is still alive. Rebecca grits her teeth, feels her jaw tighten as the three of them hug and kiss and weep together. She wishes she felt differently, but she does not. This is the story of her life with her parents and Natalie.

She remembers a time when Natalie was sixteen and she ran away to stay with some "friends" in Vermont. Actually, it was a commune led by a charismatic leader whose intentions were anything but pure. Natalie called home, begging to be picked up. Something had happened, and she had seen the folly of her ways. Of course, her mother dropped everything, insisted Rebecca leave college and drive with her to retrieve her sister. It was late at night when they arrived, and her mother thought it best to stay in a hotel and pick up Natalie in the morning. Her mother went to the bar and ordered some drinks. While they were waiting, a man at the bar started chatting her mother up. The next thing Rebecca knew, she and her mother were dashing to their hotel room where Dorothy insisted she barricade the door with the bureau. The man was on the other side, hammering and calling out, drunk. Her mother turned on the television. Loud. The Miss America pageant was playing. They braced themselves against the bureau as the man hammered away until eventually, he gave up. The next morning, they drove to the commune only to find that Natalie had changed her mind. The high drama had lessened to a quarrel with the boy she was "dating." There had been a misunderstanding. She didn't need to go home after all. Rebecca had missed three days of classes by the time this little episode was over. Yet she was sure that if something like this were to happen again, her mother would drop everything and spare no expense to fly to Natalie's rescue. And Rebecca would be expected to go along with the chaos.

Royce pulls on her arm, jerking her out of her thoughts. "Why don't we go pay a visit to the police chief? We can leave them here to have their little love fest. I'd like to get her out of this dump as fast as possible."

Rebecca has not thought of the hospital as a dump, but she can see where Royce would think so. This is not like the state-of-the-art facilities Royce has frequented any time he has had some injury, though evidently it once was so. *He is such a snob*, she thinks. *Why am I still with him? He probably cannot stand that the nurses are predominately Black.*

Rebecca has harbored thoughts like this about Royce before but always chalked them up as normal characteristics of any marriage. *There is no such thing as a perfect relationship*, she has told herself in the past. Her threats to divorce Royce have been just that—idle talk. She has had neither the willingness nor the courage to follow through. When she hears herself question their relationship this time, though, something is different. She feels as if she is standing on the edge of a precipice and has to make a choice: Turn back or leap into the unknown. All it would take is one more step, but she must make the choice herself, and she is not ready to do that. Not yet.

"Okay. I will take you there. It's not far, just in Golden Grove." She lays her hand on her father's shoulder. "Dad, we are going to go talk to the police." Her father turns and gives her a smile.

"Let's just get her home," Royce says.

Her father nods his head and turns his attention back to his younger daughter.

The ride to the police station is the first time Rebecca has been alone with Royce since he arrived. Her stomach is in knots as she anticipates what he is going to say to her. She is prepared for him to rebuke her, to reprimand her for her behavior. "I'm sorry if I upset you. If you were worried. That you had to come here and leave work. It's just—"

"Stop apologizing, Becca. What you did, finding Natalie, was good. It's wonderful. You probably saved her life."

Rebecca's eyes open wide; she takes a deep breath, braces herself, expecting the hammer to come down any second. But it doesn't.

"I say we bring her home with us to recuperate. Your parents don't have the space, or, frankly, the means to take care of her. We do. You're home. It could be a good way to heal old wounds," Royce says.

Rebecca opens her mouth to speak, but no words flow. She remembers how as children she and Natalie used to spin in circles, arms flung wide, until they lost their balance and fell to the ground, nearly sick to their stomachs with vertigo but laughing, staggering as they got to their feet like drunken sailors. That's what their father had called them—two drunken sailors, high on life. "What a great idea! You wouldn't mind having her around? It may be months, you know," Rebecca says.

"Whatever it takes. She's family."

Rebecca looks out the window, and a smile washes across her face that stretches itself down into her heart and even into her gut. She feels herself open wide, as if someone were rolling a great stone away from the entrance to a cave in which she has been held prisoner for a long time. *She is family*. Why does that sentence have such an impactful ring to it? Maybe because in it she finally hears Royce blending her family with his own.

He must know that if Natalie is living with them, that will mean visits from her mom and dad. But then he will be protected from too much contact by his work. Still, he will need to be on his best behavior. No more late nights at bars, picking up strange women and coming in at 3 a.m. Rebecca wonders if Natalie living with them will put a strain on their marriage. She snorts out loud at the absurdity of the thought. How could their marriage be any more strained than it has been for the past seven months?

"What's so funny? I mean it," Royce says.

"It is not that. I really appreciate that—having Natalie stay with us. It was something else."

"What?"

"Nothing."

"It was obviously something, Becca. If you want this thing between us to work, you have got to start sharing your secrets. No more surprises."

Rebecca is not aware that she has been harboring secrets or dumping surprises in Royce's lap. Though, to be fair, this whole trip to St. Croix was unexpected. A voice inside her encourages her to be vulnerable, to trust that she can speak her truth. Hadn't Monique recently urged her to have more confidence in herself? "I was just wondering if Natalie's presence would put a strain on our marriage. But, you know, it is already pretty strained as is."

Royce changes his grip on the steering wheel. "It doesn't have to be that way. We could go back to the way things used to be. Before ..." He stops mid-sentence, his unsaid words hanging in the air.

"Go ahead. Say it. Before Juliet died." Suddenly, Rebecca is crying. She has not thought of the baby in a while, but now that Royce is here, with all this talk of family, and Natalie's prodigal return, the emotions are overwhelming, and she finds herself blubbering, snot oozing from her nose.

"Damn it, Rebecca. Pull yourself together. We can't go into the police station with you looking like this. Why am I paying for you to see a therapist? It doesn't seem to have done much good."

The old Royce is back. And with his brusqueness, the old Rebecca resurfaces, cowering in the cave, submissive, silenced by his authority. But then something new happens. A new Rebecca, the one that has been in the field, rubbing the sticks of desperation and forgiveness together, suddenly catches fire. "I will feel any damned way I please. To hell with the police."

"That attitude may put your sister's life in jeopardy," he says.

"Well then, to hell with my sister. To hell with everything and everyone. Including you!"

Royce is quiet for a few moments. When he speaks, his voice has the energy of the calm before a storm. "Have you finished your little tantrum now, Rebecca? You need to be careful what you say."

"Why? Why be careful? You say I keep secrets. Well, I won't keep secrets anymore. I will let everyone know exactly what I am thinking and where I stand."

"You're not listening to what I'm saying," he says. "I am warning you, Rebecca. Behave."

Royce looks at her, and suddenly, she feels like a teenager defending herself in front of the principal.

"I understand you have been through a lot," he said. "This has all taken an emotional toll on you. I just don't want you to say something you will regret later on. Something you cannot take back. I am on your side, Becca. Truly I am. Put down your boxing gloves and stop fighting me."

She is baffled by her response to his words. On the one hand, she wants to punch him in the face, pound him on his chest, climb on his back, and pummel him. On the other, she wants to throw her arms around him, kiss him, and open her heart to him. She knows both courses of action are too dangerous, so she does nothing.

Royce leaves Rebecca in the car while he goes into the police station. *At least he left the windows cracked*, she thinks. But this is what Royce does best—handles these macho situations, which he solves by throwing his influence around. Twenty minutes later, he reappears with the police chief by his side. Both are smiling, laughing, as though they are best friends. The chief walks over to Rebecca's window.

"Ah, Rebecca, your husband is a most persuasive man," the chief says. "And as it turns out, we have some friends in common."

"Real-ly?" Rebecca says, the syllables drawn out in her disbelief. "It's such a small world." She wonders who Royce might possibly know that the chief would know, wonders what solution has passed between them. She is pretty sure it was some sort of bribe.

"Your sister is free to leave as soon as the doctors release her. We can conduct any further business online."

"That is great news!" Rebecca says. "Thank you, Chief. It has been a pleasure meeting you."

"The pleasure is all mine, I can assure you," the chief says as he walks back toward the concrete station.

Once they are back in the car and heading for the hospital, Rebecca turns to Royce. "So how much did you give him?"

A thin smile forms on Royce's lips. "Whatever do you mean, Becca?"

"I know you paid him off. And handsomely too, from the skip in his step."

"I made a sizable donation to the Station Renovation Fund. He wanted to name the new building after me, but I told him I preferred to remain anonymous. I do have some humility."

Rebecca doubts there even was a Station Renovation Fund; the money likely went directly into the chief's pocket. But if a cop on the take means she can get Natalie home, she will not give it another thought. She wonders, though, if Monique is aware of her father's criminal activity.

CHAPTER TWENTY

When they return to the hospital to share the good news, they find Monique is there, chatting with her parents and Natalie. An extravagant bouquet of flowers rests on Natalie's bedside table, practically obscuring her sister from sight.

"Wow!" Rebecca says. "You have some admirer."

"They're from Monique and April. Aren't they gorgeous?" Natalie says.

Rebecca feels a slight twinge of jealousy. She does not want Natalie to intrude on her relationship with the women as she has always done in the past.

"Just a little something to brighten up the room. Though I think the arrival of Mama and Papa has done that," Monique says.

Rebecca looks at Natalie. She does seem much more relaxed and animated than she was twenty-four hours ago.

"We have some good news!" Rebecca says. "Royce talked to the chief, and Natalie is free to go as soon as the doctors are ready to release her."

"Wonderful!" her mother says, hugging Natalie gingerly. "It's time to take you home."

There is an awkward pause in the conversation. No one wants to acknowledge the elephant in the room—where "home" will be for Natalie. She has no apartment waiting. The condo Dorothy and Jack live in is too small. And everyone knows Royce barely tolerates Natalie. When he speaks, his words surprise everyone—except Rebecca, who has been in on the plan since Royce mentioned it in the car.

"We would love to have you stay with us, Natalie, until you are fully recovered. Wouldn't we, Becca? We have the space, and Becca is home full-time to take care of you as you need," Royce says.

Rebecca's gaze flits from the bewilderment on her parents' faces to the doubt on Natalie's. Monique, curiously, frowns.

"This was Royce's idea. He really wants to help. I know you and he have had differences in the past, Natalie, but we really do want to be there for you," Rebecca says.

All eyes fall on Natalie, who closes her eyes and sighs.

"It would be the best thing, Natalie," her mother says. "Dad and I don't have much room in our place. Rebecca and Royce could take better care of you."

Natalie opens her eyes. "Okay. But only until I'm able to find work and a place of my own. I refuse to be a burden."

"It's settled then. Good. I see this as a positive step forward for our family," Royce says, smiling his salesman's smile.

What is he up to? Rebecca wonders.

With Royce at her side, Rebecca has found it impossible to talk to Monique. Finally, they make their escape into the women's bathroom. As they sit in adjacent stalls, Monique speaks softly. "You are not really thinking of staying in the hotel with him?"

"He's my husband. How can I not? What would I tell my parents?"

"But, *chérie*, he is a monster."

"He's not a monster," Rebecca says, flushing the toilet. "He's just domineering sometimes."

She looks at her face in the mirror as she washes her hands. She looks tired, worn, worried. Her brow lines are etched deeply into her forehead. She remembers her mother wiping the marks away with her thumbs, telling her she would never marry if she always looked so serious. Monique emerges from her stall and stands next to Rebecca at the sink. The two women look at each other's reflections in the mirror.

"I am afraid for you," Monique says. "I have known men like that. Narcissists."

"What do you think he's going to do? My parents are staying in the adjacent bedroom. Doesn't leave much room for foul play."

"And your sister, what do you know of her? Do you think it wise to bring her into your home?"

"Why would you say that? She's just been a victim of bad luck. She's harmless."

"Just be careful, Rebecca. You know you have somewhere else to stay. Always."

"I know. Thank you."

They hug before they leave the bathroom. Royce is waiting outside. He is pacing. When Rebecca comes out, he grabs her by the arm, leading her away from the older woman.

"You were in there long enough. What were you talking about? Me?" Royce says.

Rebecca laughs. "Ever the egotist. Actually, yes. Monique was saying what a great guy you are to come down here and rescue Natalie from a tough situation."

Royce smiles. She has stroked his ego at its weakest point—his vanity. He wants to be everyone's "great guy." *Here comes Royce, what a great guy! He gives to charities, throws terrific parties, puts up with a crazy, depressed wife, leaps off tall buildings, saves the day.* But in the cloak of darkness, he abuses her. Not physically. But mentally. Emotionally. His mood swings are like the Sword of Damocles, swinging over her, ready to slice her in pieces at any moment.

She hopes Royce won't see through her lie. She fears he has already picked up on the fact that she trusts Monique, after just a few days, more than she trusts him. She fixes a rehearsed smile on her face.

"I don't like that woman. There is something about her," Royce says

"Who? Monique?" she says.

"Yes. Who else?"

"I like her very much. She has been very kind to me."

"What does that mean, Becca? Did she and her lesbo lawyer friend make moves on you?"

Rebecca is startled by his comment. He has had so little contact with Monique and April together. How could he have sized up their relationship so quickly? Does this mean he can see through her lies to what she is actually thinking?

"Don't worry, Becca. I know you are too uptight to engage in any ménage-à-trois with two dykes. Hell, you won't even have sex with me, and I'm your husband," he continues. He pushes her up against the wall in the hallway.

"Royce."

"Becca," he breathes into her ear. "I have missed you. Not just the sex, though I miss that a lot. I missed you. I was so worried about you." He lifts her face by her chin and presses his lips on hers. She pushes away, turning her head.

"Not here, Royce. Not now."

"Later?"

"Maybe," she says, though she knows she does not mean it. She just wants to get him off her before anyone comes along and sees them.

"Later it is."

***

After an hour in the hospital with Natalie and her parents and Royce, who is constantly pacing and clearly not appreciating the familial scene, Rebecca suggests that she and Royce go into Frederiksted to pick up some food. She is surprised when she realizes that Royce is headed in the opposite direction, down the Queen Mary Highway, headed toward the hotel.

"Aren't you going the wrong way?"

"No."

"I thought we were going to town to get some food."

"We will. We are just taking a little detour first."

"Where to?" Rebecca asks, though she suspects he is taking her back to the hotel in the hopes that she will have sex with him. But she won't. She is determined not to let him manipulate her into having sex with him just because he came down and untangled the mess Natalie created for herself.

"Royce, I don't think this is a good idea."

"What?"

"You are taking me back to the hotel, aren't you? To have sex?" she says.

"Very sharp, Becca. Very good."

"What if I tell you I don't want to go back to the hotel? I don't want to have sex with you."

Royce steps on the gas and drives a little faster. His hands are clenched so tightly around the steering wheel that his knuckles are white. They zoom past small houses with old islanders sitting on front porches in brightly painted chairs. Chickens run out of the way of the oncoming car. An old man with white hair and a beard waves his hands at Royce, mouthing "Slow down. Slow down." Rebecca's heart races, her blood throbs in her temples, her hands sweat. She knows she has awakened the Beast.

Royce does not slow down. He races, fast and furious, until he makes a sudden screeching turn onto a dirt road. They drive along the bumpy road, hitting ruts that send her bouncing in her seat. Underbrush whips at the sides of the car. Abruptly, he stops. An ominous silence pervades. The Sword of Damocles tickles her throat.

"Do you remember that time on the way to your parents' house? You begged me to pull into the state park and fuck you. To relieve your stress. You loved it." His words, slick as a snake, make the hair on her neck rise.

"That was ... an exceptional circumstance. I'm not stressed now," she says, though her whole body is rigid.

"Don't lie, Becca. I know you better than you know yourself. This is what you need. This is what you want."

Rebecca hears thunder in the distance. Is it real thunder or imagined? She isn't sure. Maybe it is just her heart, beating furiously. A caged animal, mustering courage to escape.

"You don't know me. This is *not* what I need. This is *not* what I want," she says, meeting his stare.

Royce's eyes go black. His face is taut, barely containing his emotion. He jerks off his seatbelt, thrusts the door open, and strides over to Rebecca's passenger door, yanks it open.

"Get out."

She hears the malice in his voice, the bestial growl that precedes rage.

"No." She tries to pull the door shut, but he yanks her arm away. Pain shoots from her wrist to her shoulder. "Royce, please. I don't want to."

"Get out. Now." He reaches across her, snaps her seatbelt open. His face is so close to her; his breath is hot and thick. She pushes back against the seat, locks her legs, pulls her hands into fists, and closes her eyes, willing with all her might for this not to be happening. He snorts, grabs her by the hair, and drags her out into the dirt.

"Royce. Please don't do this. I don't want—" It is hard for her to speak because her breathing is so rapid. Her body shakes uncontrollably. Sharp rocks dig into her knees, but that is not what causes her tears to flow.

"I don't give a shit what you want. Everything isn't about you." He takes off his belt, unzips his pants, and pulls out his penis, which is already partially engorged. "Suck it," he says. "Make it hard, and I won't hurt you."

Vomit rises in her throat. She wants to tell him to go to hell. She wants to stand up and walk away, but they are in the middle of nowhere, and he has a belt wrapped around his hand. He has never threatened her like this before. She is terrified of what he might do, so she takes his penis in her mouth. When he is hard enough, he pulls her to her feet, pushes her up against the hood of the car, yanks down her panties, and enters her. He pumps aggressively, snorting and grunting, and she is crying, biting her lip until it bleeds so she doesn't make a sound. Then he is done, and he climbs off her. He pulls himself together and so does she. They get back into the car and drive in silence.

A married couple out for a drive.

The traffic is more congested now that it is late afternoon, exacerbated by a vegetable truck that has broken down in the middle of the road. Watermelons split in pieces, their juicy red fruit splayed on the road, make her stomach curl. Rebecca stares at the taillights of the car in front of them—flashing on when he brakes, off when he moves ahead. She does not dare look out her window at the hibiscus flowers or the hot pink bougainvillea against the white houses. She feels her heart might break to see such beauty now because she feels so broken, so dirty, so ashamed.

CHAPTER TWENTY-ONE

Rebecca retreats into herself, leaving Royce to take charge of Natalie's release from the hospital. He handles the doctors, he has the conversations with her parents, and he makes the reservations for the flights back to Newark. She is numb. She doesn't want to be numb. She wants to wake up out of her frozen state and breathe flames of fire. But she is so tired and depleted, she can barely move.

Her parents, so focused on their younger daughter, notice nothing. Only Royce looks at her smugly, self-satisfied.

She needs to speak with Monique before they leave. She waits until Royce has gone to sleep. She tiptoes into the living room, past her parents' bedroom, and out onto the balcony. The night air is cool against her flesh. The sky is clear and dotted with stars. She hears the waves of the ocean throbbing in the distance.

"Monique?" she says, speaking as softly as she can. "I am sorry if I woke you."

"No worries. What is it, *chérie*?"

Rebecca tells her the details of the trip from the hospital to the dirt road and what went on there.

"I feel so dirty, so ashamed," Rebecca says.

"Rebecca, he raped you. He is the one who should be ashamed."

"But I didn't fight him off. I didn't protest enough."

"He was threatening to beat you. Has he done this to you before?"

"Raped me? No."

"But threatened you? Beaten you?"

"No."

"You are not safe with him. You must leave him."

"I can't do that. We are bringing my sister home to live with us. To recuperate. I can't leave her alone with him."

"Does he own a gun?"

"He hunts. And he has his own pistol for protection."

"You are not safe. I have known men like him before."

"You don't really think he would shoot me?"

"One never knows. If he was angry enough to rape you—"

"That's just because I hadn't had sex with him in months. He was frustrated."

"Do you hear yourself? No man is entitled to rape a woman. Ever."

"I know. I just feel like I brought this on myself."

Monique snorts on the other end of the phone. "That's what they want you to think. That is how they keep you captive. It is time to be true to yourself. Take courage!"

Rebecca wants to rally, but she feels weak. The image of Royce's face, so full of anger, his body so full of rage, haunts her. She wants to forget, though she knows she never will.

"Maybe we can go back to the way things were before. As long as I was having sex with him, he was fine."

"Do you plan to sleep with him again just to appease him?"

Rebecca ponders the question. Will she sleep with Royce just to appease him? Before she got pregnant with Juliet, they used to have sex as frequently as they could—sometimes four or five times a day on the weekend. Rebecca told herself this was Royce's way of showing her he loved her. But now, she is sure she was living in denial. His addiction to sex is just another facet of his warped personality. *Who rapes his wife on a dirt road to show her who is master?* No. Rebecca knows she cannot live in the prison of her relationship as it has been any longer. When she gets home, when *they* get home, she will set up boundaries he cannot cross. Not if he wants to stay married to her.

Then she realizes how lame that sounds. Royce has all the power. He has all the money. Everything except the farm is in his name and that, she is certain, he would fight her for. He could throw her out on the street tomorrow, and she would have nothing but the clothes on her back.

She could be content living in a one-room apartment and working as a waitress if she could be free of the pressure she feels from him.

"*Chérie*, are you still there?" Monique says.

"Yes. Just pondering. Honestly, I see no way out."

"You are afraid?"

"A little," Rebecca says. "I guess Natalie and I could go live with Mom and Dad. Oh God, no. That is not even an option."

"I have a plan," Monique says.

"We can't possibly continue to stay with you and April."

"Oh no, I wasn't suggesting that. You need to go home to New Jersey, to your farm. Take your sister. Let her recuperate. Be guarded but loving in your relationship with Royce."

"Are you telling me to sleep with him?"

"Nothing of the kind. I am telling you to be true to yourself, but be prepared for backlash. Be wise. Be cautious. Don't forget that this is a man who gets what he wants. I will be in touch."

"Goodbye, Monique."

"*Bonne nuit, ma chérie. Prends garde.*"

Rebecca hangs up the phone and makes her way back into the living room. She is prepared for Royce to spring up out of the darkness and ask her who she was talking to, demand that she spill the details of the conversation. But he does not, and she makes her way back to the bedroom, climbs in bed beside him without disturbing him. They have not slept in the same bed for a long time. She lies on her back with the sheet pulled up under her chin, rigid lest she wake him, her eyes open to the darkness until she can no longer keep them open, and she falls asleep.

***

The chief is wakened by the sound of someone pounding on his front door. He looks at the clock by his bed. Almost midnight. No one should be pounding on his door at this hour. "It must be that young fool I left on duty," he says to himself. "Always sticking his nose into none of his business." But he opens his bedstand, takes his gun out of the drawer, and checks to make sure it is loaded. Just in case. One can never be too cautious.

The house is dark. He turns on lights as he goes. The knocking stops. He looks through the peephole on the front door, then opens it wide.

"Monique! You surprised me. Come in."

"I prefer to stay out here."

"Don't be childish. Come inside." He is not worried about what the neighbors might think—he has no neighbors—but, rather, who might have followed her here. She may have put him in danger. But she does not budge.

"I know what you did."

"What are you talking about?"

"I know you accepted a bribe from Royce Winslow to release Natalie Baker. I suppose I should not be surprised. You have been on the take for so many years."

"Is this what you woke me up for? To chastise me? Surely that could have waited until morning."

"You have put her in grave danger."

"What is your sudden interest in Natalie Baker?"

"It is not Natalie I am concerned about. Rebecca is the one whose life may be in jeopardy because of what you have done."

The chief stares at her, his eyes void of emotion.

"You really have no idea what is going on here, do you? You are blind to the truth."

The chief dismisses her with a wave of his hand. "So self-righteous, as always, Monique. You always have the answers. This conversation is over. I need my sleep." He turns to walk back in the house.

"Justice will be served," she whispers as he closes the door.

PART THREE

CHAPTER TWENTY-TWO

From the tropical breezes and sunshine of the island, they return to a winter storm that has nearly paralyzed New England and the mid-Atlantic states.

"I forgot how much I hate it here," Natalie says as she stares out of the limousine window. They are on the New Jersey Turnpike, which is thick with wintry slush. Heaps of snow, dyed brown by dirt and car fumes, line the highway. Still, Royce insists that the driver exceed the speed limit. Royce is a busy man. He needs to get home. When the vehicle fishtails, Rebecca's heart leaps in her throat. This is not the way she would choose to die, but she knows better than to say something to Royce. It will only make him push the driver to accelerate faster.

"It will be pretty at the farm with the snow on the fields," Rebecca says. "You'll get used to the cold in no time."

"Never," Natalie says.

"Royce will build us a fire. I'll make tea, and we'll cozy up in blankets and watch it snow through the windows."

"I had forgotten what a Pollyanna you are, Becca," Natalie says. "Is everything always gumdrops and lollipops in your world?"

"How can you even say that?" Rebecca says. She wants to throw herself on Natalie and scratch her eyes, which are already so blind. "While you were gone, we lost the baby." Rebecca swallows back tears. She refuses to break down in front of her sister.

"Oh shit, my bad. I didn't know. I thought maybe you just left it here with a nanny."

"She wasn't an it! She was a beautiful little girl. Juliet. She was stillborn,"

"I'm so sorry, Rebecca. That sucks. But I guess you can try again?"

Rebecca feels the sting of her sister's words. In the past, Rebecca would have been devastated by Natalie's comment and retreated into herself. *I shouldn't be surprised. She always has been the most insensitive, selfish bitch.* Rebecca is determined to handle things differently this time. If Natalie hasn't changed as a result of her near brush with death, Rebecca has. And maybe it isn't the brush with death that has changed her, but the kindness of strangers, of Monique, coming to her rescue. An unexpected angel arriving on the scene.

Rebecca thinks of Monique's parting words to her—*Be true to yourself, but be prepared for backlash. Be wise. Be cautious.* This advice holds not only for her relationship with Royce but with Natalie as well. What does Rebecca know about Natalie really? She has proven herself to be an untrustworthy addict with a proclivity for compromising situations. Simply put—Natalie is a fuckup. A hot mess. Why should Rebecca expect her to be any different now than she was a year ago? Rebecca knows she must be cautious and wise around her younger sister. She must have no expectations of her. But she also should stand her ground and not take any abuse from her. Or Royce. She must advocate for herself because no one else is going to advocate for her.

Certainly not her parents, who are starry-eyed at Natalie's return. They have opened their arms to their younger daughter and received her back into the family, forgiven her for the hardship she has put them through. They have expressed their gratitude to Royce for rescuing Natalie and opening his home to her, letting her recuperate there until she can get back on her feet. But to their oldest daughter, to Rebecca, they have said nothing. No "thanks for finding her" or "weren't you so clever and brave." They have functioned on the assumption that Rebecca is the rock on whom they can all rely and who doesn't require strokes of affection or approval.

How wrong they are! Rebecca flashes back to a memory of Monique hugging her in the kitchen, telling her that she is not alone in all this. That she does not have to carry everyone's burdens on her shoulders. That memory is enough to bring a smile to her face. As if the sun is breaking through the metallic gray of the clouds and snow.

"What is it now, Pollyanna? Did you think what I said was funny?" Natalie says.

"Honestly, I have forgotten what you said, Natalie. I was thinking about something entirely different."

"You look like the cat that swallowed the canary."

"Do I, now? I can't imagine why."

Royce directs his attention at Rebecca. She feels his eyes penetrate her as if trying to read her mind. She doesn't slip, as she might have in the past, into being the victim. Instead, she feels that she is wearing some kind of invisible armor, that Monique has provided her with an emotional force field with which to protect herself from their toxic comments and negative vibes.

"What do you say we order pizza tonight, or Chinese? I don't really feel like cooking," Rebecca says.

"I don't really give a shit," Natalie says.

"All right then. Royce? Is that okay with you?"

He doesn't reply but just stares out the window. Rebecca begins to imagine all kinds of things. She imagines he is thinking she is a lazy wife, not willing to fix him the fresh vegetables and protein he likes to fuel his body with. She wonders if he will force himself on her again now that the gate has been opened. She hopes he doesn't suggest they share the same bed because she doesn't want to have sex with him again. Ever. Not after the other day. She feels herself starting to sink down the rabbit hole of useless thinking and pulls herself up out of it, forcing herself to concentrate on the countryside they are now driving through. The white landscape that hides so many imperfections.

"Okay then. Pizza it is."

***

By the time they reach the farm, the snow has stopped. It is late afternoon, and the sky has taken on a peach glow, which is reflected in the white fields surrounding their house. The driveway is plowed, thanks to their reliable plowman, Rafael. Rebecca is excited to be home. She wants to put on her running shoes and go for a run on the mountain. But first, she knows she must get Natalie settled in.

"Royce, would you mind lighting a fire?" Rebecca asks.

"Give me a minute to catch my breath," he says.

"I'm sorry. It's just that the house is so cold. I didn't mean to rush you. I'm sorry."

As soon as those words spill out of Rebecca's mouth, she regrets them. She is not sorry to have asked him, nor should she be. She has no reason to apologize. She was not rushing him. She was merely asking him to light a fire. "Say what you mean, and mean what you say. Just don't say it mean," Margot has told her. She is determined to be more mindful of her words, though frankly, she is tired of feeling like she is walking in a minefield with Royce.

"Natalie, I don't think you have seen the guest room since we renovated. Come on. I will show you." She heads upstairs, Natalie in tow. At the top of the landing, she stops. Why has she given the upstairs guest room to Natalie? For the past seven months, it has been her sanctuary. Now she will have to sleep in the smaller guest room downstairs. She wants to retract her offer and is about to when Natalie speaks.

"Well. Show me."

"Sure. Why not."

They enter the room, which is spacious with a big brass bed on one side and a fireplace on the other. Worn oriental rugs cover the old wooden floors, and a comfortable velvet armchair rests in the corner by the hearth. The walls are painted a deep green, almost gray. The whole room radiates a sense of calm and peace.

"I'll have to change the sheets. I wasn't expecting company, and I haven't washed them since they were last used," Rebecca says.

"Whatever," Natalie says, as she plops down on the bed and stretches out, her fingers wrapping around the brass bars of the headboard. "I like it. Bed is firm. Room is nice. I think I am going to like it here."

Rebecca is startled by Natalie's positivity. These are the first pleasant words to come out of her mouth since they left the island.

"I'm glad. I hope you do. Now will you be okay if I take a quick run? I can't wait to get some fresh air."

"Go for it, but don't expect me to join you. I don't do running."

Rebecca smiles. She has not even considered the possibility of Natalie joining her. Nor does she want her to. Running is her time, her space to be quiet. It is the closest she comes to meditation when her mind goes blank and she is into her breathing, focusing on the next step.

"You sure?"

"Go! I'll be fine. If I need anything, I'll just ask Royce."

***

As Rebecca runs, her feet crunching in the new snow, thoughts flow in and through her mind. What will it be like having Natalie living with them? It might be good. She could be a good buffer for Royce. Maybe he will be on his best behavior now that he has an audience. Or maybe he will just disappear, coming in when he pleases, not giving a shit about what Natalie might think. He never really liked her anyhow. Why should he change now? Rebecca wonders what they are doing. If they have even spoken to each other.

In truth, she is a little baffled as to why Royce invited Natalie to stay with them. Was he just putting on a show for her parents? The doctors and nurses? Or does he genuinely care about Natalie getting better? She is sure that if she brings the subject up, he will just give her the standard Royce line—that she doesn't appreciate what a great guy he is—and ask why he can't do anything without her suspecting him of having malicious intent.

When did their marriage fall into this tangled web of misunderstanding and mistrust? The fact that he raped her on the island has only solidified her lack of trust in him. Now she questions his every move. Monique warned her to be wise. Be cautious. And she will be. She will stand outside all situations and observe, keep her eyes open to the reality of what is going on.

She catches herself running harder and faster as these thoughts race through her mind, and she purposefully slows down. She slows her breathing to an even five-flow pace and latches on to a mantra in her head. "Not my will, my heart's will." Margot taught her that one, and it always makes her feel calm. The last thing she wants to do is reenter the house in a frantic state, ready for a fight. She wants to be calm and serene. To trust that there is at least one person in the world who understands her, gets her: Monique. Even just thinking her name makes Rebecca smile. *Monique. My angel. How could I ever have doubted her?*

Turning her attention to the now-dark road, lit only by the headlamp in her cap, and a full moon that casts shadows on the road, she breathes deeply, richly, taking the cold air into her lungs. The endorphins have kicked in. She is feeling her runner's high. If only she could feel like this all the time. The idea comes to mind that she could stay in this state of bliss permanently if she were training for an Ironman. She has looked at the rigorous training schedule in the past. The days of one-hour swims, three-hour bike rides, and two-hour runs—and that was just in the beginning. Those are hours she could claim as her own, away from Natalie and Royce. Her own private challenge to cope with the challenges at home. Of course, Margot might say she was running away, substituting one obsession for another, but what does she care? Six months of training. She already has her bike set up in the attic for the winter so she can spin. And the recreation center in town has a decent pool. To focus on doing the race would give her something to think about besides Juliet or Natalie or Royce. It seems like the perfect solution to her dilemma. She determines to do it.

But then there is the fee. She remembers it costs about $1,600 to do the race and pay for lodging. Will Royce agree to pay for that? Only if he sees something in it for himself. Maybe the bragging rights that his wife is doing an Ironman. But maybe he will look on her training as taking her further away from him. That, she is pretty sure, he would not stand for. Royce demands attention. He needs to have his ego constantly stroked, to feel that he is the center of attention at all times. For a man who is as successful in business as he is, she is often amazed by his deep-seated insecurity and neediness.

She doesn't want to think about Royce. She wants to think about the race and the training and how freeing it would feel to focus on something that doesn't feel so dark and heavy all the time. She is tired of thinking, of feeling her thoughts—as if one can feel thoughts. But she knows what she means. She is tired of recycling emotions that don't seem to want to heal. Maybe if she just turns to something entirely different—if she focuses on the physical instead of the emotional and mental—she will find a reprieve. What is it Margot says? Move a muscle, change a mood. She feels her mood changing already.

The sky is thoroughly black except for the round full moon that blazes in the sky. From it, four beams of light streak out like a cross. When she enters the house, she hears laughter. At first, she does not know what it is and thinks maybe the television is on and canned laughter comes from the tube. But then she recognizes it for what it is. Royce and Natalie are laughing. Together.

She walks past the kitchen, through the dining room into the den. They are sitting on the couch together, drinking wine and laughing. Rebecca wants to hurl herself at Royce and slap his face. Doesn't he know that Natalie is an alcoholic? That she shouldn't be drinking? Especially not on the medication she is taking. But Royce wouldn't think of that. He would only think of himself and his desire to have a convivial companion. Despite all the years of her trying to educate him about the disease of alcoholism, he still doesn't get it. The first drink gets you drunk—because after that first, there will be the second and third and fifth until the drinker passes out or does something incredibly outlandish and inappropriate. Which is probably what Royce is hoping for.

When they see her, they stop laughing, abruptly.

"Care to join us?" Natalie says, raising her glass.

Rebecca stands statue-like at the threshold, arms crossed deliberately over her chest.

Natalie meets her glare with a satisfied grin, while Royce sits expressionless beside her. Rebecca watches in disgust as Natalie lifts her glass to her lips and swallows several mouthfuls of wine, places her near-empty glass on the table, and wipes her mouth with the back of her hand.

"Oh no. I can see my big sister's disapproval on her face. Well, you can go to hell."

"Good run?" Royce asks.

Inside, Rebecca is seething. But she pauses, measuring her words. "Very good. I have decided I am going to do an Ironman. I think there is one in August I can train for, or September."

"An Ironman? What brought that on?" he asks. "This is the first time I have heard of it."

"I just thought maybe doing something physical would get me out of my head."

"I can think of a number of other physical things you could do without taking on the Ironman," he says, his blue eyes cold and commanding her attention.

"What's an Ironman?" Natalie says as she finishes her wine.

"It is a race. A triathlon. A big one," Rebecca says.

"Oh, that thingy where you swim across the ocean, bike through several states, and swim till your ass falls off?" Natalie says.

Royce snorts. "Something like that. Rebecca, why does everything have to be so extreme? Why can't you just do a marathon and call it quits?"

She feels herself start to get defensive. A hard tightening in her stomach and chest. Her hands clench in fists. She purposefully relaxes her hands and takes a breath. "It is just an idea. I am going to go take a shower. Then we can order pizza."

"We already went ahead and ordered Chinese. It should be here any minute. I got you cashew chicken and stir-fry vegetables. Sauce on the side," he says.

She is surprised he remembers what she likes. There are so many sources of input coming at her from all sides. Natalie drinking. Royce laughing. Their camaraderie. She is both freezing and sweating simultaneously in her wet clothes. She needs to get out of the room into neutral territory where she can process the situation. "Thanks," she says.

Before she leaves the room, she walks over to Natalie and takes her wine glass from her. "If you are going to be living in this house, you are not going to drink."

"Bitch."

***

Rebecca looks at her face in the bathroom mirror. Is she really a bitch? She thinks not. There have to be some rules if Natalie is going to live with them. For one thing, Natalie needs to start going to Alcoholics Anonymous meetings. There are plenty in the area. Her mother always seemed to be trotting off to one when she was sober and visiting in the past. Rebecca determines that she will look up the schedule and make a plan for Natalie. It is the least her sister can do, give sobriety a shot, if she is going to stay on the farm with them. Rebecca will not abide the old Natalie, the one who stayed in bed until noon, woke with a cigarette and a shot, snorting cocaine for breakfast. Just to get things started. Rebecca will not have that chaos in her house. If Natalie wants to kill herself, she can do that somewhere else.

Suddenly, Royce's face appears in the mirror. Instinctively, Rebecca covers her naked body with a towel.

"I'm sorry. I shouldn't have given her that wine," he says.

"What were you thinking?"

"She asked if there was anything to drink."

"Did water occur to you? Or juice?"

"That's not the way she asked."

Rebecca is well aware of the strength of Natalie's manipulation. "If she had asked you to pull down your pants, would you have?"

Royce is silent.

"Oh my God," Rebecca says. "You didn't. Tell me you didn't."

"Of course I didn't. She didn't ask."

"But you would have."

"Rebecca, you are being dramatic. And paranoid. We were just bonding. I thought you would be pleased."

Monique has warned her to be conscious of his gaslighting. She knows she is being neither dramatic nor paranoid. She is also aware of Monique's instruction to maintain peace at home. Difficult as that is, she will try.

"Why would I be pleased, Royce? You gave her a glass of wine," she says, tightening the towel around her as her heart pounds in her chest.

He takes a step toward her.

She holds up her hand to stop him.

"My mistake."

"It can kill her," she says. "Drinking. On the medicine she is on."

"It won't happen again."

"Let me get in the shower before the hot water runs out."

"Becca, am I forgiven?" he asks, boyishly.

She wants to scratch his eyes out, to scream at the top of her lungs. He doesn't need her forgiveness, nor does he really want it. He wants her to make him feel all right about being such a selfish ass in the first place, for placing his own comfort first and not genuinely caring for her well-being. Or her sister's.

"If she is going to stay here, there have to be some rules, you know," she says. She is shivering now, but refuses to get naked in front of him.

"I know."

"Do you? Really? It's for her own good. And ours too. We have to protect ourselves."

"You make it sound like she's some kind of evil witch."

"You don't know Natalie."

"Point taken. You sure I can't get in there with you?"

"Royce …"

"I know. And Becca, about this Ironman—"

"It's not open for discussion, Royce. I've made up my mind. I'm going to do it."

"I was just going to say, I think it's a great idea. It will give you something positive to focus on. Enjoy your shower, sweetheart."

He walks out of the bathroom, leaving Rebecca to wonder what is really going on with him. She is familiar with the penitent Royce, the one who seeks her approval. But just as soon as that meek Royce arrives, the mean Royce is right around the corner. She prepares herself for the onslaught, though she knows their dance well enough to recognize this grace period. It will last several days, maybe weeks even. Just long enough for her to relax and let her guard down before he slams her with another assault. She is growing weary of the cycle. This time, she tells herself, she will be prepared.

CHAPTER TWENTY-THREE

Rebecca wakes the next morning in the unfamiliar bed of the downstairs guest room. The room, with its blackout curtains to keep the sun from pouring in, is dark and cold. She has no idea what time it is and guesses that when she looks at her watch, it will read 5 a.m.—her usual time for waking. She is both surprised and dismayed when she sees she has actually slept until ten. *What a waste of a day*, she tells herself, but then backs off the self-flagellation, as she recognizes that she must have needed the sleep. She wonders if Natalie, too, has slept in. She is sure Royce has already left for the office. That will leave her with a day alone with her sister, and she is not sure what they might do. Certainly some shopping for Natalie, who needs everything from a toothbrush and tampons to sweaters and jeans. Natalie brought nothing with her to New Jersey. The trauma wiped her mind clean of the present; she could not remember her recent past and had no recollection of where she lived on St. Croix or stored her clothes, of where she worked or who she hung around with. All she could conjure up was the image of herself climbing the ladder into the boat and the sound of the gunshot. Nothing else.

Which all seemed pretty convenient to Rebecca.

Questions collide in her mind like a multicar pileup on the freeway, all because of one staggering thought that she cannot shake: Natalie is lying.

Nevertheless, Rebecca will devote the day to taking care of her sister's needs, but only after she has done her morning training. Today is bike day. She will spin for an hour on the bike she has set up in the attic. To do that, she needs biking gear from upstairs. Pulling on her robe, she cinches the belt at her waist and makes her way out into the main house.

"Well, look who finally decided to show her face," Royce says as she walks through the living room into the kitchen. He is sitting in one of the comfortable chairs in the breakfast nook, a cup of coffee in his hand; Natalie sits with her legs tucked under her in the other. The coziness of the scene catches Rebecca off guard.

"Royce! Why aren't you at work?"

"Good morning to you too, sweetheart," he says.

"It's just ... you said you were so busy."

"Work can wait. I wanted to get Natalie set up in the outpatient program at Carrier Clinic. I've been on the phone with them all morning. She will start there tomorrow. Eight o'clock sharp. Right, Natalie?"

Natalie expresses her enthusiasm by putting her finger down her throat and pretending to vomit.

Rebecca is baffled. Where did he come up with the idea of Carrier Clinic, a private treatment center in Belle Mead, just down the road? Could he have possibly remembered that her mother, who was in recovery then from alcoholism, went there for AA meetings when she was visiting? And why has Royce, who has never given Natalie the time of day, suddenly taken such an interest in her well-being? Maybe he, like Rebecca, has been changed in some way by the near-death experience that Natalie went through. She would like to think so. But based on her relationship with Royce and their years together, she knows there must be an ulterior motive. Rebecca just doesn't have a clue as to what that might be.

Rebecca's next thought is a selfish one. What does this mean for *her*? Will she be required to chauffeur Natalie to the clinic every morning and retrieve her at the end of the day? Not that she has so much else going on in her life, but to be commandeered into a daily task does not appeal to her, though she has to admit that having Natalie occupied with something else all day long will suit her just fine. This way she won't have to manufacture activities for them to engage in, and she will be free to train for the Ironman as she likes. Looking at the situation from this perspective allows her to see how the benefits outweigh the liabilities. She is grateful to Royce for taking the initiative to set the program in motion.

As if reading her thoughts, Royce chimes in, "You won't need to worry about transportation. Natalie and I are going to visit the dealer today and buy a car for her. You can carry on with your housecleaning and your grocery shopping and whatever else it is you need to take care of." He takes a sip of his coffee, then looks at her, smiling. "Oh, and your training, of course."

Rebecca has a sudden twinge of guilt. Shouldn't she be the one carting Natalie around? Royce is a busy man and the breadwinner of the family. And Natalie is her sister. Shouldn't she be responsible for her recovery? "I can help. I want to help. You have work," she says.

"Nonsense. I have set today aside to tie up these loose ends. I made a promise to your parents and to the chief in St. Croix that I would see to Natalie's rehabilitation. I'm going to do that."

Rebecca is reminded of the glass of wine Royce gave Natalie the night before. How serious is he about helping, or is this all just show?

"She will need clothes."

"'She' is right here listening. Thank you all the same. I think I'm capable of going clothes shopping by myself once I have wheels," Natalie says.

Rebecca feels the familiar sting of rejection from her sister. She had thought that maybe they could start bonding over new jeans and cashmere sweaters. But obviously, Natalie has another idea.

"Whatever you like. I'm just happy to go with you, that's all. I want you to know I'm here for you too."

"Yeah. Whatever you say," is Natalie's reply.

"Well then, we've got a plan. Let's get going," Royce says as he rises from his chair. "Natalie, you ready?"

"Let me just go get dressed," she says as she untangles her legs from underneath her and lifts herself to standing. "Won't be a minute."

"Take your time," Royce says.

Rebecca pulls her robe closer to her chest. She is uneasy, and she doesn't know why, except that her day has started off on a very different note than she expected. First, there was the waking up so late. Then Royce's taking charge of Natalie's situation. Now this talk of a new car and Natalie being set loose to do her own shopping. All the while, Royce is being so solicitous, almost greasy in his accommodations. But what can she do? She can pull on her biking clothes and spin on her stationary bike for an hour. She can shop for healthy food to fill the fridge. She can call Monique and fill her in on the strange details of this morning. No, she mustn't bother Monique with every little thing going on in her life. She must practice looking at reality and seeing what is really there. But that's just it. She looks at reality and what she sees is unclear, out of focus. Perhaps she is paying attention to the wrong things.

"Why are you doing this, Royce?" she says.

"Doing what? Taking care of my sister-in-law? I told you. I made a promise to your parents and to the chief."

"I think there's more. Tell me."

"Damn it, Rebecca. Why are you always so critical of what I do? For some reason, you have labeled me the bad guy, and I can do nothing right. Nothing good."

"If you hurt her. If you take advantage of her in any way—"

"I think Natalie can take care of herself. She's one tough chick, unlike her sister."

"She's an addict and an alcoholic. She needs to recover. She needs time to heal."

"Why do you think I'm going to great expense to enroll her in the program at Carrier Clinic? I'm on her side, *your* side. Why can't you accept that? Don't you trust me?"

Rebecca smiles. "Really? You ask me that?"

Royce's face dissolves into a grimace. "Let bygones be bygones."

"You call what you did to me a bygone? You expect me to trust you?"

"What happened between us and what I'm doing for your sister are two entirely separate matters."

"And yet, you are one person."

Natalie clatters down the stairs and appears in the kitchen. She is wearing a pair of Rebecca's jeans and has thrown a black crewneck on under a buffalo plaid flannel shirt. Knee-high black boots are pulled up on the outside of her jeans, and she has draped a black cashmere wrap over the whole outfit. Rebecca hardly recognizes her own clothes in this new configuration.

"I hope you don't mind. I raided your closet."

"Not a problem, for now. You'll have your own clothes by the end of the day."

"Speaking of which," Royce says, pulling a credit card from his wallet. "Use this judiciously, but get enough so that you're comfortable." He hands the card to Natalie.

Rebecca cringes inside. She thinks of the many times she has asked Royce for new clothes or for something for the kitchen or bath and how he always made her beg to be given his card, if he gave it to her at all. He had all the money in the world, and yet he was stingy with her, doling out limited amounts on her debit card. Now here he is, freely handing over his Chase Sapphire Preferred card to Natalie, who could go out and use it for anything. Why does he entrust her with his millions and not his own wife?

Rebecca feels a resentment building inside her. Food for thought as another visit with Margot is coming up soon. She knows she shouldn't be mad at Natalie; it is Royce who is acting like an idiot, not her sister. But somehow, Rebecca senses that Natalie has a part in all of this. The word charade comes to mind, but she quickly pushes it out of her thoughts and tells herself not to be so small-minded.

"Have fun at the car dealer," she says cheerily. "I guess I'll see you both later this afternoon."

"More likely for dinner," Royce says.

"I thought you wanted to go shopping with me," Natalie says.

Rebecca is taken aback. "But you said—"

"Never mind what I said. Let's go and have some sister time. From the looks of it, you could use some new clothes too."

CHAPTER TWENTY-FOUR

The attic is cold where Rebecca keeps her racing bike on a stand so she can spin during the winter months. She can see her breath when she exhales and is grateful for the long bike pants with lining, though she is sure she will be sweating profusely by the time her hour is up. She hoists herself onto the bike seat, clips her feet into the toe clips, and slowly begins to pedal, allowing herself to warm up before she intensifies her rotations into a greater speed.

The bike is situated in front of a window in the eave that looks out over the front meadow. There is nothing much to look at, just the white stretch of the field leading to a copse of trees that borders the neighbor's property. The branches of the trees cut striking silhouettes into the empty white sky and the blanket of snow. To Rebecca, the branches look alive, as if they are writhing, reaching into the air. She thinks back to fall a year ago when the leaves were neon reds and golds and oranges. The golden autumn light shone through them, illuminating them like stained glass. Then, the branches—lead came—encompassing the glowing picture. She is glad for the memory, for the image she has carried in her heart. She feels a tenderness inside her rising like a green shoot in early spring.

Is it because Natalie reached out to her and asked her to go shopping? She sighs, thinks how pathetic she must be if she is so dependent on morsels of affection to feed her hungry heart. That is what she has. That is what she is—she is like one of those barren trees reaching into an empty sky, seeking some tendril of kindness, some wisp of love to cling to. She doesn't get that from Royce.

A sudden rumbling of feet across the roof catches her attention. The squirrels are at it again. She smiles as she increases her cadence, which had slowed to 85 rpms when she was ruminating. She needs to keep her focus, to concentrate on maintaining 90 to 95 rpms, even pushing herself to 100 for a really good workout. As she pushes herself harder, her breathing becomes more labored, and she feels her heart beating inside her chest. *Careful now, don't overdo it. This is only day one.*

Margot is always telling her "Easy does it." To which Rebecca replies, "But do it." What is the magic "it" that she is supposed to both take easy and do? Life, she supposes. When she thinks of "Easy does it," she sees Monique, who seems to glide through life, getting things accomplished *effortlessly.* At the airport, her gentle way of dealing with the security guards and police smoothed the way for Rebecca when it could have been a traumatic ordeal. It was Monique who encouraged her to ease up on her vigil over Natalie and take some time for herself. She enjoyed the day of snorkeling and was miraculously okay with the fact that Natalie came to while she was gone. But Monique wasn't all about greasing the path for comfort; she heard Rebecca's concerns about Royce and took them seriously. Monique said she had a plan. Rebecca wonders what that plan could possibly be. All she knows is that Monique wants her to stay at the farm and live her life carefully, paying attention to the reality of what is going on around her.

So what *is* going on? She is spinning—literally and figuratively. She is spinning in her relationships with Royce, Natalie, her mother. Even Margot. She feels like a piece of laundry that goes round and round in the dryer, dropping when it reaches the top to make the next revolution. The same cycle over and over again. But what she wants to do is break free. Why is that so hard? She is waiting for the timer to go off. For something outside her to say "Time's up." But she knows, from what she has learned from Monique, that she must take action. That loving herself is an inside job. She is responsible for her own life, her own happiness. And yet, she is a captive of the timer. The husband whom she cannot seem to please. The sister who is her greatest competitor. The mother whose attention is always directed elsewhere. It is time to stop. To follow another path. To move in another direction.

If only she knew how.

She looks at her watch. Fifteen more minutes to go. The whir of the wheels on the stand sounds like wings. Rebecca imagines that she is flying out of the house, down the road, across the ocean, and onto the streets of Amsterdam at tulip time.

She and hundreds of other cyclists wheel their way around fields of riotous colors. And then she is in France, whizzing past acres of lavender in bloom, taking in the fragrance of the purple flowers. Finally, her timer beeps, and she slows to a cruising speed, then to a cool down, as sweat pours down her back and her brow. She has done it. Day one of training. It may only be a start, but she is on her way, moving in a new direction.

***

The trip to the car dealer and subsequent visits to the insurance company and the DMV to obtain plates and registration eat up most of the day. Rebecca does not see Royce and Natalie until almost dinnertime when they burst into the kitchen, laughing and comfortable with each other in a way that disturbs Rebecca. The narcissist and the diva—who is playing whom? Rebecca suspects that the camaraderie being displayed between the two is based on some unhealthy neediness in them both. Natalie is sucking up to Royce because he has money and can do things like take her out and buy her a new car, while Royce is lapping up the ego-stroking attention that Natalie is bestowing on him. *Or is this me just being jealous?* Rebecca asks herself.

"Did you have a productive day?" Rebecca asks as she tears leaves of green leaf lettuce into pieces and drops them in a large wooden salad bowl.

"You could say that," Royce says.

"You should see the car Royce bought me! A Volvo XC90, with a sunroof!" Natalie says. "Top of the line."

"That's nice," Rebecca says, chopping a peeled cucumber into small chunks as she thinks of her own vehicle—a Volvo station wagon that now has six years on it. They bought her that car when she first became pregnant, thinking she might be carting a baby seat in back and possibly a dog. But that dream died. Rebecca picks up a box of cherry tomatoes and starts cutting the small red balls in half before placing them in the salad. "You took a little longer than I expected. I guess no shopping for clothes today?"

"We had to straighten out the insurance, get the registration and plates. The DMV was crowded," Royce says. "I wanted to get the car situation taken care of before Natalie begins her program tomorrow."

"Besides, I decided I don't want to shop around here. I want to go into the city to the boutiques. The last thing I want to do is to run into myself on the street," Natalie says.

Rebecca is well aware of Natalie's fetish with dressing in her own unique style. As a teen, she was ahead of the trends in dressing. As soon as she was mimicked, she would change her look. She ultimately settled on vintage boho: boots and long skirts and layers of blouses and wraps adorned with strings of necklaces and bracelets that cuffed her wrists and lower arms. Shopping at a chain store was definitely not in the picture.

"I know my stuff is not your style, but you are welcome to wear my clothes until you get some of your own," Rebecca says, though she knows Natalie will keep raiding her closet, with or without permission.

"We will be going into the city over the weekend," Natalie says.

"We?" Rebecca asks.

"I have a client coming in from overseas on Saturday. He is a big account, so I have to accommodate him. I told Natalie she could stay at our condo if she liked," Royce says.

Rebecca feels the hairs at the back of her neck bristle. Why has she been excluded? And there it is, that old narrative about not being a part of the crowd. Feeling like an outsider. She has worked on this with Margot and recognizes the symptoms—her suspicion that there might be something going on that Natalie and Royce are not telling her, her doubt that there really is an overseas client, her paranoia over her sister appropriating her life—of her distress. She makes a conscious decision not to go down that rabbit hole of doubt. She is fine. Her marriage, though a mess, is fine. Her relationship with Natalie, strained as it is, is fine. She breathes in and out. One, two, three, four. One, two, three, four.

"Earth to Rebecca. You're invited. I just wasn't sure if you would want to come," Royce says.

"We *could* go skating at Rockefeller Center," she says.

"You can go skating. The only aerobic exercise I want to get is trying on clothes," Natalie says. "And possibly lifting a fork to my mouth."

"Maybe it's better if I stay home," Rebecca says, as she imagines hours upon hours of watching Natalie try on outfits and indulge her habit. "I'll stay here and stick to my training."

"Suit yourself," Royce says. "What's for supper, aside from this rabbit food?"

CHAPTER TWENTY-FIVE

By the end of the next week, they have established a routine in the house. Rebecca is up at 5 a.m., making coffee and taking some quiet time before Royce emerges at six. She makes him breakfast—a protein shake and two poached eggs with wheat toast, the same thing every morning. By 6:30 a.m., Natalie appears, showered and dressed, ready to spend another day at the clinic. At 7 a.m., both Royce and Natalie get in their cars and drive off, she to Belle Mead and he to the dinky station in Princeton where he will take the train into New York. After they are gone, Rebecca straightens up the house and prepares for the morning's training. In the afternoon, she shops or naps or sees Margot, as she does once a week, every Thursday.

Today is Thursday. Rebecca enters the familiar waiting room and at once feels safe. There is something about the blue-gray walls and the soft music piped in through invisible speakers that calms her. Sounds of water falling, crickets, and wind. Or is it the paintings hung on the walls, their abstract shapes, that allow her mind to wander without making any decisions about their meaning? Whatever, she is glad to be here. After a brief wait, Margot calls her into the office.

"So it's been a few weeks because of the holidays. What's going on?" Margot asks.

"So much. Royce raped me. We found Natalie, and she is living with us now. I met an amazing woman on St. Croix named Monique."

"Whoa. Let's unpack that. First, Royce *raped* you?"

"Yes. On the island. I guess his frustration just reached a peak. Anyway, what's done is done. But I will never have sex with him again. I really don't want to talk about it."

"What *do* you want to talk about?"

"Me. I want to talk about me and why I can't leave well enough alone. Why do I always have to be so jealous and suspicious and trapped in my own brain? And oh, I am training for an Ironman."

"Rebecca, are you still taking your meds?" Margot says, reaching for her laptop. She lifts her readers, which are attached to a cord around her neck, and scrutinizes the screen.

"The Prozac? Yes. But it doesn't seem to be doing anything."

"Are you still depressed?"

"No, I am more angry than anything. And paranoid."

"Perhaps we need to take another look at your symptoms. Are you having racing thoughts? Suicidal ideation? A desire to spend money or engage in illicit sexual activity? Are you having mood swings?" Margot looks at Rebecca from over the top of her glasses.

"No! Why?"

"Good. I think we can rule out bipolar disorder."

"I don't think medicine is going to do anything for me. I think I just need to get over myself. Focus on making positive changes in my life. Take time to get to know and love myself. At least, that's what Monique says."

"Who is Monique?"

"A wonderful woman I met on St. Croix who helped me when I went down to find Natalie."

"We will get to Natalie in a moment. But first, what were you doing in St. Croix? I thought you were spending the holidays here with your parents. And who is this Monique? Is she a licensed counselor?"

"No. She is just a very kind, wise woman. She opened up her home to me and helped me navigate the police on the island."

"The police? My God, Rebecca, what have you been up to?"

"Not me. Natalie. She was found in a coma on a beach in St. Croix next to a murdered man."

Margot's jaw drops, and she is momentarily silenced, which delights Rebecca probably a little bit more than it should. After taking a long, deep breath, Margot continues.

"Did the police contact you when they found Natalie?"

"No. I read an article in *The Times* and flew down on the off chance it might be my sister. I met Monique on the plane. She invited me to stay with her in her villa—"

Margot holds up her hand to stop Rebecca from talking. "Rebecca, you are in a very vulnerable state right now. Are you sure this woman, Monique, was not taking advantage of you?"

"Advantage of me? How? She didn't ask me for anything. She just gave me support."

"And what did she get in return?"

"Can't people just do something nice without having it be suspicious?" As soon as the words came out of her mouth, Rebecca realizes she has been looking at Royce the way Margot is looking at Monique. She determines to be more open to his generosity and help from now on. She will not question the way in which Royce and Natalie are creating a bond. She will stop expecting "bad" behavior and give him the benefit of the doubt. After all, people can change. She has changed. As for Margot questioning Monique's integrity, she will have none of that. If she had to choose between the two women—her therapist and her friend—she would choose Monique. She deliberately turns the conversation in another direction.

"I just feel like I'm spinning. Doing the same thing over and over and getting nowhere."

"That's the definition of insanity: doing the same thing over and over and expecting different results."

"So I'm insane?"

"No. Just stuck. Talk to me about how you feel," Margot says as she places her laptop on her desk and leans forward to give Rebecca her undivided attention.

"Honestly, I feel like I'm watching a dryer going around and around with the same sock, and blouse, and panties appearing in the glass over and over and over. I'm waiting for the timer to go off, but it never does."

"Have you ever considered just opening the door and pulling out the sock or blouse or panties that are driving you to distraction?"

"What do you mean?"

"I mean, if, for example, the panties are your difficulties with Royce, separate them from the rest of the laundry. Don't wait for the perfect moment. Let go. Make a decision not to brood or ruminate over the situations that are bothering you. Take action and do something different."

"I thought I was doing things differently, setting boundaries like you suggested. But then he raped me."

"Are you sure he raped you?"

Rebecca cannot believe what she is hearing. "Of course, I'm sure! What, do you think I am making it up?"

"No, not at all. But sometimes our actions can be misleading."

"There was nothing misleading about this. We were driving down a road. He pulled over, yanked me out onto the dirt, and forced himself on me."

"Why don't you describe to me exactly what happened. Then we can see what your part might have been in it."

Taking a deep breath, Rebecca recounts the events that she believes led Royce to become so frustrated that he sexually assaulted her—beginning with the perfume-drenched shirt on the living room floor. By the time she is finished, tears stream down her cheeks.

A heavy silence fills the room for several minutes as Rebecca sobs into a tissue. Finally, Margot speaks.

"Maybe it's time to consider an alternative."

"Like what? Divorce?"

"Maybe a separation would do you good."

"I can't do that now. My sister is living with us. I can't leave her alone with Royce."

"There will always be something, won't there, Rebecca? Until you're ready to reach in and take the panties out of the dryer yourself, there's not much I can do for you."

"Are you saying our time together is done?"

"Not at all. I will be here for you as long as you need me. I'm just saying if you want to be set free, you're going to have to take some action. See you again next week?" Margot says as she rises out of her chair.

Rebecca nods and heads toward the door, then stops and turns back toward her therapist.

"Margot …"

"Yes?"

"Nothing. Never mind. It can wait."

Rebecca pushes the button on the elevator to head to the ground floor. Had she the courage, she would have told Margot that their time *was* done. That Margot, like the sock in the dryer, has become just another source of irritation. That therapy doesn't seem to be doing much for Rebecca except acting as a bandage on deeper wounds. If anything, it is keeping her stuck in a predictable cycle in which she always ends up feeling worse when she leaves than when she arrived. She has always set out for therapy in the hopes that Margot will have the solution to her problems. She arrives in the blue room with an expectation of relief. Yet more often than not, she leaves with more questions than answers and a sense of disappointment in her heart. Maybe it is time to take *this* sock out of the dryer and let it go.

***

"What is all this talk about laundry and socks in the dryer?" Monique asks Rebecca as they talk on the phone later that afternoon.

"It's a metaphor for my life. I'm spinning, like a dryer spinning clothes around, and I keep coming back to the same issues. The same sock and panties appearing in the glass."

"Oh, I see now. You are speaking of one of those front-loading dryers. Yes, I can visualize that now. The sock dropping again and again. What is it you are troubled by?"

"My therapist tells me I should just open the dryer and pull the sock out. Or, in the case of issues, like my relationship with Royce, I should just let it go. Maybe separate or divorce. I don't feel ready to do that yet." Rebecca is sitting on the sofa in the living room, her feet tucked up underneath her, with a fleecy throw pulled over her lap. Outside the snow is falling again. She has built a fire in the hearth, and it crackles and spits orange flames. She is trying something different, making the house cozy for Royce and Natalie when they come home from work and rehab.

The stew she put in the slow cooker earlier in the morning fills the house with a rich, beefy scent. When she finishes her call with Monique, she will make biscuits and a green salad. "I want to try to make this work."

"*Chérie*, that is the sock that keeps spinning round."

"What?"

"Your desire to make things work. You pursue that goal tenaciously in all areas of your life. This can be an asset, but taken to extremes, it is a definite liability. Then there is the story that you tell yourself that you are somehow spoiled goods, not worthy. These are things that cycle around over and over in your life and cause you great pain."

"So how do I let them go? Taking Prozac isn't helping. How can I pull the sock out of the dryer?"

"You don't. I am not in agreement with your therapist. I do not believe that everything requires action. Sometimes just observing, bringing our attention to something without judgement, is the best course to take. Your relationships with Royce and your sister—both problematic, are they not?"

"Yes," Rebecca says, taking a sip from her mug of tea.

"What if you just stepped back and let them be. Let Royce be the narcissist he is. Let your sister display her self-centeredness. You, meanwhile, just observe. Watch them. Don't try to please them or to avoid them. Just watch them and see what you see."

"And what is that going to do?"

"You will learn about yourself as you observe your reactions to them. You will gain confidence in yourself as you don't engage in their pettiness. The habitual responses to their words and actions will lessen, soften, and you will be stronger. So strong that when the time comes to make a change, you will be ready. But you must not force change too soon. I promise, change will come in its own time."

Rebecca sighs. She knows that Monique is right. She needs to practice detachment, with love, as they teach in Al-Anon. One thing she is sure of, she doesn't need to be paying Margot $185 a week when she can get better counsel from Monique for free. "Thank you, Monique, for being such a wise friend. You're amazing."

"It is you who is amazing, *chérie*, handling this load. But I promise, it won't be long …." Monique's voice trails off into silence.

"Long until what?" Rebecca asks.

"Until we see one another again."

After she hangs up, Rebecca stares into the fire, contemplating her friendship with Monique. They have only known each other for a little less than a month, and yet it seems as though their friendship has lasted years. Why she trusts the older woman is a mystery to Rebecca, and yet, from the first moment they met on the plane to St. Croix, Rebecca knew there was something special about her. *Or is this just another one of my socks?* Rebecca asks herself. *Am I doing what I always do, putting my trust in someone or something without really investigating first? It's funny,* she thinks to herself, *that I—an investigative reporter—should so freely accept someone into my life who I know so little about. Maybe this is me, growing. Changing. Opening up to the universe.*

Whatever it is, she isn't going to argue with fate.

***

Royce walks in the back door just as Rebecca is taking the biscuits out of the oven. "Mmm, something smells delicious," he says.

Rebecca sets the pan on a ceramic trivet on the counter and turns to look at her husband. He stands there with a grin on his face, both hands behind his back.

"Royce? Are you okay?" she says.

"Better than okay," he says and, with a flourish, produces a bouquet of exquisite flowers, which he holds out to her.

"For me?" she says.

"Who else would they be for?" he says.

She bites her tongue as she is tempted to say, *I was sure you brought them for Natalie.* She takes the flowers from him and lays them on the counter, then walks toward the dining room to fetch a chair. She will need to climb on top of it to reach the high cupboards where she keeps the vases.

"What are you doing?" he asks.

"I need a chair. I can't reach."

"You could have just asked. I can get it down for you. Which one do you want?"

"The clear one with the wide lip, in the front."

He reaches up and takes the vase down for her and holds it out. She tries to take it from him but he tightens his grip. "You know, Rebecca, I'm here to help you. When are you going to put down the gloves?"

"There are no gloves, Royce," she says, taking the vase from his hands and filling it with water from the tap. "It was just a vase. I'm used to climbing up there myself to get them. It's no big deal."

"What if you fell? And broke your arm? Where would you be then with your training? I'm just looking out for you."

"Well, thank you. But like I said. It's only a vase. It's no big deal." Rebecca wonders why Royce is making a big deal out of the situation. In fact, she wonders why he brought her flowers. "Did I miss something? Is today some kind of anniversary I'm forgetting?"

"Can't I bring my wife flowers without being interrogated?"

"I'm not interrogating you! I just wonder, that's all."

"If you must know, I had a bell ringer of a day at work. That overseas client I've been courting finally signed with me. A multi-million-dollar deal, maybe even into the billions if all goes well."

Rebecca snips the ends off the flowers before placing the stems in the vase. They are beautiful flowers: plate-sized dahlias and fragrant lilies, blue delphiniums and white buttons of feverfew. Not the standard dozen red roses of the past that Royce would bring her when they were dating. Maybe he *has* heard her over the years. Maybe he has been listening. Whatever, the gesture is sweet. Over these past few weeks, Royce has become sweeter, kinder. While Rebecca still doesn't trust him, she hopes maybe Natalie's near-death experience changed him, turned him into a new man. She is skeptical though, and wonders when the old Royce will reappear. In the meanwhile, she will enjoy his better mood and the lightness in the house, though always bearing in mind Monique's cautionary warning.

"I'm happy for you, Royce. You work hard. You should be rewarded."

He walks over to her and puts his arms around her waist, squeezing her lightly and kissing her neck. "Is that an offer?"

She tenses and shrugs him off. "Royce. I'm not there yet."

He loosens his grip on her and walks away toward his den. "I'll be here when you are. I'm going to take care of a few things. Let me know when dinner's ready."

Rebecca watches him disappear into his sacred space, which is only made available to her upon invitation.

Just then, the back door opens and Natalie comes breezing in, her face aglow. "Wow! Beautiful flowers! Someone has good taste. Are they for me? JK!"

Rebecca plumps the flowers, which now overflow the edges of the vase and emit a lovely scent. She places them in the middle of the dining room table. "You are later than usual. Everything okay?"

"I just had a few things to go over with my counselor," she says as she takes off her coat and tosses it on the couch in the living room. "I'm working on my fourth step, and she was encouraging me to write out a sex inventory."

"Really?" Rebecca says as she removes the golden biscuits from their pan and places them in a bread basket. "Isn't that fast, to be working on a fourth step? I mean, you have only been in the program for, what, two weeks?"

"They want you to move through the steps pretty fast. I think it's going to take me a while to write down all my sex exploits. Maybe not. Most of them are just vague memories of coming to from a blackout." Natalie walks to the fridge and takes out a can of seltzer, pops the tab, and chugs it down. "God, I was thirsty. And hungry. When's dinner?"

"It's ready when you and Royce are. We're having beef stew, biscuits, and a green salad."

"I gathered that," Natalie says, with an edge of sarcasm.

"There I go again, stating the obvious," Rebecca says. She feels unsettled by the energy coming from Natalie and Royce. They are both back from a full day away from outside input and emotional demands that seems to have energized them, while she is level. That's the only word she can think of to describe the way she feels. Level, from having worked out hard in the morning, spoken with both Margot and Monique in the afternoon, and filled in the spaces between with quiet rumination and preparations for their evening meal. Her life is not full of highs and lows; it is more like a steady hum of routine. She likes it that way. She will not try to match her energy to that of her husband and her sister. She will cloak herself in the serenity that she feels when she is just listening, just being, not trying hard to fit in.

At the dinner table, she watches and listens as Royce and Natalie banter about their day. About the past. And about the days to come.

"So," Royce says, between bites of a biscuit, which he eats naked, without butter, "you think this Carrier program is working for you?"

"Absolutely. The desire to drink and use has been totally lifted from me. I can't explain it. It's kind of a miracle. But I'm grateful every day."

Rebecca is surprised to hear her usually cynical sister express gratitude, but she has experienced the change that can take place in a person when they get sober, with her mother. She is happy to hear that a miracle has taken place in Natalie's life also. "What do you do all day? I mean, you are there from morning to dusk."

"Oh, you know," Natalie says as she spoons some stew into her mouth. "The usual. Group sessions. Meetings one-on-one with your counselor. AA meetings. It's kind of all jammed in there."

"What about free time? Mom said they have a great pool over there. She used to love doing laps."

"Oh yeah. There is that. They give us plenty of free time to just do what we want." Natalie takes another bite of her stew. "This is really good beef stew. What did you put in it?"

"Just the usual. Beef. Potatoes. Carrots. Onions. And a little Worcestershire sauce and nutmeg." Rebecca notices Royce giving Natalie a look, one of disapproval. She wonders where that is coming from and why Natalie has suddenly changed the subject from talking about Carrier.

"You are taking the program seriously, aren't you, Natalie?" Royce asks, his eyebrows raised high.

"Oh, yes. I mean, they are pushing me hard. Getting me to write out a sex inventory already! Can you imagine? They say it is going to help me deal with my past. And my future."

"And what do you see as your future, Natalie?" Royce asks.

"I don't know," Natalie says, looking back at Royce with a fierceness in her eyes. "What do you see as my future, Royce? At least I know I'm not going to be tried for murder, thanks to you."

Rebecca senses a tension between the two that has not been there since before Natalie disappeared on the island. She wonders if the honeymoon between Royce and Natalie is over and if this is going to be the beginning of a strained relationship. She doesn't want conflict in the house. If there is going to be conflict, then Natalie is going to have to leave. She wonders if she should say something to the two of them or just watch and listen as Monique suggested. She stabs a cucumber with her fork and puts it in her mouth.

"You have a promising future, Natalie, if you just do as you're told. The people at Carrier know what they're doing. You should trust them," Royce says.

"I do trust them! Why do you think I stayed later today, at their instruction? I'm following orders." Natalie glares at Royce.

"That is good to hear. Everyone likes a team player, Natalie," he says, as he dips his spoon into his stew, extracting a hefty helping, which disappears into his mouth.

"I am a team player, Royce. You can count on that."

Rebecca feels a buzzing sensation run through her body. She is listening with her ears but feels as though she is sensing two things going on at once. What are Royce and Natalie really talking about? Her mind drifts into its familiar pattern of suspicion and doubt. A team player? What could Royce mean by that? Yes, sobriety is a "we" effort, at least in AA, but she has never heard the term *team* used in all her years of attending Al-Anon and ACOA. She doesn't believe her mother ever talked about sobriety as a team sport. So what is this "team" Royce is referring to? She takes a deep breath and tries to look calmly at the situation. Royce is just talking in vernacular that he is familiar with. In his world, everything is about being on a team—a management team, a research and development team, a philanthropic team. Nothing is done alone, in a vacuum. He is the head of the team, always, and calls the shots. And maybe that is what he is saying about the program at Carrier. The counselors and the clients are all part of a team, with the overall program calling the shots. When she looks at it this way, Royce's words make sense. She can exhale.

"Well, whatever you're doing, it seems to be working, Natalie. You look happy and you seem lighter. So keep doing what you're doing, even if it means having to take some steps that feel uncomfortable. You will be glad you did in the long run," Rebecca says as she rises to clear the dinner dishes away.

"Thanks, Rebecca. I plan to keep doing what I'm doing. And I know it's going to pay off," Natalie says, casting a look at Royce, whose lips are pursed behind the chapel he has made of his hands.

"Anybody for dessert?" Rebecca asks. "There's frozen yogurt in the freezer."

"No thanks," says Royce. "This meal was heavy enough. I'm going to catch up on some work before bed." He places his linen napkin on the table and walks into the den.

"I've got some homework I need to get done by morning," Natalie says as she rises and starts up the stairs to her bedroom.

Rebecca looks at the dinner table, littered with salad bowls and a few plates sprinkled with crumbs. She gathers the remnants of the meal and places the dishes on the counter. She washes each dish carefully before placing it in the dishwasher, as Royce has instructed her. Something nags her as she scrapes the leftover stew into a plastic container and places it in the fridge next to a packet of shredded cheese. She can't put her finger on it. The thought is like a cloudy vision. She cannot make it out clearly. But something feels wrong as she wipes the counters clean. She will need to be vigilant, as Monique instructed. To listen. To watch. But also, not to take herself and her crazy thoughts too seriously, she reminds herself. Insanity is doing the same thing over and over again and expecting different results. As long as she is playing the narrative of Royce as a villain and Natalie as a witch repeatedly, she may never have the clarity to see what really *is*. And that is what Monique wants for her—to see life as it really is, not as she imagines or fantasizes.

She turns out the lights in the kitchen, pokes at the fire, which has now died down to embers, and takes up her perch on the sofa again, under the warm throw, losing herself in her book.

CHAPTER TWENTY-SIX

January passes and morphs into a cold, rainy February of ice more than snow. Rebecca continues with her training, getting her runs in on the track at the gym rather than on the treacherous roads outside. Still, she sticks to her routine.

Part of her routine is her weekly meeting with Margot, something she thought she would cancel. She finds, however, that with Natalie in the house bringing up old memories, there is much to talk about.

"It is not that she is doing anything in particular. In fact, she makes herself pretty scarce. It's just having her around. It's weird."

"Weird, how?" Margot asks.

"I don't know."

"That's not a good answer, Rebecca."

"It's like she brings the past with her even though she is trying to do something new and positive with her life. I don't believe her. I don't trust her. I'm waiting for the other shoe to drop and the old Natalie to reappear."

"Perhaps you're bringing your past with you into the situation. It certainly wouldn't be surprising. Your relationship with her has been rooted in negative emotions."

"Are you saying I'm somehow blinded by our history?"

"I'm suggesting that maybe your mistrust is more about *you* than her, don't you think?"

"I guess."

"You feel triggered by her presence."

"I do. She brings up all kinds of feelings of shame and self-doubt. I don't even know why."

"Go on."

"It's the way she does things. Her friendliness toward Royce. And her overzealous sharing about her program. It's not like her."

"She's changing. That makes you uncomfortable. You like to be in control, and to have her behave differently rocks your boat. You don't know where you stand."

"I don't trust her."

"Has she done anything since she moved in with you to break your trust?"

"Not yet. Not that I know of. Not that I have caught her at. But there are little things. Like the wine glasses aren't exactly the way I left them. And my brush has strands of blond hair in it. Things that make me think she's being sneaky."

"Perhaps you're being overly suspicious. It doesn't sound to me like you have any real cause for alarm."

"You're probably right. It's just my imagination getting the better of me."

"No matter what she's doing, Becca, there is only one person in this equation who you have any control over. And that is yourself. If you focus on yourself, you may find that your concerns with your sister dissipate."

"I know you're right," Rebecca says. "I will do that. I will focus on me."

Natalie's presence is not, oddly enough, putting an additional strain on the relationship between Royce and Rebecca. If anything, it is normalizing it. Now Royce leaves for the office at 7 a.m. and is home by 6 p.m.. Natalie is on the same schedule, and Rebecca has the whole day to herself. They all eat dinner together and revisit their days. Natalie regales them with stories she has heard at her meetings and topics that have been discussed at her outpatient classes. To Rebecca, her sister always seems to be pushing a little too hard to impress upon them how sober she is and how well she is doing. But as Margot has told her, her reactions have more to do with what is going on inside her than what Natalie is sharing. Royce encourages the sharing, prompting Natalie to go back further into her time on the island.

"It's weird. It's all such a blank," Natalie says as they eat salmon and asparagus for dinner. "It's like I lost a year of my life."

"You were probably in blackouts most of the time," Rebecca says.

"Could be PTSD. You were involved with some pretty bad dudes, it turns out," Royce says.

"What do you mean?" Natalie says.

"That guy who was killed. He was a notorious trafficker—drugs and girls."

"You don't say. I honestly don't remember anything about that. Anyway, I'm so glad that's all behind me now. Thank you both so much for helping me. You sure it's not too much having me here?"

"Not at all," Royce says. "You stay as long as you need to. That's what family is for."

***

Despite the counsel she has been given and her determination to pay attention to her own "hula hoop," Rebecca can't stop thinking about Natalie. Now their mother wants to come visit, to check up on her girls, but Rebecca knows her real interest is in her younger daughter.

Rebecca picks at a torn cuticle with her thumb. She would welcome some curiosity on her mother's part, but her mother asks her no questions about what she is up to—the training, the adjustment to having Natalie around, her relationship with Royce—not that she would actually share any details about her marriage with her mother. All she wants to hear about is Natalie. How Natalie is doing in her outpatient treatment. Is she getting to meetings? Making friends in the program? How are the three of them getting along?

Surprisingly, Natalie is vehemently opposed to their mother's visit. Rebecca thought Natalie would be excited to share stories of her recovery with their mother, who was now back in the program herself. But Natalie feels just the opposite.

"I don't want her here nosing around my program. She will have all sorts of opinions about the way I'm doing things. I don't know if I can stay sober with her here," Natalie said when Rebecca told her about their mother's plan to visit.

Pretty strong words and not at all what Rebecca expected. Rebecca doesn't know what to expect from Natalie. Doesn't everyone practice the program pretty much the same way? What can Natalie be doing that might alarm their mother or cause her to criticize her younger daughter, who she dotes on and for whom she scarcely has a sour word?

Rebecca answers all her mother's questions as patiently as she can, though she knows there is probably an edge in her voice. She lies about how well Natalie is doing because, in fact, she has no idea how her program and recovery are progressing. All she sees is Natalie on the outside, laughing over Royce's jokes at dinner and presenting a front of solicitousness toward her. Rebecca looks forward to her time away from them both.

Who was it who said that fish and company start to stink after three days? Benjamin Franklin. He always said pithy things like that. No gains without pains. She can relate. Natalie has been with them for almost two months now, and even though she is doing all the things Rebecca asked her to do—she is going to AA meetings, getting up early in the morning and starting the day with meditation and prayers (her sponsor's idea, not Rebecca's), and eating a nutritious breakfast—Rebecca finds herself irritated by Natalie's presence. Yes, Natalie is helping around the house, washing her own laundry. She is even exploring getting a part-time remote job so she can contribute to the household expenses, although that is not necessary. Even with all this, Rebecca finds herself on edge as she sits at the dinner table listening to Royce and Natalie banter about the most superficial things—the Super Bowl, the awards season in Hollywood, the influx of illegal aliens into the US. They talk like a married couple, at least the way Rebecca imagines most married couples talk. Except for her and Royce. They rarely talk at all. She is disgusted by the way Natalie flirts with Royce. She knows she and her sister will never be friends again.

Maybe it is because they never were really good friends to begin with. When Rebecca is in a room with Natalie, she feels overshadowed. She is at a loss for words. When she does speak, what comes out tends to be negative and critical, not at all what she really feels like saying. Natalie brings out the worst in her. There is no easy, comfortable silence. The air is always filled with the static of the past. Rebecca waits for the match to ignite and the sparkler to shoot off a thousand lights in the form of accusations and memories. To ward off the onset of such an interchange, Rebecca resorts to the most mundane topics. The weather. What they need from the grocery store. Interesting podcasts that Natalie may have come across or television shows that she might recommend.

Anything to avoid the big question she really wants to ask, which is "When are you planning on leaving and what do you intend to do with your life?"

Rebecca wants to suggest that maybe it would be a good thing if Natalie began to plan for an eventual departure. But she does not want to come across as a bitch. And besides, Royce has been so much easier to live with now that Natalie is living with them.

She gets up from the dinner table and brings the dishes to the kitchen. Natalie follows her in with the remaining plates and glasses.

"You don't mind my being here, do you?" Natalie says.

"Of course not. Why would I mind?"

"It's just that I hope I'm not putting a strain on your marriage."

"Why would you think that?"

"Well, I noticed Valentine's Day came and went without any chocolates or roses."

"Royce and I don't choose to recognize Valentine's Day. It's just another marketing scam."

"That's a bit cynical. Anyway, you aren't even sleeping in the same bed."

Rebecca stops scraping the plates and rinsing them. "That is really none of your business."

"Sorry. I'm not prying. It's just got to be hard on Royce. He's such a virile man."

"We have worked it out."

"Have you?"

"Like I said, it's really none of your business."

That night, Rebecca starts looking up sober homes in the area. Her conversation with Natalie has left her feeling uneasy. She does not want her private life on display any longer. The sooner she can get Natalie out of the house, the better.

CHAPTER TWENTY-SEVEN

In the beginning of March, almost six weeks into Rebecca's training, the weather begins to brighten. A stretch of days with blue skies and warmer temperatures lifts the pall of winter. Spring is just around the corner, or so it seems to Rebecca, who turns the heat off and opens all the windows to let some fresh air into the house, which has been closed up for months. She knows this reprieve is just that—a tease before another nor'easter blows through as it inevitably will before spring truly arrives. But she is hopeful. At this rate, the daffodils will all be blooming when her parents arrive for Easter in April.

She decides to take a long run, to push herself a little harder on this beautiful day. She pulls on a pair of running shorts and a T-shirt, laces up her shoes.

When she walks into the kitchen to fill her water bottle, Royce is at the kitchen counter drinking his protein shake. "You're optimistic," he says.

"What do you mean?"

"It's still in the forties out there. Don't be deceived by the sunshine."

"I will be all right. I'm taking a longer run than usual. I'll warm up in no time."

"By longer you mean—"

"Two hours, at least. I need to challenge myself. Up the ante in my training."

"You're determined to go through with this."

"I am."

He picks up a banana off a bunch that is in a bowl on the counter. "Here. At least have something to eat before you go."

"Thanks. Aren't you going in to the office today?" she says.

"No. I've got some things I can take care of at home. I've decided to play hooky myself on such a beautiful day. I had hoped you might join me for a bike ride."

"Royce. I'm sorry. Today is a running day."

"I know. I get it. You've got your schedule."

"Maybe when I get back, we can do something?" she says, feeling a little bit guilty that she is turning away from him when he is reaching out to her. But she knows if she lets go of her routine for him, for anyone, she may lose it altogether. And the race, the preparation for the race, means too much to her.

Already the training has helped her in dealing with Natalie. With her focus on the Ironman and not on her sister, she has pretty much left Natalie to herself. As a result, Natalie has developed a routine of her own, which leaves Rebecca wide open to be herself. She still wishes her younger sister would make arrangements to go live in a sober house somewhere, but for the time being, life is manageable. If she is honest with herself, Rebecca can see her relationship with Natalie is healing. Maybe the near-death experience really did cause a psychic change in her sister. Maybe Natalie is finally growing up into a responsible, loving, caring human being. At least Rebecca hopes so.

"I better get going while I still have the motivation," she says. "See you in a couple of hours."

Royce reaches out and takes her arm, draws her close to him. "Be careful out there. I wouldn't want anything to happen to you."

Rebecca gives him a peck on the cheek. "I'll be fine. Don't worry about me."

As Rebecca jogs down the long driveway to the farmhouse, she notices the puffy white clouds against the blue sky. She hears spring songbirds that she has not heard for a long while. Her heart lifts and opens to the beauty of the day. March 4th. She has always loved this day. March 4th. She will march forth into this day with optimism. She thinks of Monique, her encouragement and kindness. Shouldn't she be coming back from the island to the city now? Rebecca makes a mental note to call her friend and make arrangements to get together sometime soon.

An hour into her run, her legs are tired already. Although it is still chilly, she has worked up a good sweat. She is determined to keep running, but decides to turn around and head home just in case she hits the wall and her energy is depleted.

She scolds herself for not eating more than a banana. She should at least have had a protein shake. She knows better than to exercise on an empty stomach. What she does not want is to be stranded on Sourland Mountain, miles from home with no more water in her bottle. What is the worst that can happen if she turns back? She will cut her run short by half an hour. She can always take Royce up on his offer of a bike ride to round out her workout. Satisfied with that assessment of the situation, she does an immediate turnabout and heads back toward the farm, then scolds herself for wimping out and turns back to complete her route.

An hour later, she walks slowly up the gravel driveway, pebbles crunching under her feet as she goes. The run has left her feeling both enervated and energized at the same time. She checks her watch—exactly two hours since she left. She is proud of herself for pushing hard, for keeping her commitment to herself and seeing the training through. If she can run for two hours, she can double that. Four hours is more than enough to run a marathon.

Royce has stacked up the bikes beside the back door—their racing bikes and a mountain bike—she assumes for Natalie. Rebecca hadn't thought about Natalie coming with them, but it is all right. With the mood she is in right now—plus the blue sky, the released endorphins, the promise of a peanut butter and banana shake—pretty much nothing can faze her. Besides, she sees a yellow crocus blooming by the back door and her heart lifts. The long winter may be over.

When she opens the door, she expects to see Natalie or Royce, but no one is there. She fixes herself a shake and gulps it down, then heads toward the den. It is empty. By now her sweat has cooled and she is getting chills, so she climbs the stairs to get into the shower.

That is when she hears them. Natalie giggling and Royce saying, "You like that, huh? That feels good?"

"You know it does," Natalie says.

Rebecca, who has taken off her sweaty shirt and holds it in her hand, stands in the bedroom door in her sports bra and shorts. Royce and Natalie are oblivious to her presence as she watches them go at it in bed. She throws the sweaty shirt at them.

"Royce! Natalie! What the fuck!"

They look over at her, surprised.

"Oh my God, Rebecca. It's not what you think," Royce says as he extricates himself from her younger sister.

"Like hell it isn't. It's exactly what I think. You're fucking my sister!"

"To be fair, she—" he says.

"Don't blame her! Actually, *do* blame her *and* yourself! You are both assholes!"

"You said you were coming back in three hours," Royce says.

Rebecca cannot believe what she is hearing. "So now it's my fault? And I did not say three hours, I said two hours."

"I'm sure you said three."

"Don't make this my fault. Don't twist this around. You're having sex with my sister, for God's sake. I can't believe we're even having this conversation!"

All the while, Natalie just watches them, her long blond hair cascading down over the sheet she has pulled over her breasts.

"And you!" Rebecca says to her sister. "I don't even have words for you. You're a slut. Always have been. Always will be."

"At least I can give him what he wants," Natalie says.

Rebecca tries to force back the tears that have come to her eyes. She needs to get into her closet to get some fresh clothes, but she doesn't want to pass by them too closely. She is so angry at Natalie, she feels like she might spring on her like a lioness and tear out her eyes.

"I'm leaving," she says.

"Where are you going?" Royce asks.

"I'm not sure, but when I get back, Natalie, you had better be gone."

"She's not going anywhere."

"What?"

"You heard me. She's not going anywhere. If you want to leave, then leave. But you brought this on yourself, Rebecca."

Now she wants to tear out *Royce's* eyes and rip the flesh from his body. Instead, she walks calmly past them and gathers up some clothes from the closet. Then she walks out of the room. As soon as she has left the bedroom, she hears them laughing. She runs into the guest bathroom and vomits in the toilet. She puts on a fresh T-shirt and biking shorts and heads downstairs. She throws her phone and wallet into a pack, fills a water bottle, and steps out the kitchen door.

The day, which before had seemed so full of promise and hope, has become cloudy and chilly again. She pushes Royce's bike onto the ground, climbs on her own, fastens her helmet, and begins to ride.

Though her legs, her whole body, are tired from the long run, adrenalin pushes her forward up the steep hills and onto the wooded road beyond. Tears sting her eyes and blur her vision as she sees over and over again the image of Royce straddling her sister in the bed that had once been theirs. What did he mean she brought this on herself? By asking Natalie to come stay with them in the first place? She thought she was being *kind*. But then she remembers that it was Royce who asked her. Had he planned on screwing Natalie since he saw her again on the island? And how long has this been going on? Maybe he meant that her training for the Ironman had left them alone in the house for hours. Of course, Royce would see that as an invitation for mischief.

Mischief! This is more than mischief, she tells herself. This is practically incest, and here he is kicking her out of the house.

Her stomach lurches, and she pulls over by the side of the road to vomit. What if he means what he said about her being the one who had to leave? What if by the time she gets back to the house, he has changed all the locks and her clothes are thrown out on the driveway? Where would she go?

In that moment, she deeply regrets ever coming to rely on Royce because she has, she can see now, become dependent on him. She has no money of her own to speak of. No medical insurance without him. No means of supporting herself. The only place she could go would be to her parents', and she doesn't even have the gas money to get there.

How has she allowed herself to get into this situation? How has she turned her life over to this man who so clearly does not love her, who only loves himself, and who takes what he wants when he wants it to satisfy his own needs?

And Natalie. *Natalie!* Her little sister. She is as bad as Royce. In fact, they deserve each other. What will their parents say when they find out? She doesn't want to tell them. It will break their hearts. Or maybe they will side with Royce and say she brought this on herself.

The hills are steeper now, and she pumps with all her energy to climb them. Her thighs are on fire, and each rotation of the wheels sends pain shooting up her legs. At least she feels alive. At least she knows she *is* alive.

Soon she will be at the top, and there will be the long downhill home. Home. Does she even have a home? How can they live there, the three of them, together? She gives one more tremendous push, standing up on the pedals to bull her way through, and then she is at the top.

All she can hear as she sails down the mountain is the whir of the wheels. The wind whips her face, making her eyes tear again. But this time, she is not crying from betrayal or fear. Now she is angry. Her emotions are stirred into a frenzy by the landscape passing so quickly past her, shafts of sunlight in strobe, the whir of the tires, and the feeling that she is weightless. She will show them. She will not leave the comfort of her home no matter how uncomfortable the situation has become. She will let them play out their little fantasy, and she will endure it like a martyr if she must. But she will keep to her routine and enjoy the comfort of her home. It is *her* home. Royce bought it for *her*, put it in her name. If anyone leaves, it should be them.

Up ahead, the major road looms and she presses on the handbrakes to slow herself down, but her hands are frozen, paralyzed. They do not respond to the message from her brain. "Press. Press." She tells her fingers, but her hands are jelly and the road is getting closer.

It is a main road, from Princeton to Hopewell, and fairly well traveled. She is sure that at this time of day, there will be traffic. She tries to force herself to slow down, but the bike will not cooperate, and she sails across the highway and crashes into a stone wall on the opposite side of the road.

As she sits on the ground next to her crumpled bike, she thanks God, whom she long ago abandoned, that there were no cars. Her bike shorts are torn. Her knee is bloody and raw. Her shoulders ache as if she is carrying boulders. But other than that, she can move all her digits— fingers, toes. She slowly gathers herself to her feet and picks up her bike, starts to make her way back down the road, cursing all the way. She tells herself she should have known better than to take that arduous ride after a long run. She should have known she would lose strength. Now she will show up at the house, bruised and bleeding, and Royce will surely have something negative to say. Not *How are you? Are you okay?* But *I told you so. Can't you do anything right?* If only there were some place she could go.

Just then, a pickup truck drives toward her, slowing down as it nears her. It stops. A man, about her age she guesses, leans across to the passenger window. "Looks like you could use some help," he says.

"It's nothing. Just a little accident."

"Looks like more than that to me."

"It's nothing, really."

"Here. Let me put that bike in the bed, and I'll give you a ride home," he says.

From the way he speaks, he seems to know her house is only a few miles down the road. Still, she asks him, "How do you know where I live?"

"You don't remember me, do you?" he says.

She can honestly say she does not. He has a pleasant enough face, though not particularly remarkable. He could be any one of many people she has encountered in her life.

"I own the Crazy Horse. I met you when you were asking about your sister last year—when she went missing."

Suddenly, she can place him. She sees him as vividly as the day she went into the bar after Natalie had disappeared. He was drying glasses with a white cloth towel and placing them back on the shelves behind the bar when he spoke with her. He was not particularly helpful then, she recalls, and that irritated her. He might have provided the missing link to finding her sister, but he seemed to be holding something back.

"It's good you found her after all this time," he says.

"Is it?" she says, her mind flashing to the vision of Natalie in bed with Royce, that smug, self-satisfied look on her face. She wonders how he knows that Natalie has returned. Hopewell is a small town and, of course, there is gossip, but more than likely Natalie has gone back to her old watering hole and lied to her sister about her drinking. She hooked up with Royce and kept that a secret. Can Rebecca trust anything her sister has said?

"Did I say something wrong?" he says.

"No. It's just—complicated."

Cars pass by the parked truck, faces crammed in windows to see what catastrophe has occurred.

"We had better get you off the road before there's another accident," he says.

He jumps out of the cab, comes around her side, and hoists the bike into the truck bed. She does not protest. She's too tired and sore to protest. Her body begins to shake with the cold and the shock of her fall. He takes his jacket off and wraps it over her shoulders, a gesture that strikes her as unimaginably kind. She starts to cry.

"You're in shock. Let me take you home."

"No. Not there. Anywhere but there," she says.

He doesn't ask why. "We'll go back to the bar. I live in the apartment above. We'll get you something to drink."

Shivering and numb, she nods as he helps her step up into the truck. They drive in silence to the bar, which is not open yet. She has no idea what time it is. Her Apple Watch was smashed during the crash. Her phone, which she had tucked into her pack, was, thankfully, unharmed. She wonders if maybe she has a concussion, as her helmet came loose when she hit the wall. Her head is throbbing and her vision is blurry. All she wants to do is lie down and sleep.

He unlocks the bar and leads her to a table where he sits her down. "Don't move," he says, as if she intends to go anywhere or even has anywhere to go. She rests her head in her hands and closes her eyes.

She wonders if Royce and Natalie are back at it, oblivious to the fact that she might have been killed. Would they even have cared? Her head hurts so much—and her knee and shoulders. The pain is becoming more acute as she sits in the warm, dark room. How could she have been so stupid? What was she trying to do? Maybe she was trying to kill herself subconsciously? It is all moot now. She is alive and in agony.

He returns with a glass filled with amber liquid—she assumes it is whiskey—and a first aid kit.

"What's your name?" she asks.

"Jesse. Yours?"

"Rebecca. What's that?"

"Whiskey."

"I don't drink."

"This will help with the pain. Think of it as medicine."

She sniffs the glass. The pungent aroma fills her nose. "I don't think I can," she says.

"Just try it."

She lifts the glass to her lips, takes a sip, feels the liquor burn through her like fire. She sputters and coughs. He laughs.

"Pretty lightweight, aren't you? Not like your sister at all."

"Nothing like her."

"Take one more sip."

She complies and this time feels the liquor go to her head, followed by a warm, fuzzy glow.

"Better?"

"Much."

As he tends to her leg, cleaning the gravel and dirt away with antiseptic, she looks at him. He is not so ordinary after all. His dark hair curls up around the base of his neck and his shoulders are muscular and well defined under his T-shirt. He tends to her gently but deliberately, careful not to hurt her but intent on cleaning and dressing the cut as best as he can. "You should probably get stitches," he says. "I can take you to the ER."

"No. No hospital. I'll be fine. You've done a great job."

"You're going to have a scar."

"You have no idea," she says. "This is a day made up of scars."

"You want to talk about it?" he says.

"Give me another drink, and I might."

***

When she comes to, she is in a bed, not her own, not in her house. For a moment, she is disoriented. Then, as the pain shoots through her knee, her leg, her shoulder, she remembers the accident. The events of the day come back to her, right up to when he poured her the third glass of whiskey. Then she has no recollection at all of what transpired. She just knows she is in bed—presumably *his* bed. She is afraid to ask him to fill in the blanks. She already regrets what she might have said or done.

The good news is, she has all her clothes on. Then she realizes they are not her clothes but his—a pair of baggy sweatpants, a T-shirt, an oversized sweatshirt. She shudders at the thought of him undressing her and dressing her again. Who knows what might have happened in between.

She was either very drunk or in what her mother used to describe as a blackout—a period of alcohol overdosing that leads to hours of life unaccounted for with no memory of what might have happened or been said. She needs to know what happened and was said.

But not now. It is evening and the bar is busy. She hears loud conversations seep up from downstairs, music, the scraping of chairs. Jesse—that is his name, is it not?—must be at work. She will have to wait until the bar closes to piece her story together. Meanwhile, she is starving. She can't remember the last time she ate. He has only a mini fridge in his apartment, and it is empty except for some bottles of water and cans of beer. Not even so much as a celery stick or a hunk of cheese. Her stomach gurgles loudly in protest. She decides she will go downstairs, but first she will wash her face and brush her hair.

When she turns on the light in the small bathroom, she looks in the mirror. Her face is swollen, and the right side of it is purply blue with a bruise where she must have hit her head. Thank God for bicycle helmets, or she probably would be dead. There is no way she can go out in public looking like this, as if she has been abused. The irony of that thought is not lost on her. She swipes at her hair with his hairbrush, but the pain in her head is so strong that she stops, turns out the light, and goes back into the main room to wait for him to reappear.

As she sits on the worn couch, not knowing what time it is, not knowing what day it is even—it could be tomorrow for all she knows—she wonders if Royce has given her a second thought. He must wonder where she has gone. She has no friends in town, no one she could call and spend the night with. Her parents are in New Hampshire, and God knows she wouldn't ask Royce's parents to put her up for the night. She hopes he is at least a little bit concerned about what might have happened to her, though she is sure that by now he will have frozen her debit card. She supposes he could have put a trace on her phone. Maybe she should call him to let him know she is all right? And besides, she will let him squirm a little longer. Though she doubts he is doing any squirming at all.

How could he have done this to her? How could he have had sex with Natalie? And was this the first time? Rebecca shudders as she reflects on the hours she left her husband and her sister alone in the house while she pursued her training. When did the affair—she doesn't want to call it an affair. It was not an affair, for God's sake. An affair implies some kind of emotional connection, at least a vague attempt at love, does it not? But maybe she is wrong. Maybe an affair doesn't require an element of affection. Maybe it can just be rooted in lust. That is what she thinks Royce and Natalie are satisfying—a mutual need for sex that is all about animal instincts. Physical desire. She has always known that about both of them; she just never thought they would indulge in sex *together*. Not in her house. Not in her bed.

The terrible reality disgusts her. She can see them there, copulating. Naked. Taking their pleasure. She can hardly find the words to express both her anger and her deep shame, as if she is responsible for their bad behavior. She reaches into her heart to find some comfort and pulls out Monique's words about Royce. *He is a monster. I have known men like him. Narcissists. Be careful.* And what about Natalie? She is a monster too. A slut. A thief. Taking what doesn't belong to her. *If Mom only knew.* But Rebecca is sure her mother would rationalize Natalie's behavior—credit it to her addiction, to the fact that she was a "troubled soul"—and forgive her. Ask Rebecca to forgive her too. Rebecca is forgiving no one. Not this time.

Time. She wishes she knew what time it was. Jesse doesn't have an oven with a clock, just a cooktop. And his microwave doesn't tell the time. Of course! Her phone. She isn't thinking clearly. It is eleven o'clock. She can hear cars pulling out on the gravel as if everyone is starting to leave, and she hopes that is a sign the bar is closing. It is definitely quieter down there now. She gets up and peeks out the window through the blinds, checking to see how many cars are left in the parking lot. Only one or two remain.

She walks down the back stairs to the bar and looks in. There are just a few people left, nursing drinks. Jesse is back behind the bar, drying glasses with his white towel.

Rebecca remembers the first time she met Jesse. It was January 23, a bitter cold, snowy evening last year. She was cleaning up the dinner dishes, preparing to join Royce as he watched the playoff game between the Bills and the Chiefs, when her mother called, frantic. Because she had not been able to reach Natalie for the past week. "Can you please just go check on her at work for me?" her mother had asked. "I am concerned."

Rebecca, who was five months pregnant and wanted nothing more than to watch her favorite quarterback perform his magic while she tidied and nested, did not relish going out in the winter storm. But when she asked Royce if he would go, he had been so disagreeable and whiny that she drove herself to the bar.

The place was packed for a Sunday night; the noise was deafening and the place smelled like stale beer. She scanned the room quickly but did not see her sister. Maybe she was out back having a cigarette or using the restroom? To the right of the bar, a wide-screen television on the wall played what would later be called an epic game. She walked up to the bar, where the bartender was wiping glasses with his white towel.

"Excuse me," she said. "I'm looking for Natalie."

"Sorry. I can't hear you over the TV. What is it you want?" the bartender said, putting the towel over his shoulder and leaning into her.

"My sister. Natalie. I am looking for her."

"That makes two of us," he said.

"What do you mean?" Rebecca said, her stomach suddenly knotting. "I thought she was working tonight."

"She hasn't been here for a week. Left last Saturday with some guy. Said she was going to the islands." He took the towel off his shoulder and began drying glasses again.

Rebecca felt bile rising in her throat. She wasn't sure who she was most angry with: Natalie, for running off and leaving her to handle their mother; Royce, who selfishly refused to help her out; or this bartender, who seemed so complacent and unconcerned. She felt nauseous and dizzy from the noise and the smells, the unexpected information. All she wanted to do was get home into her bed. She turned to leave.

"Hey," the bartender said. "If you hear from her, tell her she couldn't have left at a worse time."

How unfeeling his words had seemed that night. Now when she looks at him, a white towel in his hand, drying glasses, she knows he was right.

Jesse looks over at the stairwell, sees her standing there. Their eyes meet for a moment. She isn't sure how to read the look that he gives her, but she tells herself it is compassion. Her thoughts are validated when he turns to the stragglers seated at the bar.

"Time's up, fellas," he says. "Let's call it a night."

Reluctantly, the stragglers leave. As the last one exits, Jesse locks the door behind him and switches the flashing neon Open sign off. She steps out onto the barroom floor.

"Well, look who it is. Sleeping Beauty," he says.

"Hardly a beauty," she says.

"Yeah, you're pretty banged up," he says as he comes to stand next to her. "You're all shades of purple. That's going to last awhile."

"Do you have anything to eat? I'm starving."

"Not much. Some stale sandwiches. How about some cheese and crackers and a Bloody Mary?"

"A *virgin* Mary. No more booze for me."

He smiles as he disappears behind the bar to fix her plate and drink. She sits on a stool and watches him.

"Thanks," she says when he hands her the food. "For everything. The clothes. The place."

"Least I could do," he says as he returns to his task of drying glasses and placing them back on the shelf.

"Jesse, did we … ? You know."

"Did we what?"

"You know. How did I get in these clothes?"

"Do you mean, did we have sex? What kind of a guy do you think I am? I'd never take advantage of a woman in your condition."

"Was I drunk?"

"Yes, you were." He smiles, chuckling slightly. "A very talkative drunk."

Her stomach clenches. She wants to ask him what she said, but she is anxious at the same time. *Time.* She has completely lost track of time.

"What day is it?" she asks.

"It's still Monday."

"I'm so disoriented."

"Based on what you told me, it's been quite a day."

She takes a long sip of her drink and bites into a piece of cheese, mustering up courage. "What exactly did I tell you?"

"Just that you found your husband and sister in bed together. And you would like to murder them both."

She sighs. "It's a shit show. I don't know what to do."

"Stay here for the night. Get some rest. Let them sweat it out a little. I will take you home in the morning—if you want to go back, that is."

"You have been so kind," she says as tears start to flow. "I'm sorry. I'm just so tired."

He comes around the bar and stands in front of her, puts his hands on her shoulders. She tenses, thinking for a moment that he might lean forward and kiss her. She lowers her head, avoiding eye contact. Her hair falls in front of her face. She feels safe behind its veil. She desperately needs to feel safe.

"You're not anything like your sister," he says.

She is caught off guard. That was not where she saw this moment going. "Is that a good thing?" she says.

"It's different. She was, is—I guess—so extroverted, spontaneous, and wild. You seem so much more responsible, in control."

Rebecca sighs. Hasn't that been the story of her life? She has been so responsible, so in control. She doesn't feel in control now. She feels like she is on slippery rocks and that she may fall at any moment. She wishes she knew what he wanted from her. Is he telling her he wants her to be more spontaneous? And what does that mean? Have sex? Her body hurts so much, she can't imagine, and yet she thinks that curling up inside his arms, letting him hold her, escaping even if it is just for the moment from the pain and fear, sounds good.

"How well did you know your sister?" he asks.

"I thought I knew her pretty well. She was predictably wild, as you say. We could count on her to be in trouble. She attracted it."

"She did. She was—how can I say this nicely—very loose with her affections. Always going home with one guy or another after work."

"She's a slut. Let's be honest."

"Those are pretty harsh words, but yes. I'd say that is a legitimate characterization."

"Why did you keep her on here?"

"She was a good worker." Jesse wipes another glass and places it on the shelf behind the bar. Then he turns back and looks into Rebecca's eyes. "No, to be truthful, I had other motives. She kept the customers coming in. For all her faults, she was the life of the party. She was good for business. Until the drugs started to get in the way."

"Drugs? What was she doing?"

"Cocaine. At the end, she was high, like, all the time. I would have had to let her go soon anyway."

"Did you ever think of getting her some help?" Rebecca asks.

Jesse looks at her, incredulous. "I was just her boss, not a therapist. What about your family? Couldn't you get her into treatment?"

"We tried, but she wasn't receptive. I just thought …You are obviously a nice guy. You helped me."

"That was different. You accepted my help. Natalie? She was on her own path. She made her choices. That guy she left with for the islands—I could see he was trouble. I warned her, asked her not to go, but she told me to 'Fuck off and mind your own business.' I was just glad to see the tail end of those three. I didn't like what they were bringing into my bar."

"What do you mean?"

"I heard them propositioning her. Offering her a lot of money if she would help them."

"Help them? Was there more than one? Were they drug dealers?"

"No. I don't think so. They looked like they should be sipping cocktails in the Nassau Inn. They started coming in a few weeks before she disappeared. They chatted her up, and she loved it. They were so out of place in here. I could sense they were up to something dark. Dangerous. When they made her the offer, she leapt at it. She couldn't stop herself. She just took off her apron and quit right then and there. Left with that one guy and never came back."

"That sounds like Natalie. Did you tell the police?"

"I did. But by then, she was long gone. I got the feeling they gave up pretty quick. They never came back to have me do one of those portrait things. Natalie was an adult. And she had a reputation. I'm sorry to sound so callous about all this."

"No. It's all right. You are just being honest. Thank you for being honest."

"You barely touched your food."

"I lost my appetite. I'm tired. Maybe we could just go to bed."

"Of course. Whatever you like."

He turns off the lights in the bar, and they climb back up the stairs to his apartment. Once there, he begins to pull out pillows and a blanket and lay them on the couch.

"What are you doing?" she asks.

"I'll sleep here. You can have the bed."

She hesitates, then walks over and stands in front of him. She feels small and fragile as he towers over her by at least a foot. He is as tall as Royce, only slighter, less threatening. "Would you mind sleeping in the bed with me? I really don't want to be alone."

"You sure?"

She nods.

"I will be on my best behavior. Though I'm not guaranteeing anything," he says, grinning.

"Please don't joke. It hurts to laugh." She begins to tremble and crosses her arms across her chest, holding herself tightly.

"Are you cold?" he asks.

"Maybe a little. More tired. And anxious."

"I'll warm you up. Get in bed."

As they lie in bed, curled up with his arms around her, she speaks softly to him. "I'm not like my sister, you know. I don't just have sex with anyone."

"Go to sleep."

She turns over on her other side, grimacing as the pain shoots up her leg.

"You can't even turn over without writhing in pain. Now go to sleep and get some rest. Tomorrow will be a big day for you."

"What do you mean?"

"You are going to have to decide what to do with your life. Are you going to return to the chaos and live with it, face it—or are you going to move on?"

"I have nowhere to go."

"You can stay here until you figure something out."

"Why are you being so nice to me?"

"To show you that all guys are not assholes, despite your previous experience."

She lies quietly and tears begin to stream out of her eyes. She is so tired and sore and frightened. "I thought you wanted me to be more like her."

"God no! I like you just the way you are."

She turns over and faces him, taking his hand. "I'm frightened. Frightened by what he will do if I stay and what he will do if I leave. He has such a temper."

"I'll be with you."

Rebecca is grateful for his support but fears how Royce might react if he were to see Jesse with her. "No! You can't be. If he sees you, he may kill you."

"Nobody is going to kill anybody. We will just go by the house tomorrow and see how you feel. Now go to sleep," he says, kissing her lightly on the forehead.

Her head begins to spin in a million directions, imagining so many different scenarios—the locks being changed so she can't get in, Natalie greeting her at the kitchen door, Royce raising his voice and hands and finally assaulting her as he has wanted to all these years. She makes herself breathe. Inhale. Exhale. Inhale positive thoughts. Exhale the garbage. Inhale. She remembers Monique counseling her to be her own person, to stand up for herself. Monique will have some ideas. She will call Monique in the morning. Finally, exhausted, she falls asleep.

CHAPTER TWENTY-EIGHT

When they arrive at the farm the next morning, two of the three cars are gone. She hadn't anticipated this, though she doesn't know why not. Royce and Natalie have both just gone about their daily business as if nothing has happened—as if she hasn't been missing for almost twenty-four hours. She gets out of the truck and walks up to the back door. It is locked. For a moment, panic grips her, but then she breathes and reaches under the rock beside the entryway to retrieve the spare key. She places it in the lock. It works. Relieved, she gives Jesse a thumbs up. He jumps out of the truck and walks over to her.

"You want me to come in with you?" he asks.

"No. I'm just going to pack some things. It will probably take me an hour or so. Do you want to wait or go do some errands? Then come back and get me?"

"So you're leaving? You decided."

"I have."

"That's very brave of you."

"I have you to thank. And I have a friend whose partner is an attorney. I'm going to call her and get her to draw up divorce papers. Beat Royce to the mark."

"Why the sudden change of attitude? Where did all this bravado come from? Not that it's a bad thing …."

"Last night you showed me I deserve more. I deserve kindness and respect. I've been living a nightmare, especially since Juliet died."

"Juliet?"

"I didn't tell you about Juliet?"

"No."

"It's a long story. Right now, I want to pack and get out of here before anyone comes back."

"Good plan."

"I will see you in an hour."

He reaches his arms out to her and folds her in a gentle hug. "You sure you're going to be all right? I can stay."

"I'll be fine. See you in an hour," she says, turning away quickly before he can see her eyes begin to well with tears.

The house feels hollow and empty when she walks in, her footsteps loud and echoing against the red-tile floor. She remembers when Royce bought the farm for her, six years ago. She was tired of living in the city all the time and wanted to find a place with country charm. The farm, with its orchard and fields, its big red barn, had that charm—although the place was too rustic for Royce's taste. Still, he had given the property to her as a gift, a celebration of her first pregnancy. Then he had immediately installed a swimming pool and spa and had demanded that they renovate the entire first floor and all the bathrooms before they move in, to make their "country" living more palatable. He had turned the barn into a fully equipped gym. They had fun importing Italian tile and creating a state-of-the-art kitchen, finding tubs that were deep enough to dive into and lighting fixtures that bridged the gap between their two lives. For a while, after the renovation was complete, she loved living here. Creating a nursery. But then that brought sorrow because the babies never came. This giant farmhouse she had once imagined would be filled with the sound of children's laughter is as quiet as a church on Monday.

She climbs the stairs to the dormer and retrieves a large suitcase and two smaller bags, then walks into her bedroom to get her clothes. There on the unmade bed are sex toys—a large dildo, vibrators of various shapes and sizes—and condom wrappers. The sheets are rumpled and the blankets tossed on the floor. Rebecca wants to vomit at the thought of their antics. But she swallows and channels her anger into filling the large suitcase with whatever she can grab and stuff in—jeans, T-shirts, shorts, underwear, socks, and some sweatshirts. She can't take everything, doesn't want to take everything, but she wants to make sure she has enough to get by.

Jesse mentioned last night that he could get her a job at the bar to tide her over until she lands on her feet again. She will need clothes for that. She throws in some skirts and blouses. She isn't sure what she will need. She wishes she had asked him to stay. Not that she would have wanted him to see the display on the bed. But her mind is muddled, and she is anxious that Royce will come in and see what she is doing and punish her for it. He never abused her physically before, aside from raping her on St. Croix.

"Listen to yourself," she says out loud. "Aside from raping you on St. Croix."

What kind of monster has she been living with? What bubble has she had around her that has kept her from seeing the truth? She throws more clothes into the case until it is filled, then closes and locks it. The case is so heavy, she can barely lift it. Besides, her shoulders are in so much pain. She will ask Jesse to come get it when he arrives.

Jesse. She has known him for what, not even twenty-four hours, and yet she is putting her trust in him? Part of her wants to run in the opposite direction from this nice man who picked her up from the side of the road, nursed her wounds, and showed her some tenderness when she most needed it. After all, what does she know about Jesse except that he kept Natalie on at the bar because it was "good for business"? No, that is not all she knows. She heard remorse in his voice over letting Natalie disappear with the mystery man. But what was he to do? As he said, Natalie had her own path; she made her own choices. And one of those choices was to have sex with Royce. *I am not going there*, Rebecca tells herself.

But what of Jesse? Why does she trust him? Why is she letting him into her life? Rebecca reflects on the past months, since she went to St. Croix. Something happened to her on that trip that opened her up to welcoming the unexpected. *Monique.* Monique appeared in her life and immediately began massaging Rebecca's rough edges. The older woman's compassion and wisdom softened Rebecca's hardened heart and allowed her to begin to believe in the goodness of the world again. Not everything seems doomed and bleak anymore. For Rebecca, there is cause for hope, even in the face of adversity. What was it that allowed her to make this change?

She takes one of the smaller bags and goes into her study. She fills it with all the books she can fit from her shelves. She will be damned if she is going anywhere without Kovach and Rosenstiel's *The Elements of Journalism* and Mary Oliver. Opening her tattered copy of *Dream Work*, she turns to one of her favorite poems.

WILD GEESE
You do not have to be good.
You do not have to walk on your knees
For a hundred miles through the desert, repenting.

Rebecca closes the small volume and holds it to her chest. When was the last time she read this poem? When was the last time she let herself feel this exquisite connection? "Tell me about despair, yours, and I will tell you mine." She has been a prisoner of her despair for years now, even before Juliet. She has lost sight of the possibilities that surround her. She knows she can't blame Royce, or Natalie, for her decline. Not any longer. Monique has shown her that and shared with her a world where trust, compassion, love, and mystery abound.

Whoever you are, no matter how lonely,
the world offers itself to your imagination,
calls to you like the wild geese ...

Why did she meet Monique? Why did she meet Jesse? She can't answer those questions, but she does know the world is calling to her, and she needs to follow that calling even though she has no idea where it is going to take her.

Royce has lost his power over her. She is sure he will just destroy everything she leaves behind, so she is careful to pack her journals, her laptop, all the tools of her trade as a writer. She hopes someday she will reclaim that version of herself.

Opening the drawer to her desk, she sees the first sonogram of Juliet when she was just an embryo. She kisses the picture and places it on top of the notebooks, closes the bag, and lugs it to the top of the stairs. It is so hard for her to move.

The last bag she fills with shoes—running shoes, boots, sneakers, flats—and her bathing suits, a towel, and goggles. She may be walking out of her old life, but she is not letting go of her new one, her training for the Ironman. As soon as she can, she will get back out on the road and in the pool, picking up where she left off. She will train on her old mountain bike until she can get a replacement for the racing bike she lost in the accident.

She sits down at the top of the stairs, satisfied she has taken everything she wants or needs. He can have all the rest—the house, the sofas, the seventy-two-inch TV. The Italian dishes. The china and silverware. The bamboo sheets. All trappings of a life she never felt was really hers.

She has about twenty minutes until Jesse will return, so she decides to call Monique to catch her up on what has happened and ask for her advice. She could use some encouragement right now. She presses the number into her phone. On the third ring, Monique picks up.

"'Ello?"

"Monique? It's Rebecca."

"Of course! How are you, *chérie*?"

"Actually, I am packing all my stuff and leaving Royce."

"Really? So you have come to your senses."

"Not exactly. I found him in bed with my sister."

Monique blows air out of her mouth into the phone. "I never liked that man."

"You know what, Monique, I don't think I did either. But I did love him."

"Where will you go? Do you need a place to stay? You are welcome to join me at my place in the city."

"You are so kind. Right now, I'm staying with a friend. But I may take you up on that."

"This friend? May I ask?"

"He's really just a friend."

"I'm no expert in these things, but April might counsel you to be careful. Royce could use that against you. You are intending to divorce him?"

"Definitely. And I don't care about the stuff—the money."

"You say that now ..." Monique leaves the rest of her thought hanging in the air.

Rebecca feels suddenly lost. All the resolve she had slides from her like water off soap. "What do you think I should do? I can't really stay here with the two of them screwing in the bedroom next to me."

"Of course not. At least, maybe not. I am no expert. But he may use it against you if you leave him. He could say you abandoned him. You really should talk to April. Do you have her number?"

"Yes. I will give her a call now."

"And *chérie*, if you do stay there with them, be careful. He is the kind to try to get you to do something foolish."

"Thanks, Monique," she says, not really grasping what that "something foolish" might be. "I will call April now."

"Very good. Just remember, I am only an hour away."

"You're in the city?"

"Yes. For the time being. That plan I mentioned to you on the island? It's about to come to fruition."

"I guess that's good news. Can you tell me more? I wish my future looked as bright."

"Rebecca, everything is going to be all right. Trust me. I would not tell you this if it were not so."

"If you say so."

"I know so. Just keep your head on straight, as you Americans like to say."

After they hang up, Rebecca takes a moment, resting the phone against her forehead before she makes the call to April. Can she stay here with them? Can she bear it? Monique may be right—if she leaves now, she will be walking away from everything, and certainly she deserves some compensation for the years she has spent with Royce.

April's voicemail picks up and Rebecca leaves a message asking that she call back as soon as possible. Then she quickly unpacks all the cases she has crammed full with clothes, shoes, books, and notebooks. It takes her less time to undo all her work than she anticipated. She still has time before Jesse arrives. She is sure he will have an opinion about her decision, but she has to think about her future and how to protect herself.

Protect herself. How? She has no gun, and she wouldn't know how to use one if she did. But Royce does. She is pretty sure he keeps it locked in the safe in his den. If she can get in and remove it, not to use it but to keep him from using it against *her*, she will feel a little bit safer. She walks downstairs to the den and makes her way to the safe, which is in the wall behind a large photograph of Royce with an ex-President, the two of them grinning at the camera, shaking hands. Two narcissists. The perfect pair.

She has no idea what his combination might be, and she realizes how foolish and potentially dangerous it is to try to break in. What if she attempts three times and then he is notified somehow that someone is trying to break in? *This is a bad idea*, she tells herself and is in the process of rehanging the picture when she hears a knock at the back door. Then Jesse calls out.

"Rebecca?"

"Back here," she yells. "Come on in."

He appears in the doorway, and she is struck by how handsome he is and how her heart leaps a little on seeing him. She hasn't felt this way about Royce for a long time. *Don't be foolish*, she tells herself. *Don't turn this into a crush. You need to keep your head on straight and not complicate things. He is just a distraction.*

"You ready?" he asks.

"Almost. Just need to hang this up again," she says.

"Here. Let me help you." He comes over and takes the picture from her. Once he has it up on the wall, he stares at it for a moment. "I know that face."

"Of course, you do. Everyone knows that face."

"Not Trump. The other guy. Who is he?"

"That's Royce. My husband."

"He's one of the guys I was telling you about, who showed up at the bar. He was there that night. When your sister disappeared. He was talking to her and the other man. I remember clear as day. He took Natalie aside, gave her something, and then disappeared. But the look he gave me on the way out when he saw me staring at them—that look sent a chill down my spine."

"Wait. Are you saying Royce knew what Natalie was doing, where she was going? That he had something to do with that?" The hairs on Rebecca's arms rise and a cold spasm runs down her spine, as if she has just seen a ghost. Then her blood begins to flood to her face and her jaw tightens.

"I'm not saying anything. Just that I saw him with them that night. In fact, he had been in the bar before, chatting her up."

"Fuck! He has known all along. That asshole!" Royce was one of the two men Jesse saw in the bar. *Two* men. Who was the other? Rebecca suddenly remembers the photo of Peter Robinson she tucked away in her desk after she returned from St. Croix. "Do you remember what the other man looked like? If I show you a picture—"

"Definitely. If you have a photo … ?"

Rebecca leaves the room to retrieve the picture. "I'll only be a minute." Her heart is pounding in her chest. What can this mean if Royce was in on Natalie's leaving? And what if the other man from the bar was Peter Robinson? What could they possibly have wanted with Natalie? She takes the photo out of the desk, anxious but excited by the possibility that she might be getting closer to the truth about her sister. When she comes back and holds the photo out for Jesse to see, he nods his head.

"Yes. That's him. That's definitely the guy she went away with. Who is he, and how did you get his picture?"

"His name is Peter Robinson. Was Peter Robinson. He was murdered. The police chief on St. Croix thought Natalie might have something to do with it. I kind of slipped the photo into my pocket when he wasn't looking. I have no idea why. It seemed like a good idea at the time."

Jesse blows a deep breath out of his mouth. "Holy shit! This is big, Rebecca. Murder? This is dangerous shit! It looks like the three of them were tangled up in something."

"It does look that way, doesn't it?" Rebecca says. "There's more."

"Shit."

"Peter Robinson was a sex trafficker. If Royce was involved with him, does that mean he is involved in sex trafficking too? Is that where he's getting all this extra money? Did he bring Natalie in on it too?" Rebecca speaks quickly, her breath shallow and fast. She feels lightheaded, as if she might faint or simply dissolve into tears.

"Let's get out of here. If he comes back and finds you trying to break into his safe, there's bound to be trouble. That's what you were trying to do, wasn't it?"

"I'm not going."

"What? You can't stay here. Who knows how deep this thing goes?"

"My friend advised me that if I leave, Royce could use that against me in court. Say that I abandoned him. I could lose everything."

"I thought you didn't care about the money."

"I don't. But I do. I care about my future. And all that you just told me, Jesse—I need time to sort it out."

"I'm not pressuring you, but I do want you to be safe. These guys are obviously criminals. And Natalie has gotten herself tied up in something. Do you think you'll be okay here with them?"

She sighs, runs her hands through her hair. "I honestly don't know. But I don't know what else to do."

"I can't convince you to come back to the bar, just for today? If you won't come with me, can I stay here with you? I'm really concerned," he says.

She shakes her head.

"Well, you know you have a place to go if things get bad."

"I will. And thanks. Thanks for all you've done."

"I haven't really done anything."

"But you have. You have been a friend when I needed one. You will keep being my friend, right?"

"As long as you need me. You know where to find me. I have to go now. I'll check in with you later, okay?"

He opens his arms to her and they hug before he drives away, leaving her alone in the empty house that feels like a prison.

Rebecca has never known time to pass so slowly or so loudly. Every clock in the house seems to have its ticker intensified, and the grandfather clock in the living room reminds her every fifteen minutes that she is getting closer to Royce's return.

What will she say to him? She wants to confront him and Natalie, but she knows that is not wise. She could quite literally be taking her life in her hands. What will she tell him about her hours spent away, which already seem so far in the distance?

She has cuts and bruises that will require an explanation. Royce probably won't even notice. If he does ask, she will tell him she had an accident and spent the night in the hospital and took an Uber home. He won't see her naked, so he won't know the extent of the damages. Just the swollen purple face.

How should she act around him and Natalie? Should she condone their behavior? Cook dinner as usual? Act as if she doesn't know their secret? She wishes April would call so she could get some counsel.

As if on cue, the phone rings. "Rebecca. It's April. I called as soon as I could. I only have a few minutes. What's going on?"

"I want to divorce my husband. I found him in bed with my sister. And it turns out he was with her on the night she disappeared with Peter Robinson to the island. I think they have been lying all along. I don't know if I should stay in the house with them or if I should leave. If I leave, will he use that against me in court?"

"Your husband is a very wealthy and powerful man. He will hire the best divorce lawyers he can to protect his assets and his name. What I can tell you about men of his kind is that they don't like to be pushed into corners. If you file for divorce, you are likely to spark some pretty ugly behavior on his part. Are you prepared for that?"

"Are you saying I shouldn't—"

"Not at all. I'm just asking if you're prepared for the consequences."

"I don't see how it can get any worse than it already is."

"Believe me. It can get worse. Walk me through how you happened on them in bed."

Rebecca recounts the previous morning, her long run, and how she came home earlier than they expected. How she found them in bed together and how they seemed to have no remorse. In fact, Royce said she had brought this on herself.

"What did he mean by that?" April asks.

"It is a long story. Basically, I stopped having sex with Royce after the stillbirth of our daughter last spring. I kind of gave him permission to find sex elsewhere, which he did. I never imagined he would sleep with my sister."

"This is Natalie? The sister we visited at the hospital on St. Croix?"

"Yes."

"Is there any chance they might have been having sex before she went missing?"

Rebecca stops breathing for a moment. The thought never occurred to her. Royce always made such a big deal about hating Natalie. But maybe that was a ruse. "I guess there may have been the possibility. I certainly never suspected it."

"She's living with you now?"

"Yes. While she's in outpatient treatment. As soon as she was healthy enough, I was going to insist she move into a sober house. At least, that was the plan. I don't know what I'm going to do now."

"What does your husband say about that?"

"He said she is not going anywhere. If anyone is leaving, it is me."

"Charming fellow."

"What should I do?"

"What did you do when you found them?"

"I went out for a bike ride, got in an accident, went home with a guy in a pick-up truck, and got drunk."

"Does Royce know?" April asks, concerned.

"Not yet. He's at work. Should I tell him I spent the night at the hospital?"

"No. His lawyers are bound to check up on that, and you don't want to be caught lying."

"He'll have a fit if he knows I stayed with another guy. Even though we didn't do anything. I know he'll go ballistic."

"Do you think he'll hurt you?"

"He might. I don't know. I didn't think he would rape me, but he did."

April is quiet on the phone for a moment. "This is a difficult situation. I hate to counsel you to stay if you think you might be in danger. But if you leave, he could argue abandonment, and you could lose everything."

"There is nothing here I want. I mean, some money would be nice, but I can start from scratch."

"Are you sure?"

"No. I'm not sure! I guess I want you to tell me what to do."

"For your safety, I would tell you to get the hell out of there as soon as possible. As your lawyer, I would say see what happens when they return tonight. It might be better than you expect."

"You don't really think that, do you?"

"No."

Rebecca swallows the fear that has risen in her throat. She feels her courage sap as her knees threaten to buckle underneath her.

"But I don't want to see you cut off your nose to spite your face," April continues. "You need to give us a little time to figure out the next step."

Rebecca is not sure what their next step will be, but for her, it is simply to breathe. She inhales a long, slow breath. Holds it. Exhales. "All right," she says.

"All right what?"

"All right. I'll stay and see what happens. I'll act as if it's life as usual. But I'll call 911 if things get ugly."

"Call me anytime. Tonight. By tomorrow we should have a plan worked out. I'll call then."

CHAPTER TWENTY-NINE

Things do not go well. Natalie arrives home after her outpatient treatment at Carrier Clinic with her arms full of grocery bags. When she comes through the back door, Rebecca is in the kitchen, preparing chicken and white bean chili, spices spread out all over the counter, the aromatic scent filling the air.

"What the fuck are you doing here?" Natalie asks.

"I live here. This is my house. Remember?"

"I'd check with Royce about that," Natalie says as she pulls out a bottle of wine from one of the bags.

"I thought you were on the wagon," Rebecca says.

"It's for Royce," Natalie says. "Besides, what I do is none of your business."

"Oh, but it is, little sister! Especially when it involves you having sex with my husband. *In my bed!* And doing God knows what else. What are you up to, Natalie?"

Natalie continues to unpack the bags, taking out steak, potatoes, sour cream, and salad makings.

"Royce will never eat that," Rebecca says.

"On the contrary, it's what he said he craved. No more of that slop you're always feeding him. Turns out he's a real carnivore. He likes red meat." Natalie licks her lips for effect.

"You disgust me. I can't believe I went down to the islands to save you, and now you do this."

"Do what? Turn your husband against you? You were doing a good job of that on your own."

Rebecca adds chicken broth to the pot, which sizzles as it hits the hot pan. She deglazes, rubbing the spoon angrily against the bottom of the pan, scratching up pieces of chicken and vegetables. "You always get what you want, don't you, Natalie? Because you're the pretty one. Mom's favorite. I'm not going down without a fight."

Natalie laughs. "Look at you, all red in the face. By the way, what happened to your face? You look like you already got into a fight."

"It's none of your business."

"Probably self-inflicted wounds to make it look like Royce beat you up. I'll testify he was with me all last night."

"Testify? I was in a bike accident. No testimony necessary."

Just then, the back door opens and Royce enters. He takes one look at the two women and heads for his den, leaving his jacket and cashmere scarf on the dining room table. Then he comes back into the kitchen, gives Natalie a peck on the cheek, and takes the glass of wine she has poured for him.

"Rebecca," he says, "what happened to your face?"

"I had an accident on my bike. It's nothing."

"Is the bike okay? That baby cost me $1,200."

Rebecca shakes her head. "Totaled."

"Damn it, Rebecca, you—"

"Thank you," she says, cutting him off, "for your concern about my well-being."

"So where were you all day after this accident? The hospital? It doesn't look to be more than a scratch."

Rebecca wants to lie. It would be easier. But she remembers April's cautionary words that Royce's lawyers would uncover the truth. "No. I spent the day, and night, with a friend."

"A friend? You don't have any friends," he says. "I've made sure of that."

Natalie laughs and pours herself some wine. She sits down on the couch in the living room to watch the show that is sure to unfold between Royce and Rebecca.

"On the contrary, I do have a friend, and he took good care of me."

"What's that supposed to mean?" Royce says.

"We didn't have sex if that's what you're thinking."

Royce slams his glass down on the counter and red wine, like blood, dapples the white marble counter. "I don't believe you! I don't believe this! You refuse to have sex with me, your own husband, but you sleep with a perfect stranger!"

"How do you know he was a stranger?"

"Face it, Rebecca, you know no one. Go nowhere. Do nothing outside of this house."

"That's not true. I go to the gym. The library. I shop. How do you know I haven't met friends there? What do you really know about me?"

"So you admit it. You're having a clandestine affair with some gym rat, and that's why you won't have sex with me!"

"Royce, that's not true."

By now, Royce is puffed up, in full anger mode, spit flying from his mouth as he speaks. "I knew it! I knew there was something else going on! Who is he? Who is this guy? I'll kill him! And then I'll kill you!"

"Royce! Stop!" Rebecca slams her hands down hard against the counter in front of her. The action sends pain up her arms into her injured shoulders. She winces. "I am through with your bullying. I am done with your threats. If you are going to kill me, do it. Get it over with! Just stop being a pussy about it and spewing out empty accusations that are not true. I'm not sleeping with anyone else, and I don't want to sleep with you because, frankly, you disgust me."

"Why, you little bitch," he says as he advances toward her.

"What are you going to do? Beat me? Rape me again? In front of your little co-conspirator? Just to show how big and powerful you are?"

"Rebecca, I'm warning you …" he says as he comes closer.

"You don't scare me, Royce. Not anymore. You're just a narcissistic, sex-driven baby who wants what he wants and pouts when he doesn't get it. Well, guess what? That does not work for me. Not anymore. I want a divorce."

Royce's hand comes down hard against Rebecca's face. She feels the hot sting reverberate in her cheek and scalp. Her jaw aches. But she refuses to cry. "So that is your solution? Beat me up?"

"No one is getting a divorce unless I say so," he says.

"Is that right? What if I told you I already have a lawyer working on it?" Rebecca knows she has said too much, put too many cards on the table, but she cannot stop herself. She feels empowered to speak and is not afraid of the consequences.

Royce's face goes entirely blank and then a ghoulish grin slithers across his face. "Already have a lawyer, do you? Who? That dyke lawyer from St. Croix? My lawyers will eat her pussy for breakfast and enjoy every bite. Now go to your room before I really do beat you up."

"I'm not going anywhere," Rebecca says.

"Suit yourself," Royce says as he loosens his tie and sidles over to Natalie, who has been watching smugly through the whole scene. He lifts her up to him, presses his lips against hers, and grinds his groin into her pelvis. "Come on, baby, let's go have some fun. All this drama has made me horny."

Natalie pushes away from Royce and looks over at Rebecca, whose face is swollen and red. Their eyes meet. Rebecca remembers the day when their mother threw the glass of wine at Natalie, how her sister had looked at her, seeking safety and support. For a moment, Rebecca thinks Natalie may relent and come to her aide. But then Natalie throws her arms around Royce's shoulders and looks into his eyes. "I'm ready when you are," she says.

Rebecca, who didn't realize she had stopped breathing, exhales. "This may have been more than I bargained for," she whispers to herself as she watches them climb the stairs to the bedroom. She takes an ice pack from the freezer and wraps it in a dish towel, presses it against her cheek. Then she calls April.

"I blew it," she says.

"What did you do?" April asks.

"I told him I had already started divorce proceedings. He said his lawyers would eat ... you for breakfast."

"You told him I was representing you?"

"He guessed. He's not stupid. Just mean."

"What did he do?"

"He slapped me across the face. Threatened to kill me and my friend if he found out who he was."

"That changes things. Where are you now?"

"Still at home. They're upstairs screwing."

"Your sister's going along with all this?"

"I don't think she knows any better. The thing is, he'll do the same thing to her. Rape her. Beat her. Leave her."

"Things are not going to get that far. Trust me."

"Right now, you, Monique, and Jesse are all I have."

"We're on your side. We're going to make this right for you. Can you stay there? One more night? Lock yourself in your room? Do you have a gun?"

"No, but he does."

April is silent on the other end of the phone.

"Now you're scaring me," Rebecca says.

"Don't be scared. Just be prepared. Keep your phone charged. Your door and windows locked. I will draw up papers tonight, and we will serve them tomorrow."

Rebecca rests her cheek against the ice pack again. "I cannot believe this is happening."

"Be strong. Be courageous. You are going to get through this. We'll talk in the morning. Just make it through the night."

Rebecca makes sure to lock the door to the guest room. She pushes the bureau in front of the door, ignoring the pain that shoots through her shoulders and back. She checks the windows to make sure they are locked too, including the small portal in the ensuite bathroom. She cannot imagine Royce will try to do anything to her during the night. But then she never would have imagined that Royce was a sex trafficker involved with a dead man with two bullets in his head. Or that he would recruit Natalie. There is so much she doesn't know about Royce, so much she wouldn't put past him now. Her imagination runs wild. What if he has organized a hit man to creep up and let himself through the window? To off her while he and Natalie screw upstairs? Just the thought of that sends chills down her spine. Royce is unpredictable, and she has pushed him a little further than usual, putting the reality of divorce out there. She is certain that, in Royce's mind, if anyone were going to be bold enough to ask for divorce, it would be him—not her. He looks on her as the weak little missus whom he controls. Her stepping out of her assigned role has unleashed the Beast again. There is no telling what he might do.

She lies in bed under a mound of comforters, but there is no comfort to be found in sleep for her tonight. Every little creak in the old house, the wind rattling the shutters, the floorboards sighing in the cold, makes her stomach lurch. Her fingers reach for the phone under her pillow. Should she call Jesse? No. What can he do for her now? He had texted her earlier in the evening, offering to come pick her up, but she declined his offer. She has no idea how ruthless Royce might be. Besides, she needs to get through this on her own, to prove to herself that she is strong. Brave. Courageous. Her eyes look out into the darkness. She tries shutting them, but they spring open again as she hears footsteps coming down the hall.

She hears the doorknob turn, but it is met with resistance. He rattles the knob again, then walks away.

Why did she decide to stay in the house? *This is clearly a mistake*, she tells herself. She should call Jesse and have him pick her up now. But how is she to get out of the room? If Royce really wanted to get in, he could have. He could bust the door down. She has known him to do such things before. But no, he was just trying to scare her. To remind her that he was—is—always there. Wild thoughts scramble in her head. She lies rigid on the bed, every muscle in her body as taut as iron. Fear grabs her by the throat, choking her with murderous hands, squeezing the life out of her. She can barely breathe.

Then she thinks of Monique and April. They said she just had to be brave for this one night. She decides to get up out of bed and wrap herself in blankets in the chair in the corner of the room. If he comes in and tries to smother her in bed, she will hit him over the head with a lamp. He won't expect her to be so clever.

The night passes with the grandfather clock tolling each fifteen minutes. She feels her eyes growing heavy, her head nodding off to sleep. The next thing she knows, a soft gray ribbon of light shines in the space between the curtains. Dawn. She has made it to morning. Why she feels safe in the morning light is a mystery she cannot explain. For some reason, she thinks Royce will behave like a gentleman by daylight. Where he might have strangled her under the cloak of darkness, he will have to find a more subtle way to kill her in the light.

She calls Monique. "I made it through the night," she says.

"Good. Now what is your plan for the day?"

"Nothing really. I think I have a therapy appointment at four. They will both be off doing what they do. Unless Royce decides to work at home." Rebecca grimaces. She has no idea what Royce's work is anymore. Not that she ever knew. She had been led to believe he was an investor, a real estate developer, a philanthropist. And maybe he is all those things. But now, she suspects sex trafficker trumps the list. It makes her nauseous thinking he could be conducting that business in their home.

"You mustn't stay there if he does. When will you know?"

"He should leave for work by seven if he is going."

"Let me know."

***

Rebecca is in the kitchen making coffee when Royce appears, dressed in a designer suit, briefcase and garment bag in hand. "Sleep well?" he asks.

"Well enough. You?"

"Like a baby."

"Lucky you."

"We will be staying in the condo tonight. Don't expect us home. I have a dinner thing."

"We? You're taking Natalie with you?"

"She's my plus one."

Rebecca thrusts the plunger into the French press, her jaw clenched.

"You're not upset, are you? I know how you hate these business dinners."

"Thoughtful of you."

"Don't forget to lock all the doors when you go to bed tonight. We don't want any intruders surprising you."

"Once again, thoughtful."

"Always thinking of you, sweetheart," he says as he comes over and kisses her on the cheek.

She flinches.

"Sorry I lost my temper yesterday. It's out of love, you know. I don't want to lose you."

Too late, she wants to tell him. But just then, Natalie walks into the kitchen, carrying an overnight case and a garment bag.

"What's in the bag?" Rebecca asks.

"Royce invited me to a business dinner. He said he was going to tell you."

Rebecca sips her coffee without responding.

"I borrowed your long black-sequined dress. I have to say, it doesn't seem at all like something you would wear. It has more of an Anjelina Jolie feel to it. You don't mind, do you?"

"Since when does it matter what I mind?"

"Rebecca, I don't want to get into it with you."

"I can't believe you! You are having sex with my husband. Taking my clothes. You are his *date* for a party. And you don't want to get into this? All I can say is, you had better be careful. Royce isn't what he seems."

"Maybe not with you. With me, he is loving and generous. Maybe if you gave him what he wanted—"

"Don't go there, Natalie. The man has raped me, abused me, lied to me. I no longer have any love for him. If you want him, he is yours. Have him."

"I don't need your permission."

"That has been made clear."

"You know what, Rebecca? I think you're jealous."

Rebecca laughs. "Jealous of what? The fact that you use sex to manipulate men? Well, sister, news flash: Royce is just manipulating you. He will dump you like all the others when he has had his fun with you."

"You don't know anything, Rebecca. Royce and I. We have plans."

"Plans? What plans?"

Royce, who has been silently drinking coffee during the whole conversation, his back against the refrigerator, comes between the two women. "Natalie, that is enough. We have to get going." He reaches into the refrigerator and pulls out a bottle of champagne, hands it to Natalie. "For later," he says.

"Can't wait," she replies.

What about your treatment program? Rebecca wants to say. But it occurs to her that maybe that was all a lie too. She watches them leave, with their totes and garment bags, and sighs. What has she not seen?

***

When they have left, she calls Carrier Clinic and asks to speak with the outpatient program director.

"Are you interested in the program for yourself or for another party?" the voice on the end of the phone asks.

"Actually, I'm just checking on my sister. She's enrolled in the program. My husband is responsible for the bill, and I want to make sure he's current." Rebecca hopes that the agent won't detect her small lie. She picks at the cuticle on her thumb with her index finger, tearing the skin until it bleeds, then silently curses herself as she presses the thumb tightly to stop the blood from flowing. Everything throbs. Her thumb, her heart, her head. She knows she is stretching the truth but justifies her actions, telling herself that she really needs to find out what is going on.

"His name?"

"Royce. Royce Winslow."

"Your sister's name?"

"Natalie Baker."

"One moment. Let me check on that for you." Soothing music flows from the phone; it does nothing to allay her anxiety as she waits. In several minutes, the voice comes back on line. "We have no one by that name enrolled in our program."

Rebecca's heart begins to beat more quickly. "Are you sure? Are there no payments from Royce Winslow?"

"Let me put you on hold. I will check again."

More music, less soothing. She opens the junk drawer and extracts a bandage from a box, wrapping it tightly around her thumb, which pulses dramatically. She closes her eyes, imagining all her fears and anxieties swelling in that beat, expanding, ready to explode. The woman comes back on the line.

"Hello? Are you there?"

"I am."

209

"I don't find anything under Royce Winslow or Royce Baker or Natalie Baker. I tried Natalie Winslow too, but there is nothing. None that I can find."

"She said she has been going for two and a half months. She even told us about her sessions."

"I don't know what to tell you, ma'am. Addicts can be very manipulative. If you like, I'll check again."

"No. Don't bother. I think I see what's been going on."

"I'm sorry I couldn't give you better news."

"You have been very helpful. Thank you." Rebecca hangs up the phone and ponders what this means. If Natalie hasn't been going to an outpatient program, what has she been doing all day? And who has she been doing it with? In her heart, she knows that Royce and Natalie have been up to no good. They have been engaged in an elaborate deceit.

She decides to run to Jesse's and puts on her running gear. She will surprise him. She doesn't want to let him know she is running there lest he try to discourage her. But she needs this run. She needs the air flowing through her lungs. She needs her head to clear of all the negative garbage Royce and Natalie have put there. She sets off down the driveway. At first, her leg is painful, and she wonders if this is such a good idea. But soon she is in her stride and the pain, though present, is not overwhelming. She focuses on breathing in the cool spring air.

What is going to come of all this? Today, April will draw up the divorce papers and serve them to Royce. He will rally his lawyers and the fight will begin. Maybe he will have the decency to stay at the condo until everything is settled, to avoid the unpleasantness of being around each other during the proceedings. The best thing would be if Royce just settled—gave her a million dollars and sent her on her way. Let her keep the house in Hopewell. But she knows he will not be so generous. He is bound to make her life as miserable as possible.

God, grant me the serenity to accept the things I cannot change,

The courage to change the things I can,

And the wisdom to know the difference.

Her mother taught her that prayer years ago. "The Serenity Prayer" by Reinhold Niebuhr. It was recited at AA meetings all over the world every day. She could use some serenity now. And some courage. And wisdom. She could use the whole package. She would love to be able to call her mother and tell her what is going on with Natalie and Royce—what might have been going on for years. But Rebecca has fallen for the belief that she brought this on *herself*. She has been so secret and guarded with her mother throughout her life, how can she possibly start opening up now? Her mother is likely to see her as the jealous sister. Natalie is her favorite. Always has been. Always will be. No matter what she does.

Rebecca arrives at the bar, sweaty and breathing heavily. She climbs the outside stairs to Jesse's apartment and knocks on the back door. It takes a few moments before he responds.

"Well, good morning," he says, clearly only just awake himself. His hair is rumpled and he is wearing only boxer shorts, his chest bare, revealing his lean though muscular body. He looks good. Rebecca looks at the floor, hopes he doesn't notice the sudden flush in her cheeks.

"I'm sorry. Did I wake you?"

"Yes, but hey. I had to get up anyway." He runs his hands through his hair. A coy smile is quickly replaced by concern. "Did you run here?"

"Yes."

"Man, you are stubborn. Do you think that's such a good idea with your leg and all?"

"I needed the endorphins. I'm dying at home."

"Interesting choice of words. Come in."

They walk into the apartment. "Can I get you some water or something?" he asks.

"Water would be great." He takes a bottle of water out of the fridge and hands it to her.

"They've been lying. Natalie never went to Carrier Clinic."

"How did you find that out?"

"I called. There's no Natalie Baker on their books. They've both been leaving at seven in the morning and coming back at six at night. I should have seen it. I've been so blind."

"You think they've been together?"

"What else could it be? On top of that, I think he's planning to kill me."

"What makes you say that?"

"I don't know. Just a feeling. The little things he's saying. The things he's doing."

"Like what?"

"Like telling me to make sure I lock all the doors and windows tonight when he and Natalie are in the city."

"Maybe you're being a little paranoid."

"Maybe. But something is going to happen. I feel it."

"If you're so worried, stay here with me. You said he's going to be out of town. And he doesn't know about me—about us—does he?"

"No. I haven't said anything."

"Then you're safe here. You can take a shower, borrow my old clothes again, watch movies, and sleep. I'll bring you food and drinks. With umbrellas. It'll be a vacation."

She feels butterflies in her stomach as he flashes a broad smile. "I have therapy at four."

"And I happen to get off at three today, so I'll take you."

"I can't hide out forever."

"You can until the next right step occurs. You'll know when it's safe to go home."

"How?"

"I'm not sure, but I'm sure you will."

She sips on her water, considering his proposition. The sweat chills on her body, and she is suddenly very cold. Her teeth begin to chatter.

"You want a blanket or something?" he says.

"No. I'm going to go. I can't avoid this situation forever. I need to stop being a baby and get over myself. I just needed to see a friendly face. Thanks for answering the door."

"At least let me drive you home."

"You don't have to do that."

"I know I don't have to. I want to."

"All right. My leg is feeling a little sore."

"Give me a minute to get dressed."

***

When they get to the farm, he walks her to the door. She is glad because in her imagination, she saw it open, an indication of prowlers inside. But there is no sign of forced entry. The crocus still blooms by the back door, and sunlight streams into the kitchen.

"You going to be all right?" he asks.

She nods. "I'm fine. I'll call you if anything happens."

"You worry me."

"What's going to happen? Royce is in the city for the night with my sister. I'll be fine here by myself. Now go—I'm feeling courageous. Don't spoil the mood."

"Can I come back later? After my shift?"

She is touched by his concern, but she knows that is not a good idea. What if Royce changes his mind and comes home early? What would he do if he found Jesse there? "Sweet thought, but I don't think that's such a great idea. You can call me though. I would like that."

"Okay then. We'll talk later."

"Later," she says. She watches him drive away, leaving her alone in the house, which feels remarkably cozy to her now. Nothing has changed except the release of endorphins. The certainty that Natalie and Royce have been carrying on since their return from St. Croix, maybe even before. That Peter Robinson was the mystery man. Which means Royce and Natalie may both be in danger, a fact that actually does not disturb her. Nothing shakes the calm she feels at this moment, knowing she has a friend close by.

She takes a long, hot shower and dresses in the most comfortable clothes she has, then goes downstairs to make herself some breakfast. It is almost noon, and she hasn't eaten anything all day. Her stomach growls as she fixes some avocado toast and two poached eggs. Why her appetite has returned, why she feels this lightness, she does not know. But she is not going to question it. She accepts moments like this as gifts in her life, the breadcrumbs that lead her through the darkness into the light. Only Hansel and Gretel ended up in the witch's house, very nearly baked in the oven. She quickly shakes that thought off and sits down at the dining room table to eat her meal.

She is facing Royce's den. Over the years, he has made it clear that she is not to go in there unless he is with her, which seems an unfair request given that the big television is there. She broke the rule when she went in search of the gun, so now, it is easier to rationalize her return. She has hours to kill, and she would like to watch a movie or some mindless show. Even as she tells herself this, she knows it is not true. She wants to go into his desk and files to see if she can find any evidence that might solidify the link between Royce, Natalie, and Peter Robinson and their dealings with one another.

She forces herself to eat her eggs and toast. Her heart is pounding in her chest. She knows she should probably leave well enough alone, but she is driven by a desire to know the truth. And so she gets up, brings her plate to the kitchen sink, and then walks back into his den.

The desk is locked, a clear indication in her mind that Royce is hiding something. But what? Photos? Lists? Letters and receipts? She is determined to get into the desk to find out. She feels under the bottom of the desk for a key to open it, but there is nothing there. She spills out the paper clips and pens he has neatly arranged in containers on the surface, thinking he might have hidden the key in there. Nothing. In a fit of frustration, she grabs a long silver letter opener and tries to pry the lock open, but she gets nowhere. Sweat is beginning to form on her forehead, and she wipes it away with her sleeve, then takes off her sweatshirt and sits down on the leather couch.

"What am I doing?" she says aloud. "He probably doesn't even have anything in there. He probably keeps it all on his laptop anyway. He's not a fool. Just an asshole." She resigns herself to the fact that she is not going to get any more information about Royce's relationship with her sister. She will have to live in speculation, which is often worse than reality.

She turns on the television and looks for a movie with Sandra Bullock. Sandra is always good for a distraction. The actress's latest release, *The Lost City*, is available to rent or buy, so Rebecca purchases the film and settles in to lose herself in some mindless entertainment until she has to go to see Margot at 4 p.m.

The movie does not disappoint. At least it helps her to pass the afternoon without thinking too much about the reality of her situation. But as she is driving to see Margot, thoughts begin to spin in her head again. Has April served Royce with the divorce papers? Should she call the lawyer or leave it alone until April calls her? What are Natalie and Royce doing now? She can only imagine.

As she drives to Margot's office, a deer leaps out into the road in front of her car, followed by two fawns with speckled coats. They stop in the road, staring at her with their wide eyes, frozen in the moment. *A sign?* Memories of driving with Monique flash across her mind, but she is quickly brought back to reality. Rebecca slams on the brakes, practically hitting her head on the steering wheel. The pain in her shoulder flares up as if on fire. She scolds herself for not paying attention. She should know better on this road. There are deer everywhere. She needs to quiet her mind and keep her eyes on the road in front of her. She calms her breath down and continues on her way.

Her meeting with Margot is emotional but not all that productive. The therapist encourages her to speak out her feelings about Natalie and Royce, to explore her anger and disappointment. "Whether you recognize it or not, Rebecca, this situation with Royce and Natalie is a trigger for you," Margot says as she opens a small bottle of Perrier and takes a sip.

"What do you mean?"

"You are reliving your grief about Juliet all over again. You are experiencing loss. The loss of a marriage. The loss of your relationship with your sister. And that is triggering the grief you still feel over the loss of your baby. An old wound has been reopened."

Rebecca considers what Margot has said. In the past, she might have been brought to tears by such a statement, but this afternoon the comments only make her mad. She is mad at Royce. Mad at Natalie. And now, mad at Margot, who seems intent on having her stay in the role of victim. She does not want to be a victim anymore. She wants to break free of that person, the person who was levelled by criticism and partiality. She wants to rise up and spread her wings like those wild geese, like the manta rays, and sail forward. What is holding her back?

"What is it, Rebecca? You look awfully pensive. What are you thinking?"

Does she dare to speak? To voice her truth? To tell her therapist exactly what is on her mind? She knows that little recovery can come from keeping things secret.

There is little purpose in her being in therapy if she isn't going to speak her mind. And yet, the old voice tells her to take care lest she say something that offends and displeases.

"I don't know …" she says.

"You do know. Something. Speak to me, Rebecca. Tell me what is on your mind." Margot smiles warmly, leaning into Rebecca with her whole body, as if trying to draw the words out of her with love.

This irritates Rebecca, who crosses her arms in front of her chest and folds one leg over another.

"I don't think this is working anymore," she says.

Margot looks startled; she has been caught off guard. "What do you mean?"

"I mean therapy. I don't think it's working for me anymore. It was good at first, when Juliet died. I needed someplace to come and just let my sorrow out. But it has been months, and I feel like I'm still stuck in that same place. A victim of my grief."

"The grieving process is different for everyone, Rebecca. Some take longer than others. And with new situations arising like the one you have described—"

"That's just it!" Rebecca says. "You bring everything back to Juliet, but I don't think that is where the problem really lies. Of course I'm sad I lost my baby. Of course I wish I hadn't had so many miscarriages. And of course I'm upset that my husband and my sister are having sex with each other and doing God knows what else. But I don't think that's the problem. I don't think that's where I'm stuck. That's just scratching the surface—the symptoms of the problem. I think it's something much deeper."

Margot makes a church and steeple of her fingers, rests her elbows on her knees, and places her hands under her chin. "Now we're getting somewhere."

"Where? Where are we getting, Margot? I feel like I'm at a crossroads in my life. I can either take positive action and move forward, or I can keep coming here and watch the sock go around in the dryer."

"You consider therapy a sock in the dryer?"

"We just don't seem to be getting anywhere. And frankly, I would rather give my $185 a week to feed hungry children in Appalachia than indulging in scrutinizing my belly button."

"I hear your passion. But are you sure we haven't gotten anywhere? Look at where you are today as opposed to how you felt when you first walked in my door seven months ago."

Rebecca is quiet as she considers her next words. It is true that she is a different person than when she walked in Margot's office seven months ago, but she is not sure if the change can be attributed to her weekly sessions. Margot has been a shoulder to cry on, but Rebecca needs more than that now. She needs someone to encourage her to blaze a new path for herself. Margot is not that person. *Monique* is. The old Rebecca, the people-pleasing Rebecca who relied so heavily on approval from her parents—particularly her mother—is finding it hard to break the tie to her therapist. Hasn't she been considering such a move for many weeks now? But the new Rebecca, the one who is filing for divorce from Royce, who made it through the night last night without panicking, is ready for change.

Say what you mean, but don't say it mean.

Rebecca untwists herself from the pretzel position she is in, leans forward, and reaches out to take Margot's hands. "You have been so helpful and supportive over the past months. But I think I need a break from therapy for a while. I want to give my mind a rest."

"Of course. You know you are welcome back whenever you are ready to begin again."

***

Back in the car, Rebecca grips the steering wheel and mouths a silent scream. "I did it!" she says aloud. "I made the break with my therapist!" Feeling pounds lighter, as though a heavy burden has been lifted, she starts the car and drives home. She hopes that someone, somehow, will tell her she has made the right choice.

She wants to call Jesse, to share her good news, but she will wait until she is not driving to do so. Her earlier encounter with the deer has made her leery, and now it is dusk and the probability of the animals coming out to play is even stronger.

She stops at McCaffrey's on her way home to pick up coffee creamer. She doesn't intend to call Jesse, but finds herself dialing his number as she stands in front of the refrigerated case of creamers, trying to decide which flavor she wants today. On the second ring, Jesse picks up.

"Hey, are you okay?" he asks.

"I'm fine. Just at the grocery store picking up a few things."

"How was therapy?" he asks.

She is pleased that he remembered she had an appointment. *It's little things like this that make a difference. Royce ...* She starts to criticize Royce for his lack of attention to the details in her life, but then realizes maybe she is being too harsh. He did remember what she liked for Chinese. And he did bring her home that gorgeous bouquet of flowers. As these thoughts pass through her mind, she sighs. Good old Rebecca. Always trying to look for the best in people .... Maybe that is not the truth. Maybe the reality is that she is not able to accept people for who they really are and seeks to make them fit the mold of what she feels a person should be.

"Rebecca? You there?"

"Yeah. Sorry. Therapy. I fired her."

"You what?"

"I fired my therapist. Don't worry, I'm not losing my mind. This has been a long time coming. I feel really good about it."

"As long as you feel good about it ..." he says.

"Now I can get on with my life. Of course, there is the problem of the little situation at home," she says, laughing.

"Glad to hear you can laugh about it, though really, it's not funny."

"If I don't laugh, I'll cry, and I am tired of crying. What do you think? French vanilla oat milk or fat-free half-and-half?"

"Definitely the oat milk. You sure you're okay? You sound borderline hysterical."

"Just giddy. I don't know why. I just feel very light and free right now. Better than I have felt in a long time. Talking to you helps."

"How about I come over tonight? Just for a short visit."

"You checking up on me?"

"Maybe."

"I don't need a babysitter. I'm fine."

"I know you are. I don't want to babysit you. Actually, I was just hoping for a good homecooked meal."

Rebecca laughs. "Well that I can provide. Do you like white bean and chicken chili?"

"Never had it. But it sounds delicious."

"It's my specialty."

"Then I'm sure to love it. How about I come over around six? I promise I won't overstay my welcome."

Rebecca sighs. She is not concerned about Jesse and his intentions. From what she knows of him, he is a trustworthy guy. It's Royce she is worried about.

"He's not coming home tonight," Jesse says.

"You sound awfully sure about that. How do you know?" she says.

"Call it intuition."

"Since when did you get all touchy-feely?"

"You got me. Honestly? If I was your asshole husband, and I knew my wife knew I was having an affair with her sister, I would take full advantage of spending the night in the city and having a good time. He is thinking about himself, Rebecca, not you."

Rebecca is silent as she lets the weight of Jesse's words sink into her mind. She doesn't like what he said, but the truth is the truth. Though it hurts her to admit it, she needs to face the reality that her marriage is over. Any chance of a relationship with Natalie has disappeared. She can only imagine what her mother will have to say about all of this.

"Rebecca? You there?" Jesse asks on the other end of the line. "I hope what I said didn't upset you."

"No. What you said ... it's the truth. I know Royce is a dick, and I don't want to be married to him anymore. But still, I did love him once. And he loved me."

Jesse is silent.

"I'm just feeling it, that's all, the disappointment and loss." She puts the oat milk creamer in her basket.

"That's only natural. But, hey, why don't I come over and have some chili, and we can talk or watch a movie and get you through this night?"

"And after this night, what then?"

Rebecca imagines Royce and Natalie walking in through the back door, garment bags on their arms, smug grins on their faces. No, Royce will be fuming because he will have been served the divorce papers, and he will want to take out his anger on her. Maybe if he comes to his senses, he will just stay in the city and leave her alone. One can always hope. She really has no idea what the future is going to bring. She could use a friendly face, a shoulder to lean on, and since Monique is not available, Jesse will do. More than do. She appreciates his quiet confidence, his gentleness and respect.

"You know what? I'm not going to think about Royce tonight. Come over. We'll have my fantastic chili and who knows, maybe I'll get you to play Scrabble with me."

"Now there I draw the line …" he says.

"All right. I will see you around six." Rebecca smiles as she hangs up the call. She is going to make it through this night after all.

***

"You know, it's weird," Rebecca says as she pushes lettuce leaves around in her salad bowl. She and Jesse are sitting at the dining room table, eating dinner. She has set the table with placemats and candles. At first, she thought maybe it was too much, bordering on creating a romantic date. But then she gives herself permission to "follow her bliss," as Monique would say. To stop editing what she is doing and to go with what feels right.

"What's weird?" Jesse says as he scoops another spoonful of chili from his bowl and puts it in his mouth.

"I'm not afraid anymore."

"This chili is really good," he says as he scrapes the bottom of the bowl for the last few bites.

Rebecca laughs. "I'm glad you like it. There's more. Can I get you some?"

"Sure." He hands her the bowl.

She feels his eyes on her as she walks into the kitchen to replenish his supper.

"What were you afraid of? Royce?"

"Yes. Him. And not being loved. And not being able to have a baby. It's funny. I feel like a bubble has burst, and I'm just not tethered down by those fears anymore. I don't know why."

"Do you need to know why?"

"I guess not. I guess I can just be grateful for the way I'm feeling right now. I am glad you came over."

"Me too. I haven't eaten this well in a long time," Jesse says, grinning at her.

They finish their dinner. Jesse insists on doing the dishes, though there are few, stating that since Rebecca cooked, she shouldn't have to clean. *Another plus mark for the bartender*, Rebecca thinks to herself. While he cleans the salad bowl and the pot the chili was in, she sits on the sofa in the living room, watching him. He looks so handsome and relaxed in the kitchen, with the dishcloth slung over his shoulder, his sleeves rolled to the elbows as he washes the chili pot. He exudes a comfortable sexuality that captivates her. It's very quiet. Only the sound of the water spilling from the faucet and the rubbing of a cleaning pad on steel. She wonders if she should maybe play some music. But no, she will opt for peace.

When he is done, he joins her. They talk for hours about all sorts of topics—their childhoods, their astrological signs, favorite movies and books, bucket lists, dreams for the future. By the end of their conversation, she feels she knows him better than she knows her own husband—and likes him better too. She has much more in common with Jesse than she ever had with Royce. Why couldn't she have met this man years ago? Her life might have been so different. But if she has learned anything from Monique in all their conversations, it is that we are exactly where we are supposed to be. A younger Rebecca might not have been open to the person Jesse is. She has needed every event in her life—her marriage to Royce, losing her babies, Natalie's betrayal, and all the moments between—to make her who she is today. At this moment, she can live with that knowledge.

At eleven o'clock, she is yawning, not from boredom but because she is ready for sleep. Jesse, who is on the verge of sleep himself, walks her to her bedroom. She climbs under the covers, without changing from her clothes, and he tucks her in. She closes her eyes, feels his lips on her forehead.

"Goo'night," she says. "Jesse? Thanks for being my friend."

"Always."

CHAPTER THIRTY

She wakes the next morning to a text from Jesse: *Good morning, Sunshine. How are you today? Hope I didn't keep you up too late last night.*

She texts back: *It was worth it. I slept like a baby.*

You ready for the day?

I'm ready. Bring it on!

Atta girl. Got to go. Talk later.

Rebecca walks to the kitchen. She has no idea what this day is going to bring, but she is ready. She fixes herself some coffee, enjoying the process of making her morning brew. Outside the kitchen window, the sky is blue and the sun is shining. The perfect day for a long run. She will fix herself a hearty breakfast before she goes so she has enough stamina to work out for a couple of hours. Aside from that, the day is open for whatever comes her way.

She is cooking poached eggs to put on avocado toast when there is a loud knocking on the door. The sudden explosion of noise makes her jump. She drops the slotted spoon on the floor and her heart leaps into her throat. Walking toward the back door, she sees a police car in the driveway and two policemen standing outside. She unlocks the door and opens it to speak with them.

"Mrs. Winslow?" the older officer says.

"Yes," she says. "What can I do for you?"

"May we come in?"

She wonders for a moment if this is a ruse that Royce has arranged to get some would-be assassins into the house. "Can you show me your credentials?" she asks.

They pull out their badges. "If you would prefer, we can stay out here," the younger officer says.

"No, no. Come in. Would you like something? Can I make you some coffee?"

"No, ma'am. Thank you anyway."

"We will sit in here," she says, motioning to the living room. When they are all seated, she folds her hands in her lap and asks them quietly, "Now what is this all about?"

"I am afraid we have some bad news, ma'am."

Rebecca's stomach lurches inside her.

"Your husband has been shot."

"Is he all right?"

"No ma'am. He is not. He is dead."

"How? When? He just left for work yesterday morning."

"For work?"

"Yes. He said he had a full day of meetings and then an event planned for last night. He said he wouldn't be home until this evening."

Rebecca hears herself mouth these words. They appear in her head like a church bell tolling. Royce is dead. Royce is dead. She doesn't know whether to weep or cheer. She feels like doing both.

"We ask because he was found in your condominium, shot execution style. With a woman."

"Oh my God. Is she dead too?"

"You know her?"

"He went to the city with my sister. It's a long story."

"She was unconscious when the housekeeper found them. She is in critical condition in the hospital now."

Rebecca is silent.

"Were she and the victim involved?" the officer asks.

"You might say that."

"We have to ask, where were you at around three yesterday afternoon?"

Rebecca thinks back to the day before. It seems like such a long time ago. She travels back through her dinner with Jesse, before that the grocery store, and therapy with Margot at four. What did she do before therapy? Watch a movie. "I was right here, watching a movie. A Sandra Bullock movie. *The Lost City*. It was very entertaining."

"Can anyone confirm that?"

"Netflix. I purchased it. And then I went to my therapist in Princeton at four. She can confirm that."

"We will need her contact information."

"Of course." Rebecca jots down Margot's name and number on a slip of paper and hands it to the officer.

"One more thing, ma'am. The detectives in New York would like to speak with you. They say they may have found information on the scene connecting your sister and Mr. Winslow to a human trafficking ring. Are you available to ride with us into the city?"

"Of course. But would you mind if I eat my breakfast first? It's poached eggs on avocado toast. I hate to waste it."

EPILOGUE

Two Years Later

Rebecca sits under a rainbow-striped cabana on a beautiful beach in St. Croix. Next to her is a baby carrier holding an infant, a little girl about two months old, with a full head of dark hair, sleeping next to her. Felicity. She chose that name because of the intense happiness she felt when she first held the baby in her arms. Though past sorrows would never be completely erased, and she knew she would grieve the loss of Juliet forever, this new little being, who entered the world smiling, opened the way for a fresh and happy life.

The baby's eyes are closed in sleep, but every now and then her tiny hands flutter as if she is conducting a symphony. The sound of the waves is like a lullaby. The sky and the sea, both infinitely blue, seem to disappear into each other on the horizon. If there are other people around, Rebecca is oblivious to them, lost as she is in her own thoughts. Two years have passed since Royce's murder, which the police pinned on Natalie. All the evidence at the scene seemed to point her way. Fingerprints on the gun. Self-inflicted gunshot wound to the abdomen. Paperwork suggesting that Royce was shorting Natalie fees due to her for her role in the sex ring. Natalie is serving time for the murder and for sex trafficking, breaking her mother's heart yet again.

Of course, Dorothy found a way to lay the blame on Rebecca. "If only you had never married that man, this never would have happened." But Rebecca knows that is not the truth. None of it is the truth. She doesn't know what the truth is, but she is certain Natalie would never shoot herself. She is too selfish. What actually happened will remain a mystery, and that is fine with Rebecca.

Up on the shore, in a seaside café they purchased with money from the sale of the farm, Jesse stands behind the bar, drying glasses with a white cloth towel. Royce left her nothing in his will; he made his mother the sole beneficiary, which sealed the bond between mother and son.

Neither Bette nor Dorothy will forgive Rebecca for what happened to their favorite offspring.

Rebecca does not mind. She has a new life. A good life. She is happy.

"Jesse. Felicity," Rebecca says. "Who knew life could be so good? Who knew love could run so deep?"

"After all you have been through, you deserve this," April says as she sits in a beach chair in the shade next to the baby.

"I couldn't have done this without you and Monique," Rebecca says. She looks out toward the water where Monique rises from the waves in her wetsuit, having swum her daily two miles to "keep her lungs healthy for singing," though Rebecca suspects there is more to that story than she lets on. "She is such a strong swimmer. Such a good person."

"Isn't that what we're here for, to help one another?" April says, as she sips on her rum swizzle.

A cascade of memories flood Rebecca's mind—Monique taking her hand on the plane, opening their home to her, giving her the courage to stand up to Royce, coaching her toward her newfound freedom. All of it seems more than a coincidence, a mystery beyond her imagination. Her heart, once so closed to the possibility of grace, is open to the certainty that there is divine justice in the world.

ACKNOWLEDGMENTS

I am very grateful for the following: the people at Warren Publishing/PipeVine Press who have worked so hard on behalf of this book, especially Mindy Kuhn, Lacey Cope and my brilliant editor Amy Ashby whose encouragement, guidance and editing have contributed significantly to making MOTHERLOVE a work that I am so pleased with. My daughter Kylie Corwin, who read early drafts of the book and offered excellent feedback that helped shape the book into its current form. Joel Holt who answered countless questions about St. Croix and provided details regarding the island. My supportive children and sisters—Nicholas, Haldis, Kylie, Felicity Myers and Ursula Costin. And most of all, my husband, Thom, who gives me the space, time and love to pursue my dreams.

ALSO BY HOPE ANDERSEN

The Book Sisters (novel)
When the Moon Winks (novel)
Where the Wind Blows (novel)
How to Remodel a Life (self-help memoir)
Postcards from a Loving God (poetry)

We hope you like this book!
Please consider leaving a review on Amazon, Goodreads,
BarnesandNoble.com, or wherever books are reviewed.
Thank you for reading!